BOY

BOY

Brent van Staalduinen

DUNDURN
TORONTO

Publisher: Scott Fraser | Acquiring editor: Rachel Spence | Editor: Crissy Calhoun
Cover design and illustration: Sophie Paas-Lang
Printer: Marquis Book Printing Inc.

Library and Archives Canada Cataloguing in Publication

Title: Boy / Brent van Staalduinen.
Names: Van Staalduinen, Brent, 1973- author.
Identifiers: Canadiana (print) 20190160632 | Canadiana (ebook) 20190160667 | ISBN
   9781459745889 (softcover) | ISBN 9781459745896 (PDF) | ISBN 9781459745902 (EPUB)
Classification: LCC PS8643.A598 B69 2020 | DDC C813/.6—dc23

We acknowledge the support of the Canada Council for the Arts and the Ontario Arts Council for our publishing program. We also acknowledge the financial support of the Government of Ontario, through the Ontario Book Publishing Tax Credit and Ontario Creates, and the Government of Canada.

Care has been taken to trace the ownership of copyright material used in this book. The author and the publisher welcome any information enabling them to rectify any references or credits in subsequent editions.

The publisher is not responsible for websites or their content unless they are owned by the publisher.

Printed and bound in Canada.

VISIT US AT

dundurn.com | @dundurnpress | dundurnpress | dundurnpress

Dundurn
3 Church Street, Suite 500
Toronto, Ontario, Canada
M5E 1M2

For my parents,
who love words.

O aching time! O moments big as years!
— John Keats

PART I
MARCH

The unopened envelope in Boy's hands is thin and light. He's not surprised. Lesser schools often pad their acceptance packages with welcome materials and pamphlets, a hopeful, last-minute attempt to sway undecided students. The best simply fold their letters twice, slide them into expensive envelopes, mail them to their selected few, and wait for the acceptances to find their inevitable way home. He turns it over a few times, inspecting every edge and seam, his eyes moving between the embossed Royal Military College seal and his laser-engraved name and address on the front. No question about what's inside. One envelope, one offer of ROTP admission — the full ride, as they say — one acceptance form. Good news.

Should be, anyhow.

— Fuck.

He draws out the consonants at both ends of the word, soft and hard, trying to savour it. But as soon it passes between his lips and teeth it feels wrong, painful, like hot coffee sipped too soon. A scalded aftertaste. He never swears — it's too much like giving in. His voice, along with the whisper of traffic on the Queen Elizabeth Way behind him, drops the short distance to the water and disappears.

Feels better, doesn't it?

— Not really.

A half-hearted response to Charlie's question, but not a lie. He won't lie to her. She came back after her death eight years ago to watch over him — the least he can do for her is find the truth. A measure of it, anyhow.

So what now?

He doesn't know. His grades have been in a steady decline over the past few months, sinking like a plane that has lost an engine. Soon, RMC will find out and the letter in his hand will become no more than a broken promise to himself. Lukewarm reality poured into the excitement he should be feeling. It's impossible to savour the tepid. All you can do is spit it out. He lays the envelope on the stone beside him and watches it a few moments, waiting for the wind to carry the bright paper towards the water. If it goes, so does the dream, right? A sign from heaven or wherever. But there's no movement, not even a flutter.

How can a single #10 envelope holding two printed pieces of paper contain the best and worst of everything? The letter was waiting for him when he got home from school, sticking out from the mailbox like an obscene gesture. He knew it was coming, knew that the board would have moved his application to the top of the pile for early selection. Impressed by the grades he carried at the deadline, the excellent essay he wrote on leadership and dreams, his exemplary volunteer and air cadet service over the past five years, and the numerous accolades and recommendations from the officers at the squadron and his teachers at school. He lined everything up just so, sending it all off with dreams of the full ride. He crushed the deadline. No one had doubted.

And it should be simple today, too. Complete the form, sign the declaration on the requisite line — *I, Boy Cornelius McVeigh, accept the offer of entry to RMC* — and send it back. Next, complete this school year, collect a high school diploma with honours, start training in July and classes in September, and sail through university towards a career in the air force. As a pilot, of course — he secured his private licence through cadets to streamline that requirement — although his six-foot-two frame will limit him to the larger, heavy-lift aircraft.

Would limit him. If only.

He looks out at the water. Lake Ontario is calm, a slate canvas under a cloudy, late-winter sky. He sits at the edge of a stone outcropping at its highest point, his pale, skinny legs dangling like an afterthought. Here, the QEW swings close to the shore, bent around the orchards and vineyards that once filled the ground between the Niagara Escarpment and the lake. His rocks — he likes to think of the knuckle of exposed dolostone as his — are part of a forgotten length of shoreline pinched between highway and lake and fringed on both sides by low trees and brush. His favourite place. No one comes here.

— What do you think I should do?

From her customary spot a few paces farther down the rocks, Charlie, too, faces the lake. Boy waits for her to speak again, but she remains silent, her expression as resolute as the stone itself. In life, even to her annoying brother two years her junior, she was the spectre of pre-teen chattiness; in death, she often drapes herself in wise, patient silence. Boy is almost grateful — it's up to him, after all. One hand on the control stick, the other on the throttle. Still, he wonders what advice she might offer. Surely she'd supply more than the common sense nuggets he'll get from everyone else when they find out. Work harder. Keep up the grades. Chin up. Et cetera.

— Well?

No response, just the same unchanging gaze out over the lake; the same defiant, folded arms; the same feet set shoulder-width apart, challenging. The same clothes she was wearing when she was killed eight years ago, a cream sweater and hip-hugger jeans both a size too large, as though she was hoping to fill them out someday. Hair in a perfect bun to impress the squadron officers and NCOs she never had the chance to meet. Their parents, Corny and Misty, had been shocked at Charlie's declaration to join the air cadets. *I want to do something different*, she said. Misty said no, but Corny talked her into it, even offering to drive Charlie every week. *Fine*, Misty said, *but you're responsible.* They never made it to the first parade — Corny swerved and flipped the car in front of a Niagara-bound truck. Charlie died. He lived.

Boy's phone thrums in his pocket. A text from Mark, a former squadron mate and his best friend, asking if the RMC letter has come through. Boy glances down at the envelope, noting the expensive weave of the heavyweight paper. Elegant. Understated. Woven through with a million expectations. He taps out a response.

— *nada. maybe tmw*

He lays the phone on the letter as a paperweight, moves his backpack behind him, and eases back into a recline against it. He feels the beginnings of a chill.

He wakes up, raising himself to a sitting position and blinking away a restive, brief sleep. He grabs his phone to check the time but the screen won't turn on. How long has he been out? Twenty minutes? An hour? It seems darker. The clouds have thickened, the temperature has dipped, and the lake has become shadowed. He shivers, sudden, deep. Through the thick insulation of his coat he feels the stubborn end of winter digging its aching fingers into his core.

It's perfectly quiet. He can hear his muscles spasming against the chill, the quick clacking of his teeth, the rustling of his clothing, but not the waves, wind, or even QEW traffic.

— Can you hear that? It's like — like —

Nothing at all.

The RMC letter is still beside him, resting at an odd angle. *Must have moved it in my sleep,* he thinks, reaching for it. He stops. It's not the angle but the position of the letter that looks so strange. It's half on, half off the rock, leaning on a short edge while the other end hangs suspended. He blinks and rubs his face, wondering if he's still sleeping and that the absence of sound and the impossibly suspended envelope are part of a strange, precise dream. It bothers him that he might still be asleep. He knows what the feeling is. *Leadership guilt,* his first drill instructor called it. *So wake up, Cadet,* Boy thinks. *Wake the fuck up. Leaders are always the first up and the first to move.*

He stands, awkwardly jumping up and down a few times to get his blood moving. He warms up quickly. He stops and looks around. Nothing has changed. Nothing moves or makes a sound.

Everything has stopped. The whitecaps on the waves have frozen themselves. Wave droplets flung into the air at the base of the rocks hang perfectly still and round, like glass marbles of a thousand different sizes. There's no wind, even though it had been constant since he arrived. He senses the stillness of the cars on the highway, their drivers stopped in mid-thought. He doesn't have to look up to know the dark ceiling of clouds has stopped its relentless scouring of the hidden sky. But why is he still moving? Why can he still speak and make sounds?

— What's happening, I —

How hard his voice is against the stillness. *Go,* his mind says. *Get out of here.* He bends over and grabs his backpack and the letter, plucking it half from the air, stuffing the envelope into the pack and shrugging it onto his shoulders. Wrong. It's all wrong.

The sound of feet on small stones drifts to him from beyond the rocks. A man appears, walking right past Charlie's ghost and looking at the sky like he's expecting foul weather. An unremarkable presence, perhaps just beyond middle age, slightly built and of average height, with greying hair and deep shadows under his eyes. He wears chinos, a chambray shirt, and a beige jacket, all with razor creases and a starched manner, as though unwrapped and unpinned just moments ago. The collar especially with the triangular stiffness exclusive to new dress shirts. Itchy.

My secret place might not be so secret after all, Boy thinks.

The man sees him and stops. A feral look hardens his features and he tenses, his eyes moving left and right. An animal caught away from the safety of its den. Boy remembers an old saying about cornered animals being the most dangerous. What about lonely ones? The man's expression says, too, that he has been on his own for a long time. Yet his hands are clean, his nails trimmed, his hair combed and parted to one side, his face clean-shaven.

Boy raises his hand slowly in what he hopes is a disarming gesture, a wave just higher than waist level. The man's eyes widen and he steps back, bringing his hands to his mouth as though he could hold back the tiny choking sound he makes. In the stillness, these tiny actions, minuscule things, ring out like gunshots and thunder. They stand for a long moment without moving, just looking at each other. The man practically vibrates, his tension just contained enough to keep him from bounding back into the scrub like a deer.

— Who are you? What are you doing here?

He's found his voice, a scratchy tremolo. Rust on old pipes.

— I was just leaving, Boy says.

— How did you find me?

— I didn't — I just come here sometimes to —

Boy stops himself, conscious of saying too much. To what? Think? Be alone? Masturbate? Why should he feel the need to put this strange man at ease? Boy could be asking him the same questions — who's the more suspicious character in this scenario? He's just a teenager who slipped around an old bit of fencing at the dead end of an unused service road. There have to be dozens of possible reasons a middle-aged man would be stomping around dead ground looking like an exhausted discount-store mannequin, and no comfortable ones. All of them enough to make him want to leave. He looks the man up and down again, noticing the starkness of the man's new clothing against the dead vegetation.

A change of clothes after hiding a fucking body, maybe.

Boy glances past the man at Charlie, who has turned away from the lake to face them and has sensed his discomfort with characteristic precision. He is beginning to feel the first roots of panic — cornered men, dangerous animals. The man sees the look and glances to the side. He sees nothing, of course, but is still trying to make sense of it all. And failing.

— What are you looking at?

Boy flushes — how could he explain?

— Nothing.

The man's eyes narrow.

— You're moving. How are you moving?

— I'm going to go.

— And talking, too — no one talks.

Oh my God, Boy thinks. He hears himself promising not to come back or tell anyone.

— No, the man says. That's not what I mean. Let me —

He steps forward, hand extended. Boy turns to run, back towards the break in the fence and his bike. Every movement too loud. The sound of his shoes against the rock beneath him. His clothing and backpack rustling. His heart. He doesn't see the ridge of stone that catches his foot, but he feels the sharpness of the one he hits his head against as he falls. A blink of sharp sound, strangely, impossibly above his eyes, a flash of white and black and quiet.

CHAPTER 2

It's late now, almost full dark; the cold feels even colder. He's sprawled out on his side, awkward, his backpack still strapped to his shoulders. He sits up too quickly, the pain in his head pouring down his neck and into his body like molten metal in his blood-stream, churning over itself a dozen times before being pumped back to his head. There are bright flashes, almost too quick to perceive. Nausea.

Yes, you're awake.

Charlie is still on the rock, again facing the water. He can hear the highway, the waves, the wind through the leafless bushes and low trees. The man is gone. Everything has started up again.

He holds his head in his hands and groans. Wait. Something is stuck to his forehead. He pulls out his phone and activates the selfie camera, squinting into the image of a white, self-adhesive bandage over his right eye. There are dark spots where blood has begun to seep through the weave and smudges beside his eye where the blood was hastily wiped away. He presses against the bandage. Instant, stinging pain as well as a deeper ache, too, like broken bone. The sensation — and the idea — triggers another rush of nausea, and he manages to lean just enough to the side to avoid being splashed by his own vomit.

Fuck, little brother. You're a mess.

— Helpful, Charlie, thanks.

There's no bite to Boy's sarcasm, just ritual. Swearing might taste dirty to him, but he's used to how blue her speech can be. When she was alive, even at the tender age of twelve, she could scorch the air, much to Corny and Misty's amusement, as though they could claim parental ownership of her expletives. They wondered where his foul streak was. He still favours composure and confidence rather than foulness, learning early that people listen better when you don't swear.

She's not wrong, though. He is a mess, likely concussed. The pain and scalp wound are a concern, but the nausea and fuzziness around his vision's periphery are much more worrisome. He should get himself checked out.

— Up you get, Cadet.

The faint path he has worn between the rocks and the end of the fence is difficult to see in the gathering darkness. He stumbles along slowly, tense against the pain but enjoying the warmth his pumping heart brings to his extremities. He tries to focus on each step — he'll worry later about what happened on the rock, he tells himself — but his mind keeps going back to the bandage on his forehead and the blood cleaned up on his face. The man stopped the bleeding and patched him up. If he is as dangerous as Boy and Charlie's imaginations make him out to be — changing his clothes after burying corpses, say — why would he do that?

Boy pedals, Corny's old ten-speed wobbling along, its orange frame filtered under the sodium street lamps into a strange, sickish hue. He passes new subdivision after new subdivision, every house delineated by the same pressure-treated fencing against the road and uniform rooflines against the darkening sky. Lots of flat screen TVs blinking in windows. Not a person in sight. Yet traffic along Barton Street is heavy, with hundreds of headlights zipping past and frequent stoplights soaring by like a bouncing, head-splitting cloud of fireflies.

Six years ago, as soon as Boy turned twelve, he made a long bike ride to East Hamilton, to the high school where 742, the air cadet squadron Charlie had hoped to join, paraded. He locked up Corny's ancient orange Raleigh and walked right in.

Two years of grief. A hole inside him slowly filling with something dense and heavy. A pocket of fluid tucked away under his heart but above his diaphragm where it seemed to weigh down every breath. Hydraulic fluid, perhaps. Red, viscous. He missed his foul-mouthed sister and had been thinking about the cadets, as well as the mystery of where Charlie got the idea, and how she convinced Sarah, her closest friend, to join up, too. A few months after Charlie's cremation, he looked around her room. On her desk was a large, resealable bag marked PERSONAL EFFECTS, the clear plastic hazy with dust. Inside, an empty purse and a jumble of things. A compact. Lipstick. Bobby pins. Comb. Small change, nickels, dimes, quarters. A cheap click pen from a random health service. Signed enrolment forms. Beside the bag was a scattered pile of literature about the cadets and how to join. He forged the necessary parental signatures, biked back out to 742 the next week, and never looked back.

No one questioned him, either at cadets or at home. Misty didn't question his disappearing every week for a few hours, the occasional training weekend away, the long absences for paid summer training. She didn't seem to notice that he never asked for money, complained about a part-time job, or brought any kids his age home to hang out. She covered her own grief with a calendar heavy with work and nights soaked in drink. Out there, she was a respected and driven realtor; at home, she drew the blinds and sipped her gin, missing most of what he was doing.

Who he was becoming, too, which these days is feeling less and less defined.

There are his grades, of course, but also the loss of the squadron. Eighteen years old, a forced resignation as of January first. Exiting after almost six years. From the moment he made those nervous stumbles on his first parade night to his earned billet as warrant officer first class, he knew all he wanted was to serve. Developed impeccable habits, hard routine. Polished and shined, always. And now? Weeknights and weekends formerly full of drill and training and command now his again. It's hard to switch off those old cadet ways. The urge to dive back into the manuals and regs and memorize. Polish buttons. Run a lint roller over his uniform blues. He's found himself in front of his closet a couple of times before remembering that everything was taken back by the squadron's quartermasters. They did let him keep his black drill boots, but there are only so many times you can spit-shine those when they don't get worn.

They'd be disappointed in him. Trying to bike himself to the walk-in clinic after a head injury? *Basic stuff, Cadet. You're mission incapable right now. You can't fly if you can't think. Get help. Ask for and expect it.* To be honest, he'd be disappointed in himself if he weren't in so much pain.

Maybe you should stop and call someone.

— It's not far.

His vision hasn't improved, nor has the pain in his head. *How much easier this would be,* he thinks, *if everything were still stopped.* A fresh cascade of nausea forces him to squeeze the brakes and skid to a halt. He drops his feet to the ground and moans. There's nothing left in his stomach to bring up, and he can't imagine dealing with another bout of dry heaving. He again recalls his extremely short contact list, reassuring himself that yes, he does indeed have to do this on his own. Mark? No car. Misty or Nick? Ha. If they're home, they're already high or drunk or both. And that's it.

How about an ambulance?

He thinks, *Not a bad idea, if a little late. But —*

— No, he says, his teeth gritted. Who calls an ambulance for himself?

Your logic is stupid.

— Maybe.

No maybe about it. You're being a fucking idiot.

A few moments later, he is again making his unsteady way towards the storefront walk-in clinic at Barton and Gray. A light snow has begun to fall, dusting the sidewalk. His progress looks like the tracks made by two drunk snakes, a never-seen suburban sub-species. Charlie keeps pace just behind, making no tracks in the snow. She appeared the winter after the accident, about the same time Corny pled guilty to all charges and was sent to Millhaven. Boy had become even more withdrawn, so in came the specialists. He admitted to the grief counsellor, a petite woman who wore only grey and tied her hair back so tightly it seemed to stretch her face, that he couldn't keep himself from staring at Charlie. The counsellor said, *Don't look right at her, then, if it makes you feel sad.* He said, *But she talks to me, too, and asks me lots of questions.* The counsellor asked if he ever responded. *Sure,* he said. *She is my sister.* The counsellor nodded. *Well, try not to talk to her in public, at least out loud — she's not really there, and people might get the wrong idea.* In her office, he could talk freely. Outside, no. Private grief was the main theme in his recovery, despite all the systems activating themselves after Charlie's death.

So much effort to help him forget his sadness, as though grieving openly, deeply, would keep him from healing. He even overheard Misty telling someone on the phone that a ten-year-old's grief isn't real. *It's just loss*, she said, *a small hole that'll heal quickly at his age*. For him, though, holes just get bigger — maybe you just get better at building around them.

When he finally arrives, he leans Corny's bike against the frosted main window. Its lock is gone, dropped somewhere between the rocks and here. He hopes he can keep an eye on it from the waiting room. An old bike, sure, but well cared for, and it would be a shame to have it stolen. Inside the house, Corny and Misty used to carry each other's drug and booze habits; in the garage, Corny repaired and cared for mechanical things as precisely as a jeweller. When he was sober enough, he'd teach Boy about gears and wiring and the intricacies of machines. Boy maintains the bike the way Corny taught him, with good oil and grease, reliable and clean tools, and an infinite supply of care.

The nurse behind the counter window takes his health card and passes over a battered clipboard without taking her eyes from her phone. The window, covered in peeling, translucent mac-tac, is only half open, so she has to angle the board at forty-five degrees to get it through. He can only see half of her face, which is pale and thin. Finally, she turns off her phone and lowers it to the counter, a secret smile fading along with the screen's dying glow. She doesn't even glance at the bloody bandage on his forehead.

— First time?

— Yes.

— Fill in both sides, bring it back. Waiting room's behind you. Someone'll call you in.

He tucks the clipboard under his arm and sinks into a pad-ded waiting chair. He squints at the impossibly small text, his head protesting the scrutiny. Standard questionnaire, a quick dash through his medical history. He's happy to lie about the family questions but pauses at one. *Have you ever ...* The cheap ballpoint, tethered to the clipboard by a filthy string, hovers over the boxes.

No.

Yes.

If yes, provide details.

During winter break last December, 742 organized an exchange with a cadet squadron in Washington, DC. Four days, a long drive, and a bus full of hopped-up cadets heading south to march in formation with their American counterparts. Mark called it the WO1 McVeigh Farewell Tour and the name stuck. The American scale of doing things was overwhelming. Tailored uniforms, patent leather drill shoes, medals, service ribbons, huge venues, and actual crowds. Boy — responsible for billet assignments — had erroneously placed himself in a female cadet's home. A Master Sergeant Morgan. She was almost as tall as him, quiet, plain. An obvious leader, too, comfortable with command. He found it hard to speak around her, and his uniform became unusually constrictive. After the final parade, she sparked up a joint behind the drill hall and Boy smoked up for the first time. The details began to get hazy. Smoking another joint when they got home, laughing a lot. Spinning. How aggressive she seemed to become after her parents went to bed. He found himself unable to say no. Another first time. Awkward apologies the following morning for taking what wasn't ready to be given. *I just assumed,* she said. *You seemed so into it.* She did not wave as the 742 bus drove away from the drill hall.

Her letter arrived about a month later. An actual letter, handwritten, matching stationery, American eagle stamp. A return address, grandly named but just an anonymous DC suburb. Bold black ink, her penmanship heavy on the vertical strokes. No first names, only rank and surname. Beyond formal.

WO1 McVeigh,
My period is a few weeks late. I took a test. I'm pregnant. I
thought you should know.
MSgt Morgan

Details, he thinks. *Right.*

He checks the *Yes* box, almost laughing at himself, a parody of things gone wrong. Sure, there's the inspirational story of a boy who rises above the tragic death of his big sister by immersing himself in the discipline of cadets and achieving the highest rank. Of sailing through high school, buoyed by the goal of serving his country with a career in the armed forces. Of earning some of the highest grades in his class, being selected first by his first-choice school, winning the full ride.

But now, the Fall. Snatched from his aspirations by distraction and necessity. It wasn't long after Charlie's death that Misty fell for Nick, the father of Sarah, also killed in the car that night; they moved in together, bonded by grief. Nick ensnared by her addictions. And then a few years later, an unexpected — Nick prefers the terms stupid and careless — pregnancy and the birth of a boy, Jay, this past summer. Misty rallying, putting aside the chemicals and booze, for a few weeks of baby care and love. Dragged off the wagon by Nick, a depression rising between the binges. Boy's duty to care for a baby half-brother, the time and effort it takes, the departure from his routines. A first sexual encounter he barely remembers, unprotected, the risk of infection, the question of pregnancy. And now, a gash on his head and a concussion courtesy of some guy he'd rather know nothing about.

You look pale.

— I feel pale, he says.

Boy's voice startles an overweight man in a greasy Ti-Cats jersey losing the battle against sleep. Ti-Cat opens his eyes, mumbles something incoherent, and begins to nod again. Charlie stands in the corner next to his chair, wedged into a corner the light doesn't quite reach. Every time the man closes his eyes, he leans closer to her before bolting upright as though he's fallen against something icy cold. A girl, maybe a couple of years younger than Boy, stares at the screen of her phone, tapping out Morse code or love letters on the cramped keyboard. Her fingers a blur. There's a nasty plum-black bruise on her throat surrounded by unblemished skin. Boy stares at it for so long that he sees it when he looks away, like the ghost image of a candle burned onto the retina.

He stands slowly and walks back to the window. Just as he is about to forty-five-degree the clipboard back to the receptionist, another bout of nausea hits and he heaves again, empty and dry. She makes a face as she takes the forms from him.

When he is finally escorted in and told to wait in a bright examination room, all he can do is lean back and close his eyes against the gleaming fixtures and throbbing fluorescent lights. Sleep is impossible. The posters on the wall and his phone aren't options, either — the text is too small for his swimming vision and aching head. Charlie, standing near the door, allows him his peace. He tries to think about lighter things to limit the strain but his mind keeps tripping back to the rocks, everything stopping, the man in the new clothing. The uncertainty of what happened. His bizarre comments. Him binding the wound and cleaning Boy's face. The absence of all movement and sound apart from his own. All sorts of questions and no responses that could be called rational.

A nurse, her footsteps heavy with fatigue, walks into the room and stands next to his gurney.

— Boy Cornelius — she checks her clipboard — McVeigh?

— Yes.

— Interesting name.

— Misty always wanted him to make a comeback, he says reflexively.

— I'm sorry?

— Misty — my mom — named me after Boy George. Singer from the eighties.

— Oh, right. I, uh —

— It's fine. Everyone asks.

She leans over him, carefully lifts the edge of the bandage, and inspects the wound on his forehead. She makes a note on his file and turns to go.

— How does it look?

— Good, although it'll need a few stitches. The doctor will be in shortly.

A few minutes later, the doctor walks in. A diminutive man, perhaps five-seven, with a few silver hairs salting the beginnings of a beard, he grabs the clipboard and stops next to the gurney. Spends a few moments reading. Nods, closes the folder.

— I'm Doctor Kamat, he says.

Boy shields his eyes and watches the doctor squeeze a bright meringue of sanitizer foam onto his hand from a dispenser on the wall. Rubs it all over his hands, palms, fingers, thumbs. If the sight of a skinny, six-foot-two young man with a military crew-cut surprises him, it doesn't show. Just another patient, albeit one who has passed the point where you call him tall for his age and instead call him just plain tall.

— You're Boy Cornelius McVeigh?

— Yes.

— An interesting name, Boy.

She should give you a fucking dollar for every time you have to explain that damn name.

— It's just a name, he says.

Dr Kamat shakes his head.

— There's no such thing. I have an original first name, too. Vena. It can be a girl's name.

— Why did your parents —

— Who knows why parents do what they do, eh? But I haven't changed it — a name sticks. So, what happened?

Boy explains about hitting his head on the rock, losing consciousness, the shard of rusty metal nearby.

— Any dizziness or nausea?

Boy nods.

— You've definitely concussed yourself. Chances are it'll just be a headache and some sickness for the next little while, but with the loss of consciousness I recommend you go to Emerg and have them check you out.

— And the wound?

— Here, let me look.

The doctor wheels over a stainless-steel cart with a bubble package resting on a green towel. He dons sterile surgical gloves and lays out the contents of the pack, more green towels and layers of sterile things, explaining each item as it is unveiled. With his foot, he drags over a low stool and sits. Boy appreciates the explanations, the discipline of what the doctor calls maintaining the sterile field. For a few moments, he is distracted from the throbbing behind his eyes. When everything is laid out in ranks, Dr. Kamat finally takes a pair of plastic tweezers and peels off the tape slowly, using a cotton swab soaked in alcohol to loosen the adhesive and gauze to clean up around the wound itself.

— The nurse was right about sutures. Five or six should do it, I think.

He has steady hands, reassuring, even as he inserts the anaesthetic needle right into the wound. A blossom of pain, once, twice, three times, before a heat and then a sense of nothing at all.

Even his head hurts a little less. After a few minutes, Kamat pokes at his forehead.

— Can you feel that?

— No. Nothing.

— Good.

The stitches don't take long, although there are few things more alien than knowing you're hurting without the pain. The curved needle biting the skin's edge, the black thread at the edge of his vision drawing the edges together. The deft flick and twirl of the doctor's hands, his relaxed posture, the ease of a subconscious task performed innumerable times. A running commentary about tensile strength and how each doctor has a preferred type of suture thread, but they all use the same knots for basic trauma such as this.

— Have you had a tetanus shot recently?

— I have no idea.

— You should have been brought in for a booster at fifteen if you were vaccinated at birth.

— Probably not, then.

— We can give you one here — I'll tell the nurse.

The doctor speaks and works at the same time. Charlie watches the doctor's hands, her brow furrowed, knotted by simultaneous interest and concern with each tied suture.

— You ticked *Yes* on the sexually active question and left blank the medical history question about untreated conditions. Did you want to talk about those?

A serious question phrased with sensitive weight. Kamat doesn't look down from the final suture as he speaks, though, perhaps understanding that although it isn't something Boy wants to talk about, it's also unavoidable. Eye contact, in such moments, must be measured by millimetres and nanoseconds. It would have been easier just to tick the little *No* box beside the question.

Would've, should've, maybe've, Cadet. Make up your mind and stick to the decision. Even when it strays from the truth. Or, in this case, the smallest uncertainty.

— I might need to be tested for STIs, Boy says.

Even saying it aloud feels strange. There have been no symptoms, no serious mood swings, no real reason to think Morgan might have been infected. But her aggressiveness, how experienced and reckless she looked the next morning even as she slept — naked on top of the sheets, stretched long, her right arm leisurely up over her head — gives him pause. How he'd felt the need to sneak out of bed, padding in bare feet to the kitchen. How her parents, already awake and bright over the breakfast table, had smiled at him and peppered him with small talk, assuming their overachieving daughter was asleep in her own bed upstairs rather than sprawled naked across the basement futon. The distraction for weeks afterwards. His grades, already feeling the strain of the extra hours spent at home with Jay, sliding further. Morgan's letter knocking the wind out of him, his continual questions about his responsibility, his role, whether or not to reach out.

A fluid coolness on his forehead brings him back into the trauma room — Kamat is wiping around the sutures with a sterile square and some leftover saline. There's still no pain, though, so Boy wonders if he should be feeling the coolness at all. The doctor dresses the wound and hands over some ointment, tape, and a small pile of gauze packages.

— Keep it dry. Ointment and fresh dressing every day until those run out, then a regular plaster should do. Watch for redness and infection around the sutures. Come back in ten days or so to get them out.

He strips off the gloves and makes a few notes in the file, slides the pen back into his pocket, and sits back, folding his arms.

21

— Have you had any symptoms? Discharge in your urine? Burning? Lumps, bumps, lesions?

Boy says no to each.

— But you recently had unprotected sex.

— Yes. A couple of months ago.

— Well, that rules out a few of the obvious suspects — you'd see symptoms for those — but you should still be tested. Have you researched your options? There's a lot of information online.

Boy shakes his head. He had never been able to get past the first set of search results. Kamat outlines a number of options, including anonymous testing elsewhere, and explains what happens if he tests positive. Boy tries to imagine the process, the waiting, the consequences, but can't — his head has begun to hurt again.

— At eighteen it's your decision, of course.

Boy looks over at Charlie, watching for the slightest reaction or indication of what he should do. But her face is a mask of stillness. He knows his own face is, too — a good cadet is calm no matter the conditions — but his insides are a soup of mismatched emotions.

— In your case, I can't recommend testing strongly enough. You're young and strong and would respond well to treatment even in a worst-case scenario. Besides, it's far better to know.

It isn't the time, Boy thinks. He thanks the doctor in the beigest of non-committal terms, telling him that he's been helpful and thanking him for his time and advice. He gets up quickly, a brief aria of pain behind his eyes, grabs his pack, and begins to walk out.

— Wait a moment, Kamat says.

The doctor gets up, walks over to a desk in the corner of the room, grabs a shiny pamphlet from a wall display, and thrusts it into Boy's hand without asking.

— We don't do the tests here — this is a list of facilities where you can go.

Boy doesn't say anything but walks out of the clinic, through the doors and waiting room and into the cooling night.

The pain comes back in full on the bike ride home, along with the tightness and swelling of stitched, stretched skin. In his own neighbourhood, one of the many faceless, master-planned communities in the east end of the city with too many cul-de-sacs to count, the streets and sidewalks are quiet. *Dead quiet, in fact,* he heard Misty say on the phone to potential clients curious about living in Stoney Creek. *Your home, your castle, safe and secure.* Which means no one is looking around or at their neighbours, either, so no one sees the families who lock their doors and retreat into chemical and alcohol security. Cars and SUVs get tucked into garages before their well-fed drivers sink into couches in front of large flat screen TVs. No one sees the gangly teenager pedalling slowly by, his orange bicycle oddly bright in the jaundiced street lamp glow.

CHAPTER 3

Boy's bedroom faces southeast, so the morning sun is usually his to enjoy as much as he wants. He's always been a morning person, first up and eating breakfast, showering, getting ready for each day. Able, almost, to chart the restless sunrise, late in winter, early in summer. Wake in darkness for school, brightness for vacation, never needing an alarm. Lately, however, it's a declining form of enjoyment, supplanted by the urge to sleep in. The halo of sun around his curtains tells him it's late. His mouth is dry; his head aches dully. The dressing has loosened, so he presses it back into place. It won't be long before the adhesive comes loose again. Once the tack is gone, it never comes back.

When he arrived home, he was tempted to leave the bike beside the garage overnight. The motor on the garage door opener burned out ages ago, so lifting it manually is hard. It's out of sight and therefore easily ignored, so Nick hasn't fixed it. He tried to take over Corny's role as leading man in Misty's maintenance production of *If It's Visible, Fix It*, but lately he's been missing performances, dropping lines. The broken light beside the driveway.

The garbage blown into the gardens. Before the accident, even though Charlie and Sarah were best friends, Nick and Misty had never met. A few weeks later, a drunk Misty admitted she snuck into Sarah's funeral, said how bad she felt for Nick, a fire-fighter and single parent. A few months later, she began calling him, disappearing in the evening for drinks. *He's sad, too,* she'd say when she left Boy alone. *He needs me and I need him.* Nick arrived one bright Saturday with a carful of clothes and never left. Misty brought all of Corny's things to the garage, piling the boxes against the wall next to the orange bicycle, leaving them to grow musty.

Corny's tools, hung with care on the pegboard above the workbench, were the only items Misty hadn't boxed up. *That way,* she said, *Nick can leave his own at his place.* The place Nick rents out but refuses to give up just in case, Boy suspects, his thing with Misty disintegrates. But Nick never goes into the garage, so Boy has the tools and the space to himself. The grief counsel-lors brought in by the school district spoke at length about the adjustment that not having a father would be, especially after the trauma of losing a sibling. It was. For all his faults, stoned, drunk, or both, Corny never left jobs unfinished. Boy missed how he and Charlie were allowed to hold the tools. So the bike always gets put away. Always. Even if it means an awkward entrance through the side door. Even through stitches and a concussion.

It took a long time to fall asleep. A couple of Tylenols answered the pain, but the mental remnants of the day were much harder to chase away. His stomach a constant presence, nausea giving way to a deep, empty hunger. He lay in bed, drifting in and out of fitful sleep — the kind you aren't sure happened at all — with images of the RMC letter, everything stopping, the man at the rocks, the clinic flashing through his consciousness like a cheap strobe light. This morning, he carries one certain thought. He has to go back to the rocks, damn the headache and stitches and concussion and nausea. The man has to be nearby. Creased and clean, like he had just gotten dressed and walked out his front door. And you don't bring bandages if you're burying bodies.

There are questions to answer.

He sits at the edge of the bed for a long moment, eyes closed, waiting for the throbbing to subside. Finally, he gets up slowly, gingerly, and puts on the jeans and shirt he was wearing last night. Leans a little too hard on the stairway banister for support as he goes down.

Misty is already at the table. An old music video, gaudy, grainy, is playing on the small TV-VCR combo on the counter. On mute. Images of pastel things and baggy clothes. On the table in front of her, a cigarette balances on the edge of a half-finished plate of smeared beans, greenish eggs, and congealed bacon. What she and Corny used to call Breakfast for Supper. Greasy pots and pans on the stove, a carton of open eggs, shy three, and a package of bacon leaking brine onto the counter. The smells of old food and cooking, mouldy dishes, the distant burnt-rope tang of smoked marijuana. She holds up a torn envelope and a sheaf of papers.

— What the hell's this?

She throws the papers on the table. The crest of the federal correctional service is visible at the top. Strange barcodes. Bureaucratic numbers. Stamps and signatures. Approvals in red. He signed and sent the forms off on his birthday. He looks at the postmark.

— They arrived months ago, he says. You kept them from me for —

— I was waiting for the right time.

She picks up her cigarette, taps the ash onto the plate, and takes a long drag. Stares at the glowing tip a long moment. Exhales. Watches him closely as she drops the butt into the dregs of orange juice at the bottom of a smudged glass.

— Why do you want to see him?

— Because you never took me.

— But he —

— Because I can now. On my own.

She frowns and reaches for the other glass on the table, a tumbler with ice and clear liquid. She closes her eyes as she drinks, breathing in deeply through her nose, the juniper cooling her sinuses. Gin ritual. As precious as sniffing a cigar or nosing fine wine. The glass of Bombay Sapphire on the rocks is pristine, the ice barely melted, without even a fingerprint marring its surface. For an instant, her face relaxes, reducing the crow's feet beside her eyes and worry lines cut into her forehead. Almost revealing the dark-haired, fair-skinned beauty she once was, whose smiling face adorns bus benches around the eastern end of Hamilton, her green eyes bringing in clients who entrust her to find and sell their homes. A stunning photo, a decade old, of a different woman.

— I suppose it's too late to ask you not to go. For my sake.

Boy laughs, harsh and incredulous. The emotion births a fresh nova of pain behind his eyes. He brings a hand up to his brow, cool against the skin.

— What happened to your head?

He thinks about lying — reality would be a strange truth to offer — but she isn't really asking. More reflex at the sight of the bright white dressing. He waves away the question. She doesn't press for more details.

There's a crackling sound from the baby monitor on the counter. An old unit moulded in a mystery shade of green. Frayed cords. Fried battery. Always plugged in, the cord and transformer hazy with dust. Boy's eight-month-old half-brother Jason — Jay — must be awake, although the sound is impossible to identify as a whimper or gurgle or coo. Boy gives Misty a look she doesn't see.

— You didn't get the new monitor yet?

— He's fine, she says.

— How hard can it be? Jump online, spend a few bucks — you don't even have to go anywhere. It's not like you can't afford it.

— I said he's fine —

— How can you know? How long has he been awake? Is he hungry?

— I've done this before.

— You'd never know.

She takes another sip, laughs.

— Next you'll joke about Nick not being the father —

— That's not what I —

— No, go right ahead. He does. Often. He —

— Jesus, Misty, listen to yourself. Think about someone else, for once.

— Oh, I do.

— Jay, for instance. Remember him? Your *baby* son?

Boy makes a show of throwing up his arms and storming out of the kitchen, although she probably doesn't notice. For a few minutes, seeing Misty awake has allowed him to think about a quicker departure, but only briefly. Baby Jay has become as much his responsibility as hers and Nick's. Why should today be any different?

Nick's snoring, a thunder escaping through the chest, makes its way into the hallway through the open door of the master bedroom. Nick is on top of the covers wearing only his boxer shorts. He walks around the house like that sometimes. *If you don't like it, don't look at it*, he says. Boy can't ignore the snoring, though. Incredible volume. A sound veil to step through with Jay wailing on the other side.

Boy's frustration evaporates as he opens the nursery door, replaced by the ineffable feeling brothers have for their baby siblings. Heartbreak, too, Jay's hungry cries have become desperate gasps, like he's trying to feed on his own dry breath. On his back, tiny fists clenched, knees to his chest, eyes screwed shut with the injustice of it all. Bright pink gums. His first two teeth, defiantly white, on full display. Boy scoops him up, ignoring the wet sleeper soaking through his own shirt, and holds him close. He whispers into his brother's ear. Jay melts into Boy's shoulder, as though he could nuzzle his way under the skin there.

Hitching breaths.

Sniffles.

Peace.

Boy lays Jay on the change table and peels off the sleeper, holding him in place with one hand while opening the cupboards and drawers. He finds a barely gnawed teething biscuit and places it in a chubby hand. A distraction against hunger and wandering hands. He finds an old package of wipes, dried with age, and a diaper that might be unused. Jay's diaper is a blown-out mess. Boy mutters an apology as he tries to clean up. Jay watches Boy's eyes and giggles, oblivious to the chaos below. A useful gift, being able to switch between emotions this way, as though the pain never happened, and the only things that matter now are enjoying his big brother and feeling clean again.

— You look good, Cadet, Boy says.

Jay smiles and wiggles in reply.

— Ba-ba-ba-ba-ba, he says.

That's right, Boy thinks. *Thrive. That's how you take control.*

Boy carries Jay down to the kitchen. Misty has retreated to the sofa in the family room, drink freshened, hand over her eyes. He buckles Jay into his reclined feeding seat, locates a jar of baby food in the cupboard, and puts together a bottle of formula. Pushes away the thought of days when the only food Jay receives is what he gets from his big brother in the morning and evening.

— We're running out of baby food, he calls over to Misty. Are you doing any showings today? Can you pick some up?

No answer from the couch. Between small spoonfuls of pureed apricots — there's little mess today, almost as though Jay knows how important each bite is — he starts a grocery list. He writes as neatly as he can. Has to make sure it can be read.

— Can Nick do it if you won't?

— You know he hates shopping for the baby. Can't you do it?

How can anyone hate anything to do with babies, Boy wonders. Nick's little girl died in the crash, too, so hesitation to bring another tiny human into the world is understandable, but *hate*? Surely there's enough goodness built into everyone to dismiss that toxic idea. Shared blood between him and Jay must mean something even as he sleeps his responsibilities away like a hangover.

— I have other plans, Boy says.

— Heading up to Millhaven, no doubt.

Caustic. He doesn't respond. No, his first trip north to the penitentiary will have to wait a few days. The rocks are calling much louder, echoes of that guy appearing, stopping — stopping what? Motion? Sound? Time? Hard to imagine. Precarious ideas leaning from their foundations, sand drip-towers built too high, too close to the waves.

— Can I leave him with you?

— Sure, you can. He's my son.

Boy glances at Misty's glass, distantly blue.

— Look, if I do the groceries, can you slow down until I get back?

— Just go. I'm fine. I'll get some food later.

— Misty —

She lifts the glass to her brow in a mock salute, the ice clacking against the sides.

— Last one, sir. Promise.

Boy cleans Jay up and brings him into the family room. He studies his oblivious mother with a serious gaze. Boy heads upstairs to shower, checking the weather on his phone. It's cold, the skies unpredictable. He'll need layers. The rocks front a lake large enough to make its own weather. And grocery stores are always cold. Misty and Nick won't remember. Saturday is just another day to forget about clocks and inconvenient sons.

CHAPTER 4

Boy shrugs his collar up around his ears. The wind is strong across the whitecapped lake, biting his ears and cheeks as it rushes up the rocks and inland. He wishes he'd brought a hat. His hair is longer than he likes it but not long enough yet to do much against the morning cold. It hasn't taken long to reach his ears, and he has to fight the urge to get a haircut whenever he catches sight of it in the mirror. He has no idea when that desire will fade. He could just keep it buzzed, but there's something about not having to. As a cadet, he always chose a step beyond the regulations, clipped to the scalp on the sides and back, never more than an inch left on top. Younger cadets inevitably followed his lead, even those whose parents forced them to enroll — they arrived hoping to keep their shaggy mop-tops and hat-head chic, wisps and bunches sticking out from under their wedge caps like scarecrow straw. But they almost always fell in, and quickly. *You look like shit. Have some pride in yourself!* Yelled in the cadets' ears during inspections.

— Did you see where he went?

East.

Charlie is in her spot down the rocks, paler in the sunshine. If that's possible, assuming the light even touches her. The hair drawn back into the tight bun draws out her face, making it look even thinner. Female cadets have more regs dedicated to their appearance. Hair short or long, bun, single- or double-braided, curled or straight, a single pair of stud earrings allowed.

Charlie loved her long hair, practising braid and bun leading up to that first parade night. Sarah taught her how to put her hair up, and Charlie had mastered the bun for the first parade, hoping to impress, along with her new but ill-fitting clothing. It held, too. Through the crash. Extraction. Journey to the hospital. Declaration.

Charlie was killed on an autumn night, late in the season, when most of the leaves had fallen. Boy remembers bare branches brushing against the family room windows. He wanted to hear about her first night as a cadet, so he made restless camp on the carpet to wait, sprawled out, surrounded by a spray of comic books. Misty had just started into her second drink of the night when the doorbell rang, accompanied by a firm but soft knocking on the front door. The two police officers on the front step were big men straining the seams of dark uniforms, their caps under their arms tiny and ridiculous. They spoke to Misty in low voices. *Thank you, but we'll drive ourselves*, she said. *Boy, get your shoes on — we have to go.* She wouldn't tell him where they were going, just pushed him towards her car. She wouldn't answer any of his questions even as she half-dragged him through the pale hospital corridor. She left him alone in the waiting room with an officer while she was escorted by the other officer and a tired-looking doctor through a double set of automatic doors.

A few minutes later she came out again and one of the cops asked if she'd been drinking at all that night, but she lied and said no. The guy nodded and didn't push it, said he had to ask. She remained quiet on their way back to the car. *It was perfect,* she said after closing the car door behind her. She stared through the windshield at the parking garage's concrete wall. Her hands rested in her lap. *What was perfect,* he asked. She said, *Everything else was* — but couldn't finish, her chest heaving, her hands taking hold of the wheel so tightly he thought maybe she could rip it from the dashboard. Then she stabbed her keys into the ignition, started the car, and drove out of the parking garage. A single tear ran down her right cheek, its shine rising and falling with the regular rhythm of passing street lights. He was ten and scared and watching his mother so closely he didn't remember until they got home and he saw the comics on the floor. He asked, *Mom? Misty? Where's Charlie? Where's Corny?* She sat down beside him. *Your sister is dead.*

All the other details came later. Sarah and the other driver dying, too. Corny thrown into a holding cell while the justice system started grinding away at a drunk driver who had killed three people. Some understanding of grief, about why Misty had obsessed about Charlie's appearance. As though Misty could bobby pin her sad thoughts to herself, to keep them from escaping like stray hairs.

Boy watches his sister. Such an unremarkable thing, a hairstyle, even one so severe and contained. And yet —

— Just get on with it, he tells himself.

And yet you haven't moved an inch.

Making excuses, then. *Excuses are like assholes, numpty — everyone has one.* A favourite epithet to dump on cadets who tried to justify failure. He jams his hands deeper into his pockets and walks past Charlie, almost to the end of the rocks. He's never had a reason to venture farther than this. He stops, pulls out his phone, and opens the satellite map, zooming in as much as possible. The map adjusts itself to face north, like he is, the little blue dot marking his location obscuring the rocks, resting on the boundary between lake and land. The Niagara Escarpment cutting east to west. Parallel ribbons of the divided QEW to the south. Vineyards and orchards to the east. Anonymous suburban neighbourhoods. This abandoned land, completely green. An undulating shoreline with notched mouths of streams, close to the highway. The satellite shots must have been taken on a late summer afternoon, the foliage full, the shadows long. Plenty of invisible places.

He thinks about calling Mark. On Saturdays, Mark is always at the squadron first thing, and with Boy's WO1 billet needing to be filled, he'll be there even earlier. In November, the CO asked Boy's impressions of a few of the senior NCOs. Boy made it clear that Mark should be at the top of the list. Pulling for him as hard as he dared without risking the old man's anger — after all, he still needed the recommendation letters the squadron's command staff had enthusiastically offered.

What would you tell him, anyway? Would you invite him here?
— No.

He isn't ready to share this spot with anyone. But, then, isn't he already sharing it with Charlie and now the stranger? Why not his best friend, his partner in command, his most trusted NCO? Because it's his secret. Secrets change when they find their way into other ears and along other tongues.
— This is on me.

He steps across the indistinct threshold between stone and rusty soil. The rocks don't *end*, of course. Somewhere below, this dolostone meets up with that of the escarpment, the continuity of geology. The quick erosion of the shale giving the outcropping its stubborn profile along the water and the ground beneath the escarpment its reddish hue. Winterbare sumac bushes dominate this part of the shoreline, growing thick almost right to the water's edge. Searching the scrub is slow and difficult, requiring a number of detours to the beach just to find a way through. Everything close to the water is wet from the waves, continuous and loud against the stone beach. Small rocks and hunks of driftwood challenge his footing.

His intuition seems enough to guide him along. Indirect sight, like blurring your vision to figure out a pattern you can't quite see. *Listen to your instincts, for sure,* his first powered flight instructor said, *but trust your instruments first.* He looks at the map one more time, steps onto the beach, and sees the shore bend to the right past another thick stand of brush. The inlet, perhaps a couple hundred feet wide, narrows quickly to a jumble of rocks that rises away from the water. There, the brush thickens, but the bare branches do little to hide the mouth of a wide concrete culvert. He stops for a moment, his stomach tight, feeling compressed, how he imagines a G-suit might feel, before stepping forward.

Everything stops again so abruptly that he stumbles. Wind. Waves. Traffic. The movement of the trees. A white pain forces his eyes closed for a long moment. When he finally opens them, he finds himself face to face with the man he came to see. But this time he looks less put together, with hollows under his eyes and the ghost of greying stubble along his jaw. He's gripping a stone so tightly the knuckles on his hand are white.

— Don't take another step. What are you doing here?

Boy is still too disoriented to speak, so he just holds up a hand. The man comes closer, the rustling of his clothes almost a roar. The stone is high, shaking. But he doesn't look angry. More desperate.

— Get out of here.

— Wait, I —

— Go away.

— Stop. Just stop. Please.

Then Boy has a thought. Redirect.

— I wanted to thank you.

The man's head tilts. Curious. Boy knows he won't throw the stone.

— Thank me? For what?

Boy points at the bandage on his forehead.

— When everything stopped, I fell. You bandaged me up while I was out.

— You were bleeding. I wanted you to go, so I —

He doesn't want you to go.

— You did it again, Boy says. How can you stop everything?

— It's not me.

— It has to be. Then, now —

— Get out of here. Please.

— Tell me how you do it.

The man tosses the stone aside. It clacks to the ground, again invisible among all the others, as the man turns away. Boy follows him to the mouth of the culvert. Which is full of things. Furniture. Clothing. Even a bookcase heavy with volumes, their colourful spines bright against the gloom.

— I don't really *do* anything, the man says.

— Well, what happens?

— It's just time.

The motion of the world begins again, the sounds thundering forward. Boy strains to hear the man's next words.

— Just time. And it stops for me when I need it to.

— That can't be.

The man shrugs and steps farther into the culvert.

Charlie has disappeared. Has she ever left him alone when he's away from the house? Boy can't recall. He follows the man inside. The man can't stop staring at Boy as he walks the length of the space. The concrete tube, which burrows under the QEW for perhaps eighty feet before abruptly ending at a pile of broken concrete and earthen fill, is eight feet high. The floor is flat and wide, the walls high, the ceiling smooth. Vault-like. Almost elegant, despite the impersonality of formed concrete.

— You've lived here a long time, Boy says.

The man frowns but doesn't reply.

And there's no denying that he lives in this cold space. A string of lightbulbs arches along the ceiling, each with a flared tin shield that blocks too much light from shining towards the lake. The bed and other furniture look dry and comfortable, unaffected by mould and moisture. Stacks of clothing on a low table: brand-new dress shirts, still in cellophane; khakis; a box of uniformly black socks; a bulk pack of white briefs. A square card table. Two chairs. No mess. Cluttered but clean.

— How — ?

— What? What's wrong?

— How do you keep things so nice and clean?

— Why wouldn't it be? Isn't a well lived-in space its own protection?

A strange tone in his voice. Wavering. Suspicious. Annoyed. As though Boy might have found something either to incriminate or embarrass him. Pride, too, concealed in the covering folds of his sharp questions. And why not? This strange place is immaculate: every angle measured and true, every stack piled perfectly, every surface dust-free. Remarkable that a subterranean retreat clad in cement would have no pebbles or dust, no particulate to irritate the throat. A minor miracle.

Like this whole area, too. He made a similar comment to Charlie the first time they found the loose bit of fencing and stood on the rocks. As though the builders of the adjacent communities had thrown up the fences at either end without caring or knowing what they were sealing off. A miracle that no neighbourhood kids have scaled the fence in search of new spots to drink, make out, smoke up. No shattered bottles, faded pop cans, brittle candy wrappers, used condoms. The culvert is free from cracks, probing root systems, slimy moisture seeping towards the floor. Minor miracle, indeed. The earth is always trying to break down what has been built and, in the end, always wins. This is why you clean your plugs and filters and fuel before even sitting in the pilot's seat; safety is in the assumption that everything has been dirtied, corrupted.

— The cement looks like it was poured yesterday, Boy says.

— I never had to worry about it.

— How long have you lived here?

— A long time.

The man becomes silent again, arms folded, contemplating Boy from near the mouth of the culvert. Boy walks towards him, feeling a cold gust of wind through his pant legs. The man shivers so quickly and violently Boy imagines he can feel it in his own muscles, and grabs a long down parka hung on a nail driven into the side of the bookcase. How cold this space must be in the winter, open to unpredictable elements from the lake. How ineffective the leafless brush in front of the entrance would be in blocking the wind. Boy's survival training tickles the back of his mind, measuring, calculating, the calories and other factors this homeless man would need to stay warm. But, then, could you really call a man with his own roof, bookshelves, and a carefully made bed homeless?

A long moment passes between them. Finally, the man shakes his head, mutters something foul under his breath, and moves towards the interior, pausing to straighten a small pewter swan on top of the bookcase then glancing at Boy to see if he has noticed.

— No one else's ever been here, have they?

— No.

— But how? Your stuff, the lights, you coming and going for years —

Boy catches himself. Another truly secret spot. Like his.

— I don't use the lights at night.

As though that could be enough.

— And you stop time whenever you go out.

— I don't know if it's time; that's just what I call it. And I told you, I don't do anything — it just happens. For me.

— There has to be a movement. A thought. An intent —

— An intent? Maybe.

— And everything stops.

— Yes.

— Sound, movement —

— Everything. The universe, I suppose.

— But not me.

— No, not you.

— Why?

— I don't know. I'm wondering, too.

Why he stopped himself from throwing the stone, of course. Curious about the gangly teenager appearing in a certain fenced-off area where no one had ever gone. Had he been watching Boy in anticipation of a first meeting, a meeting that did not go as expected? Forced to reach out when the teenager panics, falls, knocks himself out. Boy's stitches begin to itch, as though his wound is experiencing a flash of self-consciousness, too.

— What's your name?

— Mara. Father Mara, actually.

A quick response, perhaps more proof that the man had wanted to make contact.

— You're a priest, Boy says.

A shrug.

— Pastor, actually. Someone I met under a highway called me Father. And yours?

— Boy.

Mara gives a fleeting smile, quick as snapped fingers, and tilts his head.

— No, really. It's Boy. Misty always —

Mara nods, his whole bearing becoming more relaxed. The easing of tight springs.

— It's a good name.

Mara moves near the entrance. A naked wooden chair has been placed there, all alone, and Mara sits, looking at the white-caps on Lake Ontario. Boy would bet that this chair always faces the lake. There is another chair, all right angles and chipped paint in a garish green, tucked neatly under the card table. All the furniture is like that. Precisely placed for one person to make the best use of it. Ordered. Yet completely mismatched. A strange sort of balance. Unbalance, too. Claustrophobic. How solitary and lonely this place is. Only one person is meant to know it so well.

— What kind of name is Mara? I've never heard it before.

Mara takes a deep breath but doesn't turn.

— It's just a name.

No, it isn't, Boy thinks. *If you have that kind of name, you know about it.* An echo of the clinic doctor's words.

— Does it mean anything?

— Why do you need to know?

— Did someone —

— Stop asking me so many questions!

Mara's voice is low, acidic. His eyes are closed, fingertips digging circles into his temples. Boy falls silent. Boy shifts too, from brief discomfort to puzzlement to suspicion about why men seek out lonely places to dwell. Why priests can't stay where they want to stay. Why they run.

— I should go, he says, moving to the mouth of the culvert.

— No, wait. Stay. We can — we can —

Mara seems to run out of words, so he shifts in the chair and sweeps an arm towards the back of the culvert. He tries to smile, but his teeth seem far too white, his eyes too eager. There was an officer in the squadron in Boy's first year who had teeth so white they were either fake or irrationally cared for. An airline pilot with odd schedules, he came to parade nights unpredictably. He gave lectures on wind shear, humidity and frangible materials, how the compass was never one hundred percent accurate on its own, its deviation measurable. A short man, he would eschew the lectern and stand next to the desk, removing his uniform jacket and draping it over the chair. His hands never left his pockets, never stopped moving. He made them sit at attention for the entire class. Not knowing if he would be there was a strange dread they all felt. There was rejoicing when he was asked to leave, even though they had to retake the lectures; it was assumed nothing was learned. Mark and the other younger cadets still joke about it with words like *creepy, sex fiend, weirdo, pedophile,* and the dozens of other terms that have become far too easy for kids to use.

Mara sees Boy's expression and lowers his hand.

— What's wrong?

— Nothing. I have to go.

— All right.

Boy walks out, down the jumbled stones and back through the scrub. By the time he gets his bicycle from its hiding spot, Charlie has reappeared. She stays with him as he rides to the grocery store and parks the bike in the rusty bicycle rack, moves straight to the baby food aisle, and fills the basket with jars and pouches. Jay prefers the sweet vegetables — carrots, squash, peas. Diapers are next. Number threes, an upgrade: Jay has been testing the limits of the twos. Selecting baby food is involved enough to make him forget about those final moments in the culvert. But they come back as he walks towards the checkout line. What Mara's words might mean. Why the priest hides. Boy left and the feeling of danger had passed by the time he had his bike on the road. Here in the store, only minutes removed, he's back to the curiosity that took him to the rocks rather than being filled with fear. This gives him pause.

— Why am I not more worried?

Do you think you should be?

— I'm not sure.

He nearly collides with a man at the tail of the checkout line holding bags of oranges, lemons, and limes. Startled, the man turns and pulls an earbud free. From behind, the guy looked young, perhaps in his early twenties, but his hand, throat, and face are a constellation of liver spots, his skin sallow. Tinny, high-tempo music bleeds from the small white speaker.

— I'm sorry, what?

— Nothing, sir. Just talking to myself.

The man grunts, replaces his earbuds, and turns back to the conveyor.

Boy never asked Misty for cash, so he pays with his debit card, also buying two bags to balance on his handlebars for the ride home. About halfway, at a busy stoplight, he and the traffic are forced to wait while an old man and his walker inch their painful way across the intersection. Without realizing it, he begins to watch for everything to stop again.

CHAPTER 5

Boy wants to tell Mark everything. It's what happens when you encounter the impossible and you have so few in whom to confide. He watches the other high school students bounce between the cafeteria's collapsible tables and flimsy chairs, and he feels apart. From all of it. Gossip. Study. Drugs. Social media. Trivialities. But this isn't new; he's always been a non-person here, the tall, strange kid who sometimes wears a uniform on days other than Remembrance Day. Easy to ignore while the drama plays out among the rest of them. Not invisible, but maybe blurred against the background. He feels old. Would Mark understand? Mark, Boy would say, you know how time is a constant, that death is permanent? What if I told you they're all moveable? Could you imagine?

Imagine.

Boy skipped all his classes yesterday. Misty was nowhere to be found when he woke up. Jay had again filled his diaper and then some and ate a double portion of everything at breakfast — cereal, formula — like he knew a draught was coming. An hour later he needed to be put down again. Boy stayed. Changed and fed and napped him all day. Universal truths: babies must not be allowed to starve, sit in their own filth, or be kept from good sleep. It's supposed to be built into a caregiver's genes. Boy tried to pull up schoolwork from the school's online portal, but instead found himself surfing parenting sites, trying to calculate due dates. Conception has a certain timeframe, but there's no way to know when the first day of Morgan's last period was. A mid-August to mid-September baby. Morgan giving birth either in the middle of his move to Kingston or his first weeks at RMC. He was sick then, dashing to the bathroom and kneeling in front of the toilet, dry heaving until his stomach felt like knotted rope. He went back online and found the contact page of Morgan's CAP squadron website, as he's done a dozen times since receiving her letter. She never asked for help or for him to be involved, so he hasn't written back. The return address on her envelope too intrusive, contacting the squadron unnecessarily formal. He hasn't called. He doesn't know if he's being respectful of her privacy or neglectful towards the unborn baby.

He glances at the digital clock above the cafeteria doors. Lunch is nearly finished. He begins to gather his things when he sees Mark sneaking into the far end of the hall, heading straight for the serving line. He'll fill his tray with greasy and sugar-filled things, smear them with ketchup and hot sauce, and somehow swallow all of it. He watches his friend load up at the condiments counter. Then Mark looks over and cringes. Caught.

— Hey, Boy says when Mark sets down the tray.

— Hey.

— Just because I won't eat that shit doesn't mean I won't be seen with you.

Mark gives a pained little smile as he dunks a deep-fried zucchini stick into a sauce with the consistency of bad pea soup and stuffs it into his mouth. Frowns.

— Cold, he says.

— They've probably been sitting there since breakfast.

Small talk as camouflage. Mark grunts but doesn't say anything more, unusually intent on his food. Fascinating. Boy had even dropped in a mild profanity, certain that Mark would comment. Mark, new to the squadron, had been placed in Boy's flight and idolized him even though Boy was only a few months older. *You don't swear — all the other NCOs swear like sailors*, he said the first time they had lunch together in the cafeteria after realizing they went to the same high school. Most of their fellow students would be surprised to know Mark is a senior and decorated cadet NCO. He never wears a uniform away from the squadron, unlike Boy, who felt duty-bound to wear the colours. Mark is good contrast, a nuclear child, elder brother to a pigtailed sister, son to doting parents with clean smiles. Into sports and girls and working out and making Mom and Dad proud. Boy's the fragmented one. Used to being ignored. The weird kid who's into all that cultish, paramilitary stuff. With a drunk, murdering father doing time and a mother who shacked up with the first man who showed interest. Mark doesn't care about any of that, choosing friendship and scorn by association without complaint. He sticks. Boy's growth spurt in grade eleven mitigated the physical challenges and bullying — six-foot-two and skinny is still six-foot-two — but not the whispers. Mark carries enough extra weight that no one pushes him around.

Boy digs into his pack, pulls out the letter, and slides it in front of Mark. His friend reads the note without comment.

— So that's what all this is about.

— All what?

— Your fucked-up school year, all the skipping you've been doing, the tanked assignments.

— Well —

— Pretty low, using your baby brother as an excuse.

— That's not true. Misty's away a lot, and —

— And yet all the teachers still think you walk on water. Every last one.

— They don't, believe me. What do you think I should do?

— Seriously? You're asking me after —

He stops, looks down at the table.

— After what?

Mark shakes his head, lifts his chin at the clock above the door, its digits glowing redly.

— You should get going, he says.

— What about you?

— I'm not going.

— What? Mark Anderson, Mr. Perfect Attendance, going rogue?

— You just don't get it. Go to class, Warrant.

— What's going on?

Mark pushes the greasy plate around the tray. A moment passes.

— I didn't get it, he says.

— Get what?

— The promotion. CO thinks I'm not ready.

Boy sits back. That hurts. Mark must be as devastated as Boy himself would be. If the CO said he isn't ready, the decision will have been passed down. The colonel tells the major, who tells his captain, who tells the lieutenant. A few months ago, the lieutenant would have told Boy, then the most senior NCO and Mark's immediate superior. Boy wishes he could have been the one to tell his friend. Now the entire chain questions Mark's readiness. Which will follow him around for the next year until he, too, resigns. *Isn't ready* so often meaning *never ready*.

Mark looks him in the eye.

— You must have told the old man the same thing.

— What? No way — I pulled hard for you.

— He'd rename the squadron after you if he could. You must have said something.

So this is why Mark wasn't at their table at the start of lunch. Why he tried to sneak away.

— No way, Mark. I recommended —

— Stabbed in the back by your best friend. How shitty is that?

Mark is bitter enough to spit. *Come on*, Boy thinks, *get past this: you'll see I had nothing to do with it*. Mark continues to stare him down, his face clouded. Boy is suddenly angry with life's unpredictable path, how everything else keeps getting in the way.

— Think what you want, he says. I pulled for you.

— You're full of shit, McVeigh.

— And you're not the only one with problems.

He stands and snatches his books from the table, ignoring the surprise on Mark's face. Walks away.

— Fuck you, Mark says to his back.

Charlie moves beside him. Boy won't look at her — her face's neutrality will just make him feel worse. Already feeling guilty for the outburst, weighing his pride against turning around and apologizing.

I don't swear, Boy thinks as he passes under the clock. *I won't.*

Mark's empty spot has been filled by a transfer student who appeared just after the Christmas break. Kyle. He daydreams, hunched over a binder filled with untouched paper, his subconscious habits revealing themselves. At this moment, a pimple on his scalp, pinched and worried with one hand, fingers licked clean. If he'd arrived two years ago, he'd have been called husky and shunted to the JV football squad as a linesman. Now he's just fat and bored. Spends his time trying to get noticed by an indifferent senior class. He tried out for the rugby team a few weeks ago and was cut in the first round. A humiliation multiplied by every set of eyes witnessing the last painful lap of the endurance test on the track, every drop of vomit splashed across the coach's shoes. Every smartphone recording the run, every hit to the remixed and slow-motion video uploaded to the web. Boy had no idea about any of it until a few days later when he corrected Kyle on a point of chronology in the middle of Mr. Essère's history class. *Piling on the embarrassment,* Mark said at the time. Now Kyle singles Boy out for a strange kind of torment, dull mischief, knocking books and things out of his hands, bumping into him in the hall. Comic and cliché all at once — the fat kid trying to bully the beanpole — if it wasn't so annoying.

Mr. Essère, a short, balding teacher with a particular fetish for demonizing the Catholic church, has decided to take the class back to the early Canadian history they learned in middle school. His diversions from the curriculum are legendary. His eyes are always wide open, his eyebrows high, and what little of his hair remains is wispy and untamed. Like an absent-minded university professor who napped too long in the wrong department meeting and somehow ended up teaching high school. Boy hasn't thought about terms like Upper Canada or voyageur in years, but a new book on the subject has Essère all worked up, waved around like scripture as he paces and sermonizes. There is a tense moment when a girl asks if the material will make it into the final exam. Essère stops mid-wave and glares at her, like he's thinking what a lovely mark the heavy hardcover would make between her bright, keen eyes. The bell eventually cuts him off, preventing him from assigning homework. The class leaves, spilling gratefully into the hall. Essère asks Boy to stay back a moment, follows the last student to the door, closes it. He sits behind the desk and produces a sheaf of papers. Boy stands and waits, pack slung, hands in his pockets.

— Do you recall the surprise quiz I gave a couple of weeks ago?

A silly question. You don't forget quizzes, especially surprise ones with essay responses. Ones based on readings you didn't do. Ones where Boy could have piled on enough vague material to squeak out a pass, had he not stopped writing precisely four words into paragraph number two. After a weak introduction.

— Sure, Boy says.

Essère pages through and pulls out a single sheet. Hands it over.

— Not your best work, I think you'd agree.

— Yes, sir.

— I haven't marked it. I wanted to see if there's anything you needed to tell me.

An opportunity for mercy. But the truth is so simple and complete — it was a failing effort of the purest kind — that even the possibility of a lie is as alien as a far-off planet. He fingers the bandage on his forehead, now just a self-adhesive plaster that doesn't quite match his skin tone, worrying an edge that has come unstuck.

— Something to do with your new accessory?

— No, sir, I just didn't do the readings.

— Surely you could have written more. You had the entire class period.

— I had nothing to write.

Essère leans back, the old chair squealing in protest, and folds his arms. Says nothing. Waiting for Boy to grab hold of the mercy bar, dig out the old family difficulties chestnut. A little reedy voice goads him to grab it. Drunk mom. No-good dad. Baby needing big brother. Unprotected sex. Unmade decision regarding STI testing. Teenage daddyhood.

But Boy, tired and unwilling, just waits. The teacher sighs.

— You're not giving me much to work with here.

— Is that all, sir?

— How are you doing in your other classes?

Boy opens his mouth to speak, once, twice, but closes it. Moves his eyes around the front of the room. The walls and bulletin boards are bare. An occasional yellowed bit of tape and greasy dot of blue-tack remain, but even Essère's photographs are gone. Rectangles of slightly less faded paint, the faintest of dust outlines from the pictures that had been there the longest. The teacher's desk is as cluttered as ever but somehow Boy knows that all the drawers have been emptied of their ancient stationery, rusted paperclips, capless pens, stashed memories. The new airiness in the room and the bare walls seem to shrink Essère behind the desk. Diminished in this space. *Low*, he thinks. *The man looks low.*

— Are you moving?

The teacher glances at the bare walls.

— No, not really. The school is over capacity, so I can't have my own classroom anymore.

— Halfway through the school year?

— Not until September. But once I got thinking about it —

— You couldn't stop thinking about it.

— Right.

— I'm sorry — you've been in this classroom —

— Forever, it seems like.

— How does that make you —

— Uh-huh, nice try, McVeigh. We're talking about you here. Your other classes?

— They're fine.

Essère leans forward, the chair groaning in relief, and places his elbows on the desk.

— They're not, actually. Everyone has noticed your slide in performance this semester. We're all concerned.

A loaded question, then. The teachers, all rooting for the star pupil, the one who had it all lined up. Decorated cadet, leadership potential, stellar grades. A victory, helping align at least one promising candidate from this year's crop of misfits. Conversations come back to him — his teachers' underpaid, careworn faces only smiled, where the word chosen was *when* and never *if*. How quickly would his star status decay into the trite phrases that define disappointment? *Squandered his chances. Let his grades slip. Let opportunity get away. Didn't apply himself.* It would happen as quickly as it takes to glance away from an embarrassment. Toilet paper stuck to a shoe. Underwear tucked into nylons. An open zipper. Forgetting would take longer, but it was inevitable — you can't expect teachers to dwell on the bad ones when a new, shiny batch arrives every September.

— You can't afford to get a single zero in my class, Essère says. Not when you're so close to the end.

Old voices, old command. *Buck up, Warrant. It isn't their battle.*

— Well, aren't you going to say anything?

— Is that all, sir?

A pause.

— I suppose it has to be.

— Thank you, sir.

Boy heads for the door, Essère's disappointment cool on his back.

His first zero. Essère was right about the impact it would have on his class grade. The math of grading is simple, its weights and grades. A quiz doesn't weigh much on its own, as long as it has a mark, high or low. But a zero — a nothing in the truest sense — has improbable gravity, a black hole sucking the other marks down into it. Ms. Vos, his English lit teacher, had used those exact words a few weeks ago. A hard woman in her thirties for whom a failing grade is a just and fair result for slacking off, she used to be among his most vocal supporters. *A black hole, Boy, I'm not kidding,* she said to him. *You can see your marks plummet right there on the screen.* Her advice was to always hand something in, even if it's drivel. But her support extends only so far as the effort he is willing to put in — lately she has been at the low end of the cool spectrum.

He walks past Vos's room, which is a few doors down from Essère's, the narrow window above the door handle dark, reflecting the hallway light. She must have gone home early. His reflection flits across the narrow safety glass as he passes, a blink, too fast to catch without stopping. Which he'll do sometimes if he's alone, one backwards step at a time, just to see if he can frame himself before his backpack touches the lockers behind him. It never happens. The hallways are just too narrow.

He stops — something has changed — listening to the sounds of the school. The hum of industrial lighting above him. The distant echoes of opening and closing doors. Muted voices through wooden doors, the soft ocean roar of a student body contained.

Charlie.

She's not in her customary, indifferent position — behind, when he walks, somewhere beside him when he doesn't. He last saw her —

He rolls his eyes and turns back, exasperated, before catching himself. A strange thing, to be annoyed when a dead sister lags behind. Essère looks up, his red pen suspended above another student's best efforts, when Boy barges back into the classroom. Charlie has moved from her shadow at the back of the class and stands exactly where Boy had stood mere moments ago. Staring, her gaze indecipherable. The teacher puts down the pen, not looking particularly surprised to see that Boy has returned.

— Can I help you?

— No, I —

Talk to him.

— I did already, Boy says. It's no use —

Essère's expression stops him. There are methods to deal with the continual presence of dead loved ones, but only one that keeps others from thinking you're crazy. You don't talk about them with language that suggests you can see what might not be there. That you believe in that kind of thing. You don't tell the history teacher you've come back to fetch your dead sister who's standing a breath away from him. And you don't respond when she speaks.

— What's no use?

— Nothing, sir. Sorry to have bothered you.

Boy hesitates, though, watching her stare at his teacher. She was never afraid of staring. Especially at anyone different than her. Not around their subdivision, but there were ample opportunities to go where families didn't care so much about a good, scrubbed, proper image. Corny discharged himself from the military back in the mid-nineties when he met Misty, marching out of the army and into her life, into their mutual thirst for chemical escape. They always brought the kids along whenever they went into the city to score, giving Charlie the chance to stare. Gangs. Homeless. Colourful new Canadians. Endangered steelworkers and pensioners watching their east-end neighbourhoods change. Sometimes they'd make it as far as the city core, where need was on full display all the time. Baby brother Boy didn't care about what was outside, as he had his foul-mouthed sister for entertainment. *Damn, that woman is skinny! Where'd that guy get the fucking shopping cart? They're all black, Corny, all of them!*

Her staring was one of the few things about her Corny and Misty always reacted against. Too much generated attention. Good parents don't let kids stare, and parents caught away from the suburbs don't need to create memories. Their life was a careful production. Misty maintained her facade as the successful, go-to real estate agent with the clothes and car to match, drugs and real drinking happening only behind closed doors and windows. Corny, who worked odd jobs, followed her lead and remained invisible in their suburb. In the city they were protected by short memories and illicit trade, but the master-planned communities in the east of the city required a different sort of performance. Keep your house shut tight. Ignore your neighbours. Take the kids along when you go out — who knows how dangerous the nosy, pimply neighbour girl brought in to babysit could be?

He stands at the classroom door a long moment. Charlie doesn't budge. He steps into the hall just far enough to see if she follows. She doesn't.

Take the goddamn opportunity. You know he wants to help.

— You're welcome to stay, Essère says, amused, when Boy reappears in his doorway.

Why is she choosing now to act weird, he thinks. Ever since that first interaction with Mara, she's departed from her own routine, the normal, passive presence Boy is used to. Not quite comfortable, of course, but at least familiar.

— I had to come back. May I have a late slip for my next class?

— Because you never spend your spare period here, studying.

There's an unfamiliar twinkle in the teacher's eyes, as though he is thoroughly enjoying Boy's discomfort.

— I'm glad you came back, Essère says. It has to come from you, you see.

— Sir?

— Your extra credit, of course.

Essère launches into his prepared spiel. He's been waiting for this, of course, the project centring on an obscure rebellion in Upper Canada early in the nineteenth century. Boy watches him get worked up, standing and pacing as he describes what he hopes Boy will uncover. Halfway through, Charlie turns and moves out the door and disappears, waiting for him, he's sure, just out of sight. Boy listens as best he can, caught between his teacher's goodwill, his pride versus the shame of his own ineffectual efforts, and the ease with which he's being manipulated from all corners, presently alive and long dead.

I should have gone to the back of the line, he thinks. Students wait behind him, impatient to board the bus, to escape to wherever they go after school. Bunched up like pack animals, the boys slouched and grubby, the girls bright and chatty.

— How far out do you go?

— Barton and Fruitland, the driver says.

— Are there any buses from there —

— On or off, kid. I got a schedule to keep.

Boy apologizes and feeds the exact fare into the fare-box.

Charlie has situated herself atop the cowling above the wheel near the front door, sitting cross-legged and staring at the bulkhead behind the driver. Boy selects the first set of forward-facing seats, takes off his pack, and folds himself into a space designed for shorter people. After just a moment, he shifts to the aisle seat, hoping to stave off the familiar cramps known by the tall in a world of economical spaces. Doubly claustrophobic, his own body, everyone else's, all wedged in together. He hates this. He walked out to find Corny's bike vandalized, its airless tires pinched sadly beneath their rims, the paint job scored with a sharp object down to the steel frame. But kids who slash both tires on another kid's bike — and leave all the other bikes on the racks untouched — aren't thinking about convenience or personal phobias. Boy simply walked away, unable to deal with this latest injustice, the bike locked and bright and sad behind him.

A girl from his history class drops herself into the empty window seat, flashing a spark of a smile, uttering a low thank you. Like Kyle, she's new to the school, appearing without fanfare a few months ago. Never volunteers answers. Writes down everything Essère says. Boy half studies her features in his peripheral vision, trying to remember her name. Something Asian. She pulls out her phone and begins smashing tiny jewels that cascade from behind a menacing countdown timer at the top of the screen.

He pulls out his own phone and starts a text message. Abandons it. What to say? Mark will come around eventually, but Boy wonders how he'll take the news of his RMC acceptance. Mark will face his own application next year with a stain on his record. Indelible and malignant. Unavoidable. Damning. Like the members of the admissions committee will have developed tumours on their retinas.

The bus fills steadily, the students trundling on to their customary spots, a distinct pecking order. Status grows as you move to the back, the volume rising accordingly. Backpacks are never removed, not even in the seats. Gum, forbidden in school, is cracked with great enthusiasm. Swear words restrained all day are freed, savoured like the clashing teeth of first teenage kisses. Headphones for every pair of ears, phones in every hand, yet the conversation never ebbs.

A backpack thuds into his shoulder. A flaring of pain and a soundtrack of harsh laughter. Kyle makes a show of righting himself, having faked a stumble just to swing the pack at Boy. He raises his hands as he tries to elbow his way to the back, pushing younger students aside. A momentary victory in his battle for acceptance. But you can't just change the sociology of the bus with one gesture. The laughter dies quickly and he finds himself in a crush of bodies, stuck in a purgatory of grade tens and elevens. Boy tries to rub the pain away as it spreads, hot, from the starpoint of impact.

— Are you okay?

His seat partner asks this without taking her eyes from the streaming jewels on her screen. He feels bad for not knowing her name. Sympathy from almost strangers, or something like that.

— I'm fine, thanks.

— A walking cliché, right?

— Right, he says.

The girl frowns and goes silent, still fixated on her game. Boy can't find any words to say. Finally, the bus pulls away, carrying its load of everyone's hormones and dreams. Bright conversation fills the bus to capacity and sifts out through its windows and doors, a noisy overpressure. He's disappointed in himself for not finding anything to say to his new ally, another dropped chance at solidarity in the charged, too warm atmosphere. He hopes he feels better after he disembarks, that the long walk home will cool him down.

CHAPTER 6

When he gets home, he throws his pack into the closet and heads into the dark kitchen, pulling out his phone. *Just do it,* he tells himself. *Text Mark. You were an ass to him. Reach out. Apologize.* He taps out a quick text.

    — *sorry about what happened at the caf, buddy*

He puts the phone down on the countertop and stares at it, willing Mark to text back.

It lights up and buzzes, startling him despite his anticipation.

    — *nice to meet you*

By the time the bus made its turnaround at the old city hall at Jones Road, it was mostly empty. Only Boy, his seat partner, a goggle-eyed grade nine boy, and a couple of sleepy workers from Eastgate remained, disembarking in that stunned silence marking the end of the day. The girl almost bumped into him, absorbed in a heavy phone call from her father. His voice, tinny and strident, seemed to echo for a few moments after she ended the call. Boy asked if she was all right. *I'm okay,* she said. They found themselves walking together in the same direction. He introduced himself. She laughed and said she knew who he was. *I'm Shi*, she said, pronouncing it with a curious assonance, like the *sher* in sherbet but farther back along the tongue. She had to spell it for him. He asked about the phone call, and she explained that her father is a pastor establishing a new Chinese congregation in the eastern suburbs. He ordered her to play hostess for tonight's council meeting. She told Boy she hated to be taken away from her homework, but her eyes said there was more to it. Boy hadn't wanted to pry, so they talked about other things. They parted ways with a new comfort in their conversation, traded numbers, agreed to meet up sometime to study.

— *you too*

His stomach groans. He hasn't eaten since lunch. He rubs his eyes against the harsh glow of the screen, stretches, and turns towards the refrigerator. Stops. Something is different. He turns on the lights.

The kitchen is spotless. The counter gleams like it's been polished for a commercial. There are no unpleasant smells in the air. Even the appliances have been wiped down, now free from grease, fingerprints, the usual caked-on food. In the family room, too, every smudged glass, dirty plate, and junk-food wrapper has been tidied. He can't remember the last time he's seen these spaces so clean, and why would they be? Misty has eschewed every sort of visitor since Corny went to prison. Nick, too, folded himself into their lives without bringing anyone along, content to revel in the attention Misty gives him and the substances they use to escape together. Without thinking, he pats himself down as though for inspection, feeling for loose threads, unbuttoned pockets, before shaking it off.

He opens the fridge and finds a pizza box decorated in garish splashes of red and white, a folded note taped to the top.

I knew you'd hit the fridge first! Nick cleaned up a bit for our
anniversary — isn't he great?! He took care of everything! We've gone
out for the night!
  M.

A long moment passes where all he can do is stare into the
open refrigerator at the pizza box, stunned by an unexpected
rush of affection. A clean house. Actual foresight about his needs.
There is a sudden, internal gnashing of emotions, stalling and
ripped apart, like reversing the props at altitude and watching
the engines tear themselves away and plummet to the earth. He
imagines Charlie punching him on the shoulder, making his eyes
water. *Fucking wimp*, she'd say. *It's just pizza.* Boy takes out the
pizza, closes the fridge door, and sits down cross-legged with his
back against its cool white surface. Opens the box and inhales the
smell of burned pepperoni and greasy cheese. Starts eating while
staring at the kitchen from floor level without really seeing the
kitchen at all. How can the smallest of gestures shatter a person
so thoroughly? As though perspective is just a matter of finding
the right fast food in the right box at the right time.

Or maybe Charlie would be right. It really is just lukewarm
pizza. He's so tired. Life is tiring. He laughs, a little manic, a little
out of control. The gleaming kitchen takes in his laughter, hollow,
and does not reply.

Boy is in the front hallway a short while later, staring out the open
front door.

The late March sun is low, almost touching the roof of the
house on the other side of the cul-de-sac. Daylight savings has
purchased an extra hour at the end of day, but he'll still be making most of his trip in darkness. A large metal flashlight and

headlamp rest heavily at the bottom of his pack, along with a bottle of water and leftover pizza in tinfoil for Mara. He had decided earlier, before seeing his bike's slashed tires, that he had to go back to the place beyond the rocks. His plan — spurred on by the sense that the universe had sent him something probably best not to ignore — had been to get home, grab something from the cupboards to eat, and head right out. Which didn't happen. Meeting Shi had been an unexpected and welcome diversion, of course, and Misty's note, well, who saw that coming?

There's a noise behind him, soft and indistinct. He turns his head back towards the interior of the house. The sound again. Plaintive, not yet committed to a full cry. Not fully awake.

— You can't be serious, he says.

He closes the door, drops his pack, and heads upstairs. Jay smiles, recognizing Boy's familiar, silhouetted figure against the cracked yellow light of the doorway. He gurgles an enthusiastic greeting, sated by his late nap, oblivious to having been left behind. The pizza had been warm, so Misty and Nick's exit couldn't have been long before, but Boy was about to leave, too. He has to shake off the image of his brother waking up later in a darkened house with no one to respond. This can't have been the first time. He turns on the lamp in the corner.

— Hey, Plug. Did you have a good sleep?

Jay flutters and giggles, loving the attention. Not caring about being called Plug, the semi-insulting, semi-affectionate term NCOs use for younger cadets. He's figured out how to pull himself up on his own, his head and shoulders above the railing. Too big for the infant setting — the crib should have been adjusted months ago.

Jay reaches his arms out. Pick me up, big brother.

Boy pockets the phone and leans over, his foot striking something on the floor which skitters under the crib and against the wall with a plastic clatter. *Probably the broken baby monitor*, he thinks, lifting Jay from the crib and carrying him over to the change table.

Nick didn't get here in his cleaning frenzy. Old baby wipes litter the top of the table. A sodden diaper is wedged between the pad and the wall, almost spilling its cargo. The container of zinc oxide diaper cream lies open, a dried wipe stuck to a smear of cream on the edge. Boy shuttles Jay from arm to arm as he readies the change table, trying to create a clean space, and digs into a drawer for a clean diaper.

— Are you hungry? How about something to eat? Let's go to the kitchen and see what we can find for you, okay?

He scoops Jay up and heads downstairs. Jay holds tight, nestling against Boy's neck, trading with his big brother the sure warmth of carrying and being carried.

The cupboard is almost empty. He always stocks it in precise ranks, lining up the baby faces and cartoon images of food on every tiny jar. Only a single pouch of pureed vegetable-fruit medley remains at the back, fallen to its side like a forgotten casualty. The rest of the food jars he purchased just the other night are at the back of the fridge, pushed back by the ungainly pizza box. Open. Meats and vegetables with a spoonful or two scooped out. Every fruit down to the dregs. Jay must have been fussy about his food, Misty giving him bits of everything rather than balancing out the portions. He has no idea when they were opened, so there's no option but to waste them all. The bag is heartbreakingly heavy as he lowers it into the bins in the garage.

Jay's steady, babbling monologue doesn't let up for the entire walk to the supermarket. Boy leans into the stroller — a cheap one with small wheels and a plasticky seat — and lets his brother's voice chatter into the night, occasionally lost in the rush of passing vehicles. White noise against white noise.

It's cold, clear. There's still a sunset glow strung across the horizon yet the first stars are alive, bright against the gradient sky, orange to white, cerulean, cobalt, indigo. An easterly is pushing the haze from the steel mills away from Stoney Creek and towards the city, so reflections are sharper, lights brighter. The sounds are crisper, too. His breath is a yellow fog under the street lights. *Even the pavement shines a little*, Boy thinks. Charlie appears when they leave the house and goes with them, sometimes right behind, sometimes across the street, moving in parallel.

Boy stops, pulling on the stroller straps, checking the zippers and snaps on Jay's snowsuit.

— Almost there, buddy. Not long now.

There's an agreeable reply from somewhere beneath the layers.

As they enter the store, Jay is silenced by the heavy clunk and whir of the automatic sliding door. Boy smiles as he leans down to remove his little brother's tiny toque and mitts and unzip his snowsuit. Jay is mesmerized by the lights and bustle, his mouth hanging open at the bright palette of the produce section.

Boy tells himself he won't dwell on Misty's abandonment. Even though it would be easy to do. A simple matter of seeding resentment, grown like a crop, harvested when convenient. On the walk, he had glanced over at Charlie and tried to imagine the magnitude of her foulness in such a situation. Would she let loose at Misty, scalding her as thoroughly as she was capable, or would she wait to share it with Boy? He never saw Charlie curse their parents even when she was at her angriest — which was often enough — preferring instead to find Boy in his room and whisper her vitriol in the darkness. Forcing him to stifle his giggles in his pillow.

There's a light, startling pressure on his arm.

— Are you all right, young man?

A frail woman in a beige coat and clear rain bonnet stands next to them looking concerned. He and Jay are in the baby aisle, yet he can't remember having arrived. Charlie waits at the end, looking at the three of them without expression. Jay has flipped up his snowsuit's zipper tab into his mouth and is worrying it like a puppy. The shelves are full of baby food, busy and bright, a dizzying food festival of competing brands.

She must be a thousand years old.

Ha, he thinks. *Not that old.* But certainly old enough — there is almost no weight to her touch, like she has laid a white cotton parade glove on his arm instead of a hand. Her other hand is clamped to the handle of her wheeled walker, its brakes set, its aircraft-grade aluminum frame effortlessly bearing her nothing weight. Powder-coated in a surprisingly bold, space-age red.

— You were talking to yourself.

A reedy voice. Almost invisible.

— What did I say?

— Most of it was gibberish.

— And the rest?

A pause. She takes her hand back and releases the looped brake handles.

— Bad words I'm not comfortable repeating. But I wanted to make sure you were all right.

— Tell me, ma'am, I —

But she has already turned and walked away. He shakes his head and reaches for the baby food, piling the jars and packages on top of each other in the cargo basket under the stroller's seat. There is a brief flaring of pain behind the bandage on his forehead.

At the checkout at the front of the store, Boy rubs his left temple, trying to get at the pain, now a low ache migrating around his cerebrum, shifting whenever he gets near it. An after-effect of the fall, of course. But the blackout? Who knows.

There are only two registers open. The express checkout has a long, snaking line of college students and late-night snackers. At his register, he and a few other shoppers with fuller carts shift impatiently from foot to foot while an elderly gentleman at the front of the line insists on paying with coins. Remarkably, despite his nap, Jay looks as though he could drift off at any moment.

— It's Boy, isn't it?

Boy turns.

— I'm Dr. Kamat. From the walk-in clinic.

— Right. Hi.

Kamat is wearing jeans and a T-shirt under a down-filled coat. His small hands, skinny legs, and puffy coat make him look like a strange inflatable toy. He, too, has his phone out and is leaning on the handle of a full grocery cart.

— I'm sorry I didn't notice you sooner, Kamat says, stuffing the phone in his coat pocket.

— It's a slow line.

— How are you?

— Fine, thanks.

— And who's this? Kamat asks, nodding at the stroller. Your son?

— Jay. My brother.

A shadow flickers in the doctor's eyes, his head tilts a degree or two, and his eyelids narrow for an instant. Boy wonders about the look. Is it the familiar — oh, you're from *that* family, that's *your* dad — or more generically concerned? Perhaps another home situation where an eighteen-year-old fills the conveyor belt with baby food. Or doing the math between their ages. Where a brother slinks into walk-in clinics asking about STI tests. Who probably cut himself as an excuse to get there. Misdirection.

Blood camouflage. Kamat seems to catch himself, though, and shoos the expression away with another smile. The clerk crashes closed the cash drawer and begins scanning his jars. *Not quickly enough*, Boy thinks, pushing the stroller through. It takes him three tries to get his PIN number right on the keypad.

— Well, it was nice to see you, Kamat says.

— You, too.

Boy heads towards the open exit, moving through the open sliding door — which doesn't close behind them, like it's been propped open — and into the parking lot. Only a few cars dot the asphalt expanse, lonely against the acres of parking lines and cart corrals, a motley herd of metal horses huddled together for warmth. Jay is sleeping and heavy, the dead weight of innocent sleep, and Boy distracts himself from the awkward encounter at the checkout by avoiding the pavement cracks.

— Boy! Wait!

He stops and looks back towards the store. Dr. Kamat is running after them, his marshmallow coat open and bouncing around him.

— You forgot your debit card.

Boy takes his wallet out and opens it, running a finger along the empty card slot's ridge of leather.

— Your receipt, too. You left so quickly.

Boy accepts the card and receipt and slides them into the wallet.

— You left it in the chip reader, Kamat says. I said I'd run it out.

— Thanks. Where are your groceries?

— Still at the checkout waiting for me, I guess, he says, laughing.

But Kamat doesn't go back. He zips up his coat against the cold and puts his hands in the pockets. Looks intently up at the sky, now full dark, like the first star is his for the taking.

— You'll be all right?

— I think so.

Boy lays his hands again on the stroller's foam handle and takes a step towards home.

— More protein, Kamat says.

— I'm sorry?

— For your brother. I noticed that you had all fruits and vegetables in there. It's important to make sure he gets protein, too.

— All right, thanks. I will.

Kamat gives Boy another long look, as though he is waiting for him to say something. Boy waits, too. There's only a slight breeze and the darkness has brought down the temperature so their breath hangs in the air between them for a moment before drifting away. *The test*, Boy thinks, understanding. He wants to know. Boy is touched by Kamat's concern, but when there is no news to give …

Boy says nothing.

Finally the doctor, perhaps remembering his groceries, perhaps understanding, turns back towards the store, wishing them a good night over his shoulder. Charlie moves slightly aside so he doesn't have to walk right through her.

And good health, too. A doctor should wish you good health and a long life.

CHAPTER 7

The app on Boy's phone estimates that the walk to the rocks should take thirty minutes but it takes more than forty-five. He hates being late. Even when there's no one to chastise him about not accounting for baby brother time and stroller speed. Still, it's important to be precise. Hearing his own voice in his mind this time, standard response to cadet tardiness at parade night. *No one trusts the cadet who's always late, right, Numpty?* But who's watching? Who cares? Maybe this new lack of precision is appropriate, given his current status. Why mark the time when you're just suspended between everything?

At the start of the school year, to raise money for charity, the student council threw a carnival on school property. One of the city's steel mills had kicked in sponsorship money and publicity, so for a single day, the school was overrun with carney booths, rides, hemp-obsessed vendors, and food trucks scattered across the football field in a savoury sprawl. Boy volunteered his squadron to run the bumper balls, where kids were zipped into capsules suspended in the centre of large plastic spheres. Soccer balls thrown in, the kids charging at each other, eyes down, before being bounced away. Boy feels like that. Distanced from his life by bizarre plastic sinews. The motion of contact but not the impact, protected in some ways, helpless in others.

Misty and Nick never came home last night, foiling Boy's plan to present them with a dose of his most righteous indignation. He brought Jay into the house and changed him for bed, somehow managing to lever his limp, sleeping form through all the preparations without waking him. The new baby food remaining untouched downstairs.

From his stroller, Jay makes a series of sounds that might be an attempt at saying Mama. Boy kneels in front of the stroller with his back to the chain-link fence and tucks the extra fleece blanket around his brother's legs.

— Ba-ba, Plug, he says. Ba-ba. More like Boy, so I can come running.

You'd come running no matter what words he uses. Misty said I sure did.

True. But maybe Jay will say his half-brother's name before anyone else's. He reties the strings dangling beneath the comical ear flaps on Jay's favourite toque.

— There. Ready to go in?

A brilliant smile, cheeks carrying the blush of newly ripe apples, eyes watering from the cold. Of course he's ready. He loves his big brother with unquestioned and total trust. Boy still pauses a moment. Maybe this is a mistake. There are still too many questions about the strange man in the culvert. His gift, if you could call it that. He could do anything. Without consequence. Bringing Jay feels like he is delivering fresh game to the mouth of a wolf's lair.

You've thought this through, I imagine.

— He doesn't feel dangerous.

And that means what?

Exactly. It doesn't make sense that Boy should base any decision on such muddy logic. Acting on his instinct feels completely un-instinctual — a pilot always relies on his instruments — so even coming this far again is pulling at Boy's conscience. But he's still curious. Memories of their encounters nag at him. Tight, itchy, like the stitches on his forehead. He has to be here.

— He let me leave both times. Should mean something.

It might.

Might not, too.

He unbuckles Jay from the stroller and eases him into the chest carrier, a piece of Euro-baby-care probably as old as he is. Jay, starfished by snowsuit and strapping, tries to wave his arms and kick his legs but can't. He makes a few half-hearted, muffled objections before pacifying himself with a convenient strap-end. Boy collapses the stroller and hides it under the bush he normally uses for Corny's ten-speed.

His phone buzzes in his pocket.

— *where are you? what are you doing?*

He smiles. Mark wrestling with how far to carry his anger, knowing Boy didn't sabotage the promotion, deciding to reach out. A text from calculus class, hiding the phone under the table while the teacher drones on. Boy taps on the text box to respond, but stops. The little cursor blinks with impatient certainty. Unlike him. He puts the phone away.

Another good plan.

— I know, I know, he says.

He'll always just wait for you.

In a way, Misty and Nick's absence has made it easier to come. Clean exits are so rare. He lingers sometimes, helping out. Protective. Skipping school to care for Jay is a new kind of dropped stitch in their haphazard knit, though. Missing school at all, actually, and he knows Mark is worried. More echoes of the Washington trip. The final morning, before the long bus ride home, Boy mustered the cadets for a quick inspection. Distracted, exhausted, Boy had butchered his orders. Later, near the border, Mark tapped his shoulder, waking him from a fitful sleep, and asked him if he was all right. *I'm just tired, Sergeant — go check on your people*, Boy snapped. He never apologized. It cuts at him like a chipped tooth's edge draws the tongue.

He backs through the loose fencing, covering Jay's head with a protective arm, and walks towards the rocks. A light southerly blows around him, carrying the breathless roar of Toronto-bound traffic on the QEW. Almost warm. Teasing spring. Charlie remains outside the fence line, moving through the brittle grass, her loose clothing untouched by the wind. As present as a sculpture, yet as perplexing as the last dream of a long night. Along the shore, in the lee of highway and bush and rock, the lake is flat calm. Tiny waves form about fifty yards out, fleeting goose-flesh brushed about by the wind. When he gets to his spot on the rock, Boy steps carefully to the edge. Conscious of his new weight. The innocent shifting of a big brother's centre of gravity. Jay becomes still and he begins to pant, puppy gasps just loud enough to carry to Boy's ears. He smiles, imagining his brother's eyes and mouth wide open. The scale of what he is seeing for the first time. Without the words to express himself. Only big, wondrous breaths.

— You have to go. I don't want you here, Mara says.

His hands are a strange boxer's pantomime, loosely clenched and limp, like they're uncommitted to whatever fight lies ahead. *Firm up*, Boy thinks, remembering squadron gym days and a bored boxing instructor. *You'll break your hand*. Mara's eyes move from Boy to Jay. He takes a long deep breath, brow furrowed. Pondering, no doubt, another unplanned appearance, visited this time by a baby in a sling in addition to the gangly teenager. His hands dip slightly, his look softening.

— Do it again, Boy says. Stop time.

— No.

— I came back for this.

Mara turns back into the culvert, shaking his head before disappearing into the gloom. Boy, with a sidelong glance at Charlie for strength, follows Mara in. His eyes take a few moments to adjust. Mara is at the back, where a large bookcase partially obscures the fallen dirt and stones at the end, displacing the bed, which now lies to the side, parallel to the culvert wall. The bookcase is a simple piece, a cream-coloured laminate. Stacks of old books, cloth and leather hardbacks, rest on the floor.

— I said go.

— You don't want me to. I saw that the last time.

— You didn't see anything.

— I did. And now I'm here.

— The baby as leverage, I suppose.

— I just have to take care of him today.

— Your brother.

— Jason. Jay. We call him Jay.

— Where's your mother?

An instant of hesitation, as though he could possibly have a reason to hide this from someone like Mara. Someone so random. So disconnected.

— I don't know, actually. They just left.

— Who's "they"?

— Misty and Nick. Misty's my mom.

— Nick's your father.

— No.

Mara shakes his head and kneels in front of his books, moving them between piles.

— You have so many books, Boy says. Have you read them all?

Mara ignores him and begins filling the lowermost shelf. Right to left, an odd system. Undecipherable mutterings, just under his breath, accompany each book. *Talking himself through the process, maybe*, Boy thinks. As far as he can see, the stacks of clothing, supplies, and books he saw the last time are in the same places. The books beside the bookcase seem different, perhaps new additions to the culvert collection. Boy picks one up from the closest pile by leaning awkwardly over and reaching around his brother. Jay giggles and tries to grab Boy's sleeve. He holds it high, just out of Jay's grunting reach, but doesn't open it. Most of the gilt lettering has flaked away from the cracked brown leather. The dusty, browning pages look as though they would as easily crumble as reveal their secrets.

— This is no place for a baby, Mara says.

— No place for anyone, I'd think.

A sudden laugh, tight, echoes against the concrete walls. But not bitter — more restrained.

— True enough.

— I've been wondering how a priest who can stop time ends up here.

Boy says it while watching the older man, who continues loading books onto the shelves. Meticulously so, the spines perfectly aligned. When a spine is nudged out of true, Mara begins each shelf again from the beginning.

How does anyone end up anywhere?

— How does anyone end up anywhere?

— Oh, my God — you see her, too.

Mara turns slightly to face him.

— See who?

— Charlie. My sister, she's —

But he stops at Mara's expression, a single raised eyebrow, a doubtful crinkling of his crow's feet. Amusement? Mocking?

He can't see. I don't know how that happened, but he doesn't see me.

— No one, Boy says. I was just talking to myself.

— You should be careful with that — people don't understand.

— You would.

Mara allows a tiny smile and goes back to aligning his old books.

— Don't forget, I'm the one living under a highway.

— But with your — your —

— You want to call it a gift. It isn't.

— Well, what is it?

— I told you.

— You said maybe the universe stops, but I don't think so. I'd have noticed it before.

— I used to do it only at night.

— Why?

— To use the darkness, I suppose. But recently —

Mara stops, considering. He seems about to say something more but waves it away as though it's a bothersome insect.

— Anyhow, I don't use it often. It has to ripple.

— Ripple?

— Change always creates other change.

But what exactly is changed? *Know your things, your people,* his flight instructors drilled into them. *Computers can do the heavy lifting, but you still have to know how to put it all together yourself. Timing, schedules, fuel, load.* And yet things and people become weight, load, souls, and pax, the paradox of more responsibility through the objectification of terms. But time is time, right? Its complexity constant? Too constant, perhaps, to contemplate how it could be interrupted. Boy becomes aware of Mara, now finished with the bookshelf, watching him closely.

— It's probably not time anyhow, Mara says. There's just something so unfathomable about how time could possibly stop.

— If not time, then what happens?

— You have to call it something.

From his jacket pocket, Boy's phone buzzes once, twice, and a third time. Mark always sends texts in bursts, as though a barrage will drive a quicker response. Mara frowns at the sound.

— Everyone has those things. Out all the time, like people are afraid to escape.

— It's my buddy Mark. He's just worried about me.

— You should be in school.

— I should, yes.

— How old are you?

— Eighteen.

— In grade twelve.

— Yeah.

— And taking care of a baby who should be at home with his mother rather than missing classes near the end of an important year. Why?

— It doesn't feel like a choice.

— Don't you have any other family?

— No.

A fair question. Everyone has someone, right? Or at least a logical *why* if they don't. But aside from the accident spinning them apart, there isn't a why. Just vaguely explained reasons for Corny cutting ties with his wealthy parents long ago and no mention of Misty's family. Time fades so many childhood details, especially the unpleasant ones, but Boy has a sense of flight, of running away as a theme in the argument, played out over two kids, Misty entrenched in the family room, Corny building walls in the kitchen. He and Charlie had talked a handful of times about what having large families must be like, the vanishing contrails of conversations by kids just trying to make it through. In the end, a single sentence suffices, about a drunk mother shacking up with the grieving father of the other girl killed in that accident while a father fades in prison.

Mara listens but doesn't speak.

Jay squawks and squirms. Tired, hungry. The snacks are back in the stroller. Boy moves towards the mouth of the culvert.

— I have to go — Jay isn't good at waiting for his food.

— All right.

As he steps onto the stones leading down to the shoreline, he stops, cocking his head. The signature, throaty rumble of Rolls Royce Merlin engines. The old RCAF Lancaster is up on a fundraising flight, the paying passengers enjoying another era. He looks up as the plane passes overhead, engines straining against gravity, patiently lumbering out over the lake.

— There was a guy at my old church who looked at planes like that, Mara says. Do you fly?

— I do. Did. I have my single-engine licence. Through cadets.

— An expensive hobby.

— It's subsidized. And I'm a good saver.

— What a blessing. The licence, I mean.

— I suppose it is.

— Will you keep flying?

The question sits wrong. Blessing? After missing his shot at RMC? He hears himself asking Mara why he chose this place, when he could have gone anywhere. Mara becomes visibly rigid under the coat.

Careful, little brother.

— I won't tell anyone, Boy says. I like that no one comes here.

— Why do you skip school? I'd think a kid your age with a pilot's licence would be thinking about university. Engineering. Sciences. Something.

— I would be, but —

How much to say? He was about to admit that his grades have slipped, that RMC now might be out of reach, but then he'd have to get into Misty's issues, Morgan's letter, and everything else. No, not now.

— But what?

— Nothing, Boy says.

Jay squirms and stretches.

— I have to go.

— Then go.

Boy watches Mara's back as he moves deeper into the culvert, partially swallowed by the shaded interior.

— Can I come back?

Boy blinks. He didn't mean to ask. The urge was to issue an imperative, to tell Mara he'll be back as soon as he is free again. As though it's a foregone conclusion that Mara's mysteries are his to solve. A flush of embarrassment moves up his throat.

Then, from within the darkness, a faint reply.

— Yes. Do.

Issuing an imperative.

— Thanks for the drink, Boy says. And thanks for coming.

Mark laughs.

— If we're meeting here, during the day, and you can't pay, it must be serious.

— They only take cash.

As he and Jay left the rocks, Boy texted Mark and convinced him to meet. Even from their spot in the farthest corner, the coffee shop is busy and loud, with chatting customers, smooth jazz wafting over the sound system, and the near-constant hissing and clunking from baristas working their machines. There's a long line of customers, noses buried in their phones or studiously avoiding eye contact. They all look tired. Mark is skipping class for the second time, his eyes flitting from patron to patron, as nervous as a sparrow pecking for crumbs on a busy sidewalk.

— Think any of them might be truancy officers?

Boy snorts.

— If we lived in the sixties, maybe.

There are a few bursts of small talk, but for the most part they sit quietly, sipping their drinks. Jay is playing quietly with toys on a blanket laid out for him on the floor, occasionally crawling over to Boy or Mark and lifting himself to a standing position, leaning against the chair and their legs for support. Misty and Nick are still AWOL, so Boy loaded him up in the stroller, which he accepted without complaint. Again. Boy watches his brother play and babble, amazed at his determination to develop his skills despite the lack of stimulation he receives at home. Jay looks up and smiles at Mark, drooling — Mark passes a napkin across the table.

— I can't believe Misty and Nick would just leave Jay all alone.

— It's happened before. Before Jay.

— Shitty thing to do, regardless. A baby …

— Yeah.

— Sorry I was such a dick, Mark says. I know you'd never badmouth me around the squadron.

— No, I wouldn't. You should have gotten that billet.

Mark shrugs.

— Woulda, shoulda, coulda —

— You'll get it next year, Boy says. You'll be the most senior warrant then.

— These things have a way of following a guy around.

They do, indeed, Boy thinks.

They fall into a comfortable silence. Boy meant to ask for advice about Misty and Nick, Jay's needs, perhaps about Mara. Charlie didn't respond on the way over. Jay thought he was being talked to, responding with sober snippets of baby talk in between distracted bouts of watching his breath turn to steam in the cold. Charlie, now standing in the corner, has maintained her silence, like she hasn't taken in a single word her brother has said.

— Essère's worried about you, Mark says.

— I know.

— I think they all are.

— That's what Essère said, too.

— Doesn't seem to bug you much.

Boy lifts his cup and breathes in the steam, watching his sister. Thin and vigilant. Forever twelve. Undecipherable eyes. She'd be twenty now, off at university somewhere. She used to scoff at the idea of university, saying the military would give her a home. Even at ten, Boy could tell it was a passing idea, like cadets would have been. Something to throw yourself into headlong until something else comes along. How easily he moved through activities and ranks, the structure and chain of command tangible, predictable realities. Boy fell in love with it straight away. Charlie might have lasted a few months out of solidarity with Sarah, but her foul mouth would have been a poor fit for the rigidity and etiquette expected of her. Her brand of intelligence masked by her swearing and temper. Boy and Charlie shared that intellect, although he used his openly while she had let people guess. Received from Corny, his ability to dismantle and reassemble problems. She would have graduated from high school with honours. Boy imagines her strutting across the graduation stage, diploma clenched between her teeth, middle finger raised. A fond rush of sadness swells behind his eyes. If only.

— If only what? Mark asks.

— What?

— You zoned out for a minute and then said "if only" while you were staring off into nowhere.

— Oh.

— I'm worried about you, too, to be honest.

— Thanks, but I'm okay.

Mark looks unconvinced.

— No, really, Boy says. I'm good.

— You're not. Look at you — taking care of baby brother in the afternoon, skipping school when you should be working to keep your admission, and you aren't talking to me.

— I'm talking to you.

Mark shakes his head.

— No, you're being an asshole.

Jay looks up, knitting his brow at the edge in Mark's voice. Mark tut-tuts under his breath, makes a bright face, and reaches over to pick Jay up. His brief anxiety assuaged, Jay lets himself get tickled, perhaps deciding that cheerful intervention is the best salve for a far-too-serious moment.

Later, on the walk home, Boy tries again to call Misty. Still no answer.

In the end, although Boy still hadn't told him anything, Mark relented and they departed on amicable terms. Enough grace in such moments to repair rifts and restore balance, but a finite supply. Once again his friend meets him where he is, and once again Boy leaves Mark with far less than he's been given. Boy takes a different route home, along new side streets. Charlie has again chosen the far side of the road. They pass school kids of all ages heading home, earnest grade-schoolers with purpose, meandering teenagers looking for anywhere else to go. School buses rattle by, younger children looking out the window, the older ones mere shapes behind them, turned in towards aisle gossip or buried in their devices. He feels detached, as though the other students and familiar afternoon sights are already foreign to him. But who knows where he'll end up next year. The sealed RMC envelope still gathers creases at the bottom of his backpack, a constant reminder of an accomplishment he should be proud of, yet the acceptance from RMC seems to be fading. Not completely, though. Like a dream that frightens you enough to keep you from going back to sleep. Carried around for the rest of the day as fatigue and a sense of dread you know isn't real but still worry about.

— If you could stop everything, like Mara can, would you have to worry at all?

He lives in a culvert. That's fucked up.

— You could do anything.

No, I don't think so. You couldn't redo the past.

When they arrive home, as he reaches into his pocket for his keys, a bright line of pain slips across the back of his hand. Paper cut. He pulls out a folded pamphlet advertising the locations of the various anonymous STI testing sites around Hamilton. Has it been in his pocket the whole time? He sucks away the tiny button of blood that has appeared along the paper cut's edge and stuffs the pamphlet into his pack. Over time, it will make its way to the bottom, where it will wrinkle and crease, just like the two letters already there.

CHAPTER 8

That night, Boy puts Jay on his play mat in the family room with toys, grabs a drink from the fridge, and sits in front of the mail that has accumulated over the past few days. He sifts through the envelopes — the mailbox was stuffed full — and stops at a thin white letter bearing the provincial crest and addressed to him. He reads the single page, folds it, slides it back into the envelope, and places everything back on the table. He makes a single, forced laugh, loud in the quiet house.

Jay flinches and looks over at Boy with his eyes wide and filling. Boy holds him close as the sniffles begin.

— Sorry, buddy, that was right out of the blue. You're okay, I promise.

Declined for financial aid because of the household's net income. He applied as a safety net, knowing he was likely to get the full ride from RMC but unwilling to leave anything to chance. The estimate of the household income was too high — Misty had pushed and sold more homes before the pregnancy took. She was angry when he asked for the information. *I pay my goddamn taxes,* she said, *so why the hell do they need to know?* It took her awhile to calm down, yelling at him and at the straw man, that it took some nerve asking her to put anything on paper. A second gin and tonic relaxed her enough to agree, but only if everything else was filled in first and she could be the one to seal and mail the envelope off. She completed the form but forgot to seal and mail the letter. Boy saw the figures anyhow. Knew he'd be declined.

Within moments, Jay is squirming to be put down again. Boy sits next to him on the floor with his back against the sofa and reaches for the TV remote. Jay takes in the TV's sounds and images for a moment but turns back to his toys looking, Boy thinks, almost disgusted by the intrusion. Boy feels it, too, the jabbering and frenetic sounds from the TV — a large, flat screen monster Nick convinced Misty to buy — almost immediately grating. He powers off the unit, leans his head back against the cushions, and closes his eyes. Trying to decipher the soft background sounds of the house. Refrigerator. Furnace. The clicks of a cooling TV.

Jay is having none of it. He crawls over and uses whatever clothing he can to lever himself up to a standing position. Boy smiles but keeps his eyes closed, which Jay takes as permission to begin climbing, contentedly grunting with the effort. Boy feels the bulk of his growing half-brother's weight on his lap and the lighter pressure of love on his shoulders. Jay, now quiet, is probably studying his face, just waiting for the moment Boy will open his eyes and look at him, practically bursting with anticipation.

— Boo, he whispers, popping open his eyes.

Jay squeals and falls onto Boy's chest, shaking both of them with his laughter so thoroughly Boy almost doesn't feel Mark's text arrive.

— *misty home yet?*

— no

— what next?

I have no idea, he thinks. One night isn't that long — she has disappeared before, and for longer stretches, but always well into a binge where the signs have built up alongside her intake. But only before Jay was born. For all her faults, she is at least staying home these days. Until now. Like she's trying on for size a departure on her own terms.

His phone thrums. Another text, this time from Shi.

— big bio test this week

— yeah. you ready?

— almost. want to review at lunches this week?

— will that be enough time?

— yes if we actually study

He laughs. Jay is startled again but doesn't cry this time — he just stares at him for a long, sober moment, an oddly mature expression on his face.

— And if Misty doesn't come back? What then? Do I drop out of school to take care of you?

But Jay doesn't respond. He just squirms to be put down and is back to his toys in an instant.

Later, while feeding Jay a bottle of formula, creaking back and forth in the old wooden rocker next to the crib, Boy tells him a story. It is, he realizes, the first time he has ever done so with such intentionality. A departure from the mechanical necessities of speech. He talks softly, first working through his own issues but soon transitioning into cadet adventures, gear inspections, screw-ups on the parade floor, the buzz of promotions, the memory of his first solo flight. Jay is transfixed, eyes wide, with an occasional, milky grin around the bottle's nipple. Somewhere around Boy's final approach, Jay's eyes droop and close. He sleeps through his burping and is a rag doll when laid in the crib.

Boy goes downstairs to the front hall and opens the closet door for his backpack. Homework. Maybe starting the extra credit assignment for Essère's class. As he kneels beside the closet, there's a soft knock at the front door. An elderly woman stands in the dim spill of light from the hall.

— May I help you?

— Hello, Boy.

Boy flips on the front light. Sees her coat first. A rich carmine, with subtle champagne buttons, and precisely tailored to her thin but upright frame. She has short white hair, carefully styled, and perfect makeup. Polished and poised, as though always ready for a camera to be pointed her way.

— I'm sorry, ma'am. Do I know you?

A momentary downturn of her lips, then a smile. Straight, white teeth.

— We have met, although you were quite young. My name is Cynthia McVeigh.

— Oh my God. You're Corny's mom.

— Your grandmother, yes.

— Right.

She shivers, startling both of them. *Now the coat makes sense*, Boy thinks. A coat you wear between your expensive car and building doors that are always held open.

— Please come in.

— Thank you.

She takes precisely three steps along the hallway runner and waits while Boy closes the door. She does not turn, forcing him to move in front of her. She has recovered her bearing. Classic command tactic. *Make your subordinates come to you.* Boy clasps his hands behind him and stands straight in front of her, meeting her gaze. *Always wait for them to speak.* A long moment passes where they appraise each other in the bright hallway. Finally, she nods and laughs quietly.

— Good. I am impressed.

— May I help you?

— *She's* not back yet.

Not Misty. Just a pronoun with a dropped tone in place of an identity. And not a question.

— How do you know that?

— Or the firefighter, I forget his name —

— Nick. No, they're not back yet. Again, how do you know?

Instead of replying, she begins to unbutton her coat, the red of which seems to have deepened in the incandescent glow from the hallway chandelier. She takes it off and holds it out. Boy moves past her and takes a hanger from the closet, tempted for an instant to hand it to her. But courtesy is a powerful instinct. He hangs her coat without a word. He follows her down into the kitchen and family room area.

— I really shouldn't be so surprised, but this is a lovely home.

— It's not usually so neat.

— No, I meant in an all-around sense — secure, cozy, warm. From the outside, it just looks like every other house in this neighbourhood.

Which is intentional. Camouflage. Still, he has never thought of the home as anything other than home, as a place in which to grow, eat, shower, work. Leave and come back to. Even now, as Cynthia is clearly appraising the place, he has trouble imagining it any other way. Fixtures are just fixtures. Furniture there to be used. She moves around the room, studies every shelf and chair. He has the familiar, polite urge to offer her a place to sit.

— Can I get you anything?

— I'll only be staying a few minutes.

She'll get to her purpose soon enough. He watches her, trying to discern a family resemblance between her and Corny. He can't see it — the eight years between his ten-year-old impressions and an eighteen-year-old cadet's precision are a chasm.

She glances at his forehead.

— Should I be worried about that bandage?

— What? No, I just tripped and fell.

He realizes too late that his hand has gone to the bandage. He drops it to his side.

— I'm fine, he says.

— I saw the light upstairs go out.

— I'm sorry, I —

— In the baby's room. After you put him down for the night. It shouldn't be you.

He shrugs as if to say, Who else?

— I've been watching the house from my car for a while now.

— From your car? Why?

— We only live five minutes from here. Did you know?

— No.

— After Cornelius went away, your mother said we weren't to visit or even call.

Went away. A useful way to refer to a son in prison.

— I can't remember you coming by before, either, he says.

— No, we didn't, but that was more implicit than explicit.

He and Charlie had occasionally wondered aloud about their grandparents but stopped short of asking Misty or Corny. Here, though, stands an actual grandparent, a strange reality when both parents had cut even the tiniest reference to them from every conversation. Might this be the time to ask? No. Too much like an intrusion into the corridors of a life other than his own.

— May I ask why you're here?

— I'd like to help.

— I don't think Misty would want that, Mrs. — Gran— What should I call you?

The briefest mote of pain causes her features to sag for an instant, but she recovers with a deep breath and a shallow laugh.

— A good question. I was Mrs. McVeigh until Carter died. And Grandmother's a stretch, don't you think? How about Cynthia?

No way he'll call her by her first name — certain habits too ingrained — but he nods anyhow.

— You're wondering why we weren't around, she says.

— Corny and Misty were never much for family talk.

She takes this as permission to explain. Cornelius — she uses the formal version of his name like a sommelier might say the name of a favourite wine — had cut them out of his life shortly after he and Misty were married eighteen years ago. They'd eloped — Misty's word for running off to the justice of the peace at nine in the morning — the morning after he resigned from the military, a few months after returning home from active duty overseas.

— Wait, he says. He served overseas? Corny talked about leaving the army, but —

— No, he didn't talk about it. He couldn't.

— Where — ?

— Peacekeeping. Bosnia. Or Croatia, I can't recall.

— I had no idea.

— He had a rough time.

— How long was he in the military?

— Four years. Five, maybe.

— He would've been about my age when he joined up.

— All he wanted to do was join the infantry. You have bigger plans, I understand.

Boy turns away from Cynthia, pulls out a chair from under the kitchen table, and sits. *Jesus*, he thinks. *Corny was an infanteer.*

An actual soldier. He never talked about what his role was in the army, or what things he might have seen. A number of things fall into place: his precision, tidiness, even his religious haircut at the beginning of every month. Encouraging Charlie to join the cadets. Cynthia takes another chair and begins to describe how he changed during his service, how his training had given him a hard edge, how excited he'd been that his unit had been selected for duty overseas. How proud Cynthia and Carter had been, even though they would have preferred university for their son rather than mud and guns. But her tone changes as she talks. His sudden discharge. The questions. Drug use. A civil marriage ceremony precisely one week after meeting Misty.

— As if to rescue him from whatever he became over there. And his mood was so ... no, wait, it was more than that. His whole being was in shadow.

A different story than the one he and Charlie had pieced together from the bits they were given. Light-hearted. How ' Corny was brought into Misty's life after she graduated from college. That they knew right away. Corny sweeping her off her feet. And so on.

— And then he just stopped talking to us. We tried to reach out, to visit, call, and so on, but he — although I think it was more her — just went away.

— But not too far.

— Might as well have been across the ocean.

Why does this feel like cold water down his back? He and Charlie never trusted the story, not really, but never confronted Misty and Corny about it, either. Why had he never been curious about the backstory? Boy had never known either parent to be anything other than codependent. Always that way, brought together by mutual need. Addictions already saturating their personalities. For Misty, this is certainly still the case and might always have been, but Cynthia's words highlight a definable point where Corny changed. His weaknesses welded to him after his military service like plate armour.

— I had no idea, he says.

— No, you wouldn't.

For Cynthia, it's much easier to blame the outsider, a daughter-in-law not of her choosing. But Corny had his own burdens. Few bear more than soldiers, as though they can never fully release the seventy-five-pound pack they carry into conflict. Boy feels a growing sense of solidarity with his absent father and a growing sense that this woman clearly disapproves of the choices Corny made. The kinds of choices Boy might have to make, too, if a life of service is the destination. He looks at his grandmother, stiff in the kitchen chair, and sees that it isn't Corny's service or Misty's insertion between parent and child she wants to share. She's waiting for something. Permission?

— You said you'd like to help, he prompts, hearing a new sharpness in his tone.

He wonders, *Why am I angry?*

— Carter and I have been saving money for your education.

— So?

— Since you turned eighteen a short while ago, you're now entitled to it.

His first instinct is to ask how much they've saved, but he bites back the question.

— You're also entitled to Charlie's money.

— That sounds —

— Boy, it's important to us — to me, now — that her money be used to help you, so you won't have to worry about money while you're completing your studies.

She takes a deep breath and sits back, her eyes glistening, and he sees why she needed to get it all out at once. Cynthia is not a woman accustomed to emotional displays. The heartbreak of a granddaughter's life cut short. Investments that should have grown for eight years, given to Charlie in her own name at the proper time.

— I'm not sure what to say, he says.

— Say you'll accept this gift — gifts — and use them well.

And there it is: how many of her hopes he'll be carrying. Waiting until his eighteenth year so he can manage the funds away from parental control. *What hope*, he thinks. *What trust.* That he might not be going to RMC next year, that he might be unable to carry what Cynthia — his grandmother — is offering, settles on him like the weight of an atmosphere. He feels her watching him and waiting.

— Thank you for this, he says. I'll do my best.

She breathes a deep breath and gives a bright smile.

— I know you will, Boy.

Her voice is lighter. Unburdened. And he sees.

— Corny's your only child. I'm your only grandchild.

— Yes.

— He never told us.

— I know.

Boy has never seen Misty so angry. Her usual method of expressing displeasure is passive-aggressive torrents of guilt or gin-soaked sarcasm. When she and Nick arrived home a few moments ago and discovered Cynthia, she threw her overnight bag at the wall, knocking a gaping hole in the panelling.

— You expect me to fix that?

— Really, Nick? Now? Get the bags and we'll deal with it later.

— Fuck that —

Nick's eyes are as shadowed as Misty's, as though neither has slept. He drops his duffel bag in the centre of the room and stalks out to his SUV, leaving the front door wide open. The sound of his tires as he rushes away, whistling in like the cold, is loud against the still neighbourhood night. Misty barely notices.

— Leave, Cynthia.

— So that's who you've replaced my son with.

— I want you to go.

— I'm glad I was out there. The boys need me.

— You've been watching us? For how long?

— What kind of mother abandons a baby?

— Get out, and stay away from my kids.

— And for what? Booze? Drugs?

— Get. Out.

Boy just watches, hoping Jay won't have to pay for everyone's raised voices. *Wait, watch, and learn, Cadet. Speak only when you have something worth offering.* Misty spits her words. Cynthia's are more controlled, though full of disdain.

— Carter was right about you. You've never been fit to have children.

— It's not my son in prison.

— Don't you —

— My son didn't kill two little girls.

Boy feels Misty's words in his stomach. Her eyes glittering with rage, Misty stands over the older, smaller woman, goading her. For a long moment, Cynthia just looks at the floor, her jaw trembling, before getting to her feet and moving towards the door. *Misty has no idea what she just said*, he thinks. *She just invoked the memory of her dead daughter — my sister — to win an argument.*

— I can't believe you just said that about Charlie.

— That bastard took everything from us.

The monitor crackles with Jay's first tentative cries.

— You better take care of that, Misty says, nodding at Boy.

She moves across the room to the liquor cabinet. He shakes his head and goes into the hall, refusing to watch her pour herself a drink. He hears it, though, the sound of ice and glass as distinct as Jay's crying. He opens the front door for Cynthia as she puts on her tailored gloves.

— I'm sorry, she says to him.

— Yeah.

She pulls out a small card from her pocketbook. It's heavy cardstock, cream-coloured, engraved with her name and contact details in an elegant, looping script.

— That was my fault, she says. I just meant to tell you about your money and leave the card with you. I didn't mean to stay so long.

— Thank you, but I don't think I'll —

— Call any time. Day, night, whenever, especially if —

She looks down the hall towards the bright kitchen and stops.

— Okay.

Jay cries again, this time with the sure knowledge of hunger. Boy heads up the stairs to comfort his brother as Cynthia lets herself out, the front door closing with a hush against the cold.

CHAPTER 9

The normalcy of the clock radio going off is almost a relief, apart from the morning show's inane babble. He set the alarm for eight minutes past the hour, enough time for the news to pass so he can wake up to music. But the cheap time circuit has since shifted backwards just enough to land him in the middle of chatter. The clock's digits are a red blur across the room. Tinny, crackling sound. He yawns his way out of bed and shuts it off, then turns it on again for tomorrow morning. Automatic. Assuming his life isn't thrown from the sidewalk again, making him scramble in the slush to find it.

Last night, Jay needed an entire bottle of formula to go back down, sucking back his consolation prize as though he'd never eat again. Boy slept for a few hours, only to be woken up again when Nick returned, drunk and looking for a fight. Jay woke up. Nick stumbled into Jay's room, yelling at him that he was being too loud, why wouldn't he be quiet, and to shut up already. Boy had to leap from his bed and stand between Nick and Jay until Nick finally left, muttering to himself. Nick has never hit Jay, but last night Boy wondered yet again when he might. The frightening ease with which Nick seems able to drink away the knowledge of a baby son, becoming again the guy without children. Mercifully, Jay fell back asleep quickly. Not Boy — it was impossible to tune out the muffled, mixed soundtrack of Nick and Misty's make-up sex and the Cars bleeding through the walls.

He grabs some clothes and heads to the bathroom to shower, studiously averting his eyes from the master bedroom's wide-open door. He can smell their sleep, a stale fug wafting into the hall. Nick's crepitant snoring as grating as the sound from the clock radio. He steps into the tub and puts his head under the steaming spray. Stands there a moment, the only sounds the hissing of the water and the distant roar of plumbing. Feels good to slip back into routine, albeit briefly. How elusive establishing rhythms can be for anyone with goals and challenges beyond the immediate. Constant adjustment. This year especially. He reaches for the soap and laughs at himself, the necessity of introspection — why can't the day's first trip into the bathroom just be about getting clean?

There's a text message from Mark waiting for him when he gets back to his room.

— *u @ school 2day?*
— *u 4get how 2 spell?*

He taps *send*, imagining the expression on his friend's face. Mark won't laugh out loud. Maybe a frown, puzzled by the levity. Perplexed, even, by the delay. Boy sends a confirmation in plain text to reassure his earnest friend. Mark's response is almost immediate.

— *great see you in 1p*
— *we'll be meeting shi at lunch to study bio*
— *???*
— *new girl, history class*
— *howd you meet?*

He doesn't respond, savouring his playful desire to leave Mark hanging. On the way downstairs, he looks in on Jay. Snoring gently. Face-down. Bum in the air. Such perfect oblivion. Boy pauses, watching his half-brother sleep. Misty is home, but can he leave Jay in her care all day? *Maybe I should stay*, he thinks, *until* —

Jay stretches, rolls onto his side. A lion cub stretch and sigh. Silence. Boy smiles, eases the door closed, and heads downstairs for his breakfast. Jay will somehow find a way to be fine on his own, like always. The kid has built-in lion strength. Maybe he'll even teach Misty a thing or two.

Boy opens the door to head outside. Cold air moves through his jeans, cooling his legs.

— Boy, wait.

Misty is in the hall, holding her thin, flimsy robe closed in front of her with one hand and prodding at her hair with the other. The thigh-length robe has no tie to keep it closed. Not that it would help much — he can see the outline of her dark panties beneath and the hint of cleavage just above her protective arm. He closes the door and looks away.

— We need to talk, she says.

— I've got school.

— Stay home. I'll write a note for your teacher.

— A note? You can't be serious.

— Of course I am.

— I'm eighteen, Misty. I can write my own notes.

— Just let me get dressed — we'll talk and you can do whatever you want afterwards.

— A day off, then. Like yesterday.

— Yes. No. I — what are you talking about?

— No, that's fantastic. Really. Everything else can wait.

— I don't understand.

And she really doesn't. She just looks at him, the puffiness under her eyes brought out by dried-out makeup and whatever chemicals remain in her system. She shifts her weight, foot to foot, bare feet cold and impatient on the tile, holding herself together, now with both arms across her chest. As pale as a moment of missed opportunity.

— Jay, he says.

— What about him?

— Who do you think took care of him after you left the other night?

— You didn't like the babysitter?

Boy just tilts his head and gives her a look.

— But Nick took care of everything. The plane tickets, the hotel, the passes. He said the babysitter —

Boy shakes his head. After a second or two, she raises one hand to her mouth, her eyes widening.

— Oh my God —

A rogue wave of regret thunders into her and she sways on her feet. He steps forward by instinct, awkward in boots and coat and backpack, ready to catch her. But instead of falling, of losing herself, after an instant she lifts her chin, looks at him, and becomes still. A new spark brightens the arced edges of her irises. Her hands drop to her sides, loose and assured, forcing him again to look away from her breasts, their telling lines and dips and swells now clearly visible through the thin fabric.

— I'll do better, she says.

A kind of apology. Should he savour it or graciously lay it aside? You never know until it's offered.

— But we still need to talk about Cynthia, she says. You'll tell me if *she* comes here again.

Her voice has gained an edge.

— She just wants to help, he says.

A snort.

— I'll put some clothes on, she says. Wait in the kitchen. I'll be down in a minute.

Alone again, overdressed and overheating in the front hallway. Too stunned to roll through the things he's wanted to say since they left. About negligence. An unworthiness to be placed in a position of responsibility. Broken trust. The suffering of a baby boy who still grins at the world. A lifetime, maybe, of things that need to be said when you're given just the right moment. When you don't squander it.

He stalks out, hoping to find equilibrium on the long walk to the bus stop. Just down the road, he passes Cynthia keeping warm in her expensive car, a wisp of engine exhaust coiling upwards from the rear. Here again, or here still? He gives her a low wave and receives a slow nod in return. Charlie, who normally falls in with his movements as soon as he leaves the house, is instead waiting beside the idling car and watching Cynthia. She remains in place, a signal he now recognizes. Like he should stop and talk or get into the passenger seat, as though maybe Cynthia could drive them both to school like nothing had ever happened.

There's a new beginning here, brother. Stay.

— Sorry, Charlie, he says. Not today.

He keeps walking, ignoring the sound of the car window being lowered, crisp in the still morning air, and Cynthia's voice, frail in its volume, asking him to repeat himself, assuming his words were meant for her.

Boy spends much of the day worrying about Jay, revisiting his decision to leave him at home. There's much grace in not remembering babyhood — the falls, the messes, the tears — but when does a child begin to retain memory for the long term? To recall a mother's lacklustre attempts at care?

Halfway through English lit, Mark gives him a worried look when he pulls out his phone and googles the questions. He loses the remainder of the period learning how children remember everything but the earliest memories tend to fade. Crystallizing their ability to remember by age ten or so. Still, the earliest pieces remain, even from infancy, although it is reassuring that the traumatic doesn't weigh more than the benign. Sort of. Surely it depends on how the volume of memories is allocated. The more there are, the more the likelihood of remembering.

A sharp slap on his shoulder. He looks up, annoyed. Mark standing in the aisle getting ready to smack him again. He looks around — the class is empty. Ms. Vos watches them closely from the front. He hadn't even heard the bell.

— We'll be out of here in a second, Miss, Mark says.

Vos waits on the tall reading stool, arms folded loosely, back straight, legs crossed. One foot rests on the crossbar, the other bounces restlessly in front of her shin. A file folder and the marked teacher's copy of the class novel are balanced on her knee. Boy slips his phone into his pocket, turning his body to shield the attempt.

— Don't bother, she says. You've had it out for the last half hour.

— I was just —

He stops, feeling too tired to lie, too troubled to tell the truth.

— Just what?

— I'm sorry.

Mark fidgets next to him, edging towards the door.

— That's all I get? she asks. No grand excuse for missing hints and tips for the unit test next week?

— No, ma'am. I'm sorry.

She stands, places the materials on the corner of the desk, and smooths her skirt. She walks over to the windows and partially draws down the blinds, dimming the light in the classroom. The boys watch as she lowers each blind to its own level, no two the same, staggering their heights, a bar graph against the light. Finally, she moves over to them, standing between Mark and the door.

— You can go, she says to Mark.

— That's all right, I don't mind.

— I'm only writing a late pass for one of you.

— Right, he says.

As he leaves, awkwardly manoeuvring by her in the aisle, he pauses at the door and looks back. Boy shakes his head.

— I'll see you in class. Save a seat for me.

Mark nods and disappears. She folds her arms again and looks down at Boy.

— I'm glad someone's keeping an eye on you.

— Sorry about the phone. It won't happen again.

— No, it won't. If you can't be present in my class, there's no point in being here. Just stay home.

Really? Can she say that?

— Miss —

— I don't want to hear it. I'm thinking about everyone else in the class now. If one student is allowed to get away with texting all class, they'll all do it. You have a week of detention, starting tomorrow.

— What? I —

— Report to the detention room at the start of lunch.

— It was just a mistake.

— And there's a consequence for it. You'll use the time to work on Essère's extra credit project.

— I haven't decided —

— Yes, you have. You don't throw grace away.

It's not his fault, not his problem, he wants to say, but doesn't.

— We all put our names on those recommendations. Did you know your squadron's commanding officer came here and asked us to help get you into RMC?

Boy shakes his head.

— I do dozens of recs every year but this is the first time I've had a general ask me for help.

— A colonel, actually —

— Be quiet and listen.

He looks down at his hands.

— When a teacher like Essère, who's done nothing but defend you, starts speaking about your potential in the past tense, it makes me angry.

She stops and takes a deep breath, watching him intently, as though deciding whether to say what she wants to say. Her next words are so quiet he has to lean towards her to hear.

— You *will* have detention, and you *will* do Essère's assignment while you're there.

Oh, so that's the method, he thinks. Treat him like a soldier, order him around like a recruit and appeal to his need for routine, structure, direction. The image of the classic drill sergeant appears in his mind, standing over and screaming at the man on the ground doing push-ups, questioning his manhood, his sense of honour, his everything. And then it's Vos standing there, tall and lean and waving a book at him. Boy throws back his head and laughs, surprising Vos back a few steps where she waits, her arms folding and unfolding, trying to regain a veneer of authority that's been torn from the grain.

— Stop laughing, she says. I'm serious.

He stands, roughly gathering his things before facing her. His face feels as though it has flushed to a hundred degrees above normal.

— You know this isn't about you at all, right!

— Get out of my classroom.

He thinks, *But it's not your classroom, is it? And this isn't my life. We're all just shuttling around temporary spaces assigned by others.*

Vos remains in the aisle as he brushes past her and leaves. Students from her next class are waiting in the hall, huddled excitedly around the slit window and probably listening to every word. He pushes through and walks to his next class, not bothering to look back and check on Charlie, make sure she's able to negotiate the gauntlet, as if she needed his concern to do so.

Later, in Essère's class, Boy has the urge to call home and check up on Jay, concerned about leaving his brother alone with their mother. What a thing — that a mother can't be trusted to care for her own son.

— Mr. McVeigh? Do you not agree?

His teacher is looking at him expectantly.

— Sir?

But he's just playing it out, really, already knowing he must have spoken aloud. Damage control. I'm sorry, sir. Yes, I'm fine. No, it won't happen again, et cetera. *Shit.* Mark isn't even looking at him, focused instead on his margin doodles. Kyle, off to his right, is chuckling and whispering to those around him.

Good one, brother.

Oh, yes, Boy thinks. *A fine moment indeed.*

He picks up his pen, leans over his binder — the page is empty — and looks at the whiteboard. Essère returns to his lecture. Mark finally looks over, and Boy dismisses the episode with a slight wave while keeping his eyes forward. But a few minutes later, his thoughts have again wandered and his phone has found its way out of his pocket. Hidden from the teacher's view by the student in front of him, the phone rests like a rock outcropping on the tundra of his nonexistent notes. Things fall apart, Vos would say. The centre cannot hold. And Misty will do better.

Not fucking likely.

Hiding her weaknesses from the world is an art and science, so why should it be any different now? Before Jay, Misty was as good at timing her drinking and drug use around the things that needed to get done as she was at those things themselves. She was so much in demand that she set her own schedule and her clients always deferred to her. Savouring the dance and danger of it. As effective at camouflaging the sags, shadows, and spots with her attitude as she was with the makeup she could cake on. Nick found his way into their lives less than a year after Corny killed Charlie and Sarah and immediately reduced his hours at the fire hall. Misty became even more energized, as though she felt a primal need to care for Nick like a new dependant. They partied right through the pregnancy while Boy immersed himself in cadets and school.

He found out that Jay had entered the world by text message. *Your mom needed a csection*, Nick wrote. *Stay home. I'll call.* But he didn't. Boy texted and called, asking if she and the baby were okay, but Nick didn't answer. Boy rode Corny's old bike so hard to the hospital he worried he'd bend the pedals. Charlie stayed behind him as he rode and didn't speak the entire time. Not on the visitors' list, the nurses wouldn't let him in until Nick came out. Shuffling along the corridor like he was in mourning, not saying a word to Boy. Misty was asleep when they arrived, pale and drawn. But the instant Boy's eyes rested on the baby, a tiny, wide-awake burrito swaddled in blue-striped receiving blankets, Nick's insensitivity and Misty's neglect evaporated. Unnamed and flawless. Hands clenching and unclenching. Eyes clear and dark. Boy likes to imagine Jay's first thoughts after he was cut out from his mother. *Screw you, Mom, Dad. I'm here and I'm perfect. Get ready.* Nick collapsed in the reclining chair, half asleep by the time his head hit the vinyl. *I heard a little rumble before you came in — I think he shit himself,* he said without opening his eyes.

A few days later, they came home. Nick closed the front door behind them hard enough to startle the baby awake. When he began wailing, Misty lost it, too, burying her face in her hands, her whole body shaking. *Shit,* she said again and again. *Shit, shit, shit.* Later, while nursing, she directed Nick to empty the liquor cabinet and dump the bottles. He refused, poured a drink for himself in front of her, and disappeared up the stairs. Misty named the baby Jason after a week or so of them getting used to each other, a nod to a slasher film from the eighties. She said, *A horror baby, get it? He's our horror child.* Boy decided that his half-brother would never hear the name's association from his big brother's lips. *Jay,* he said. *That can work.* The booze never got discarded.

The bell rings, startling him. He pockets his phone and looks around as the other students bustle and rise. Essère raises his voice, exhorting them to remember an upcoming test, attempting to shout down the swelling sea. Boy tucks his binder under his arm, grabs his pack, and moves for the door, apologizing to the students he pushes aside. Essère cuts him off on his way out of class, blocking the rest of the students. The teacher pauses a moment, as though gathering his thoughts, as the captive crowd behind Boy grows.

— My offer is still good, he says. Think about it.

— I said I would, sir.

— Did you? I don't recall. Anyhow, don't take too long.

The teacher stands aside, releasing the flood of student bodies. Boy stuffs his things in his pack and heads towards the exit, tucking away the lost school day, too. In the hall, he feels a tap on his shoulder. It's Shi.

— I'm glad to see you're all right, she says.

— It'll be fine — Essère's always had my back.

A smirk.

— I'm not talking about him. You stood me up today. At lunch.

— I don't —

— Didn't write, didn't call — enough to give a girl a complex.

— Shit, he says. Studying. Lunchtime.

— Right.

— I don't know what happened.

— Judging by how out of it you were in there, I'm amazed you remembered to get dressed this morning.

— One of those days, I suppose, he says. How about tomorrow?

She gives him a look, her expression inscrutable. Waits.

— Uh, the library's always quiet at lunchtime this time of year, he says.

— Sure, sounds about right. Tomorrow, then.

— Great.

And she walks away, shaking her head. He pulls out his phone to check the time.

Pathetic.

— What? Why?

Charlie doesn't respond, just remains in her spot, watching. More waiting. A few seconds later, as a few late students brush by on their tardy way to class, he understands. *I should have apologized,* he thinks. *How self-absorbed am I?*

And tomorrow is Saturday.

He groans out loud and moves to follow Shi. But his motion is arrested as a hand grabs the rear of his collar, pulling him back, his throat bitten by the teeth on his coat's zipper. Another hand grabs the pack strap over his shoulder and spins him around, slamming him up against a locker. Kyle. The late stragglers rushing to their classes stop to watch as Kyle — face red, eyes raging — pins Boy against the cold metal, reaching up to hold his forearm across this throat.

— You told them, didn't you? They're always watching me now, you fuck.

Kyle is thick and strong but a few inches shorter, so Boy isn't worried, just surprised. Kyle glares at Boy through slitted eyes, breathing heavily through his mouth. Boy doesn't know what to do. Fight? Flight? He is aware of the looks they're getting from the other students, hungry, waiting for a scuffle. *Kyle is certainly committed*, he thinks. *That's funny.*

For the second time that day, Boy can't stop himself from bursting into sudden and inappropriate laughter, his Adam's apple bobbing, painful against Kyle's arm. Kyle's surprised look — perplexed with a salting of confusion — is funny, too. He sees Mark waiting for him just down the hall, looking concerned but not doing anything, and he can't keep anything in any longer — it's just too hilarious. Shaking with laughter, Boy uses one hand to remove Kyle's arm from his throat, his other to push him aside as easily as a well-balanced door. He registers Kyle's embarrassment as the crowd's mood shifts from fight-hungry to entertained. Boy rearranges his pack on his shoulders and wipes his eyes. Kyle walks away, his shoulders hunched. Boy resumes his movement towards the exit and smiles at his sister.

— That was something, wasn't it?

Fuck, yeah, that was something.

— Let's get out of here.

He's forgotten about Shi and making up for his terrible screw-up. He doesn't see Mark opening his mouth and closing it, as stunned as everyone else. Or hear the whispers, the nascent rumours about the tall army geek who laughed away a beating and then started talking to himself.

After school, Boy walks to the rocks. It begins snowing on the way, though the weather report had called for a cold and sunny day, a flight-perfect high-pressure front supposedly keeping clouds away. Boy pulls back the fencing, the snow on his shoulders and hat floating down to vanish against the centimetre already on the ground. Lake-effect snow, the clouds hitting the cold air over the city and releasing the moisture they picked up over Lake Ontario. Terrible visibility. The snow fast and opaque and muffling the sounds from the traffic on the QEW. He rubs his hands together and breathes on them for warmth. In his rush to leave this morning, he forgot his toque and gloves. He turns his ankle a few times on the stone beach and stumbles, scratching his palms on the gritty, wet stones. His hands begin to ache. He stuffs them into his coat pockets, clenching and unclenching his fists to keep the blood moving.

Mara has rigged a few sheets of heavy, translucent vapour barrier across the culvert's mouth and against the weather. Snow gathers in the plastic's hanging folds, mottling the dim light from inside. Boy calls out a greeting. Mara holds back the plastic carefully, keeping the snow out.

— You can hang your coat, he says. There's a hook —

— On the side of the bookcase. I know.

It's warm. Mara is dressed in his usual khakis and collared shirt. Boy shrugs off his pack and coat, thinks about removing his sweater, prickly against his neck.

— You're sweating. Let me turn down the heater.

Mara points a remote control at the heater. The roar diminishes.

A remote, no less. Mara moves away from him and back to the small kitchen table and chair against the wall. He sits and picks up the book laid on the table, spine up, and resumes his reading. Boy looks down at the heater, plugged into a yellow extension cord that zigzags along the floor to the back of the culvert. There, it rises to a junction box awkwardly duct-taped to the concrete. Both cords are still kinked and stiff, brand new, flagged with sheaves of superfluous safety tags.

— I'll get masonry anchors at some point, Mara says, watching Boy over his book. No baby brother today?

— He's at home.

Mara nods and turns his eyes again to the pages in front of him.

— That's better, he says. Good, I mean.

— You've been busy.

Mara dog-ears the page and lays the book on the table. He shifts in his chair and crosses one leg over the other, watching Boy move around the culvert.

— How did you stay warm before, without the plastic?

— I had a small heater.

— But without anything covering the entrance —

— After you left, it occurred to me how silly it is to always be cold.

Boy stops again in front of the bookcase, tilting his head to read the titles there. Non-fiction dominates the collection, connected to Mara's former life — faded biblical commentaries, glossy modern studies of bible books, and biographies of historical religious figures. A few of the names look familiar — Augustine, Aquinas, Lewis, Pope this, Pope that. The bottom shelf is fiction — classics from Tolkien to Brontë to Dickens.

— Asimov? he asks, pulling an old hardcover from the shelf.

Mara stands and walks over. He takes the book with gingered hands and replaces it in its rank, lining up the spine perfectly with its neighbour.

— The End of Eternity, Mara says. A first edition.

— What's it about?

Mara smiles and returns to his chair.

— I'll just let the title do the work.

— It's about stopping time.

— No. Yes. And more.

— May I borrow it?

Mara shakes his head.

— As I said, it's a first edition.

Mara seems content to sit with his legs crossed and his hands on his knees and watch him. Boy doesn't know what to do next. He feels that instinctual discomfort with being watched by strangers.

— Please, sit, Mara says. You look like you're going to faint.

— I'll be fine.

Mara reaches under the table, pulls a plastic bottle of water from a small wooden chest, and holds it out.

— You're probably dehydrated. Relax.

Boy sits, defying the voices in his mind yelling at him not to. His knee bumps against the leg of the table, threatening to knock the bottle over. A small but intense point of pain where knee meets wood. He flashes out a hand to steady the bottle.

You're not being smart right now.

— I'll be fine, he says again.

— Now you sound like you're convincing yourself, Mara says.

Charlie is just a shadow on the other side of the plastic sheeting and Boy looks over at her, willing her to come inside as backup.

— Look, if you're uncomfortable, I don't want you here. You can't be here if —

Mara is on his feet now, grabbing Boy's things, muttering that he should go, that he could come back another time. The haunted look Boy saw at their first meeting is back, a blend of

surprise, guilt, shame. He worries that his chance to learn is
slipping away.

— Why do you live out here?

Mara stops, Boy's coat and pack in his hands, suspended.

— I have to, he says.

— Why?

— I just do.

— But you could live anywhere. Money's not an issue. You
could just take things you need. Like you already do, I think.

— It's not about the things. Or the place. It's —

Mara puts the pack and coat down but says nothing.

It's about people.

— You can't be around people, Boy says.

— It's still a choice. This place is my choice.

— What are you running from?

Mara shakes his head and returns to his seat.

— From everything, maybe. If I can stop it, maybe I just need
to avoid it, too.

— No one could touch you.

— It's not that simple.

— But it is, really. If anyone found you, you could just get away.

— How many times?

— What?

— How many times would I have to do that?

— As many as you needed to, it —

— They remember. And I can't erase memories.

And patterns form. He could put himself in a cardboard
box under a highway or in a mansion, but there are leads and
sightings and the thousand clues a person deposits as he moves
through the world. Stopping time might give Mara room to run,
but memories are long. Connections never fully get erased. All
you can do is run to wherever people aren't. And yet —

— You could just disappear into the woods somewhere, Boy says. But you put yourself here in this culvert. This is a city of half a million people. Thousands of cars must drive above you every day.

Mara moves the book around the small table, lining it up with one corner and then the next. It's an old leather volume, with a faded maroon cover and gold writing on the cracking black spine. *INCOGNITUS IN PSALMOS*. When he moves his head, the light catching his features, there is the faintest trembling of the jaw, the pursing of lips, the deep breaths and swallowing. Until the clenching of jaw muscles banishes all those other tells, setting his face again, hard against the shadows.

— There's someone nearby. Family, Boy says.

— Yes.

— A parent? Brother or sister? Wife?

At the mention of the last one, Mara gets up again and motions towards the entrance.

— You should go. I don't want to talk about it.

— Does she know you're here?

— No.

— Are you still married? How long?

Mara scratches his stubble-lined cheek — not shaved this time — and allows a small, sad smile.

— A long time. A very long time.

— Do you ever make contact?

— I write letters, mail them when I go out and get supplies.

— Never in person?

— There are things you can't go back to.

The image of Mara moving around Hamilton, dropping letters into different mailboxes to mask his trail, doesn't seem quite right. Boy can't see Mara travelling great distances. He says his wife doesn't know, but surely the postmarks tell the story clearly enough. His expression when he speaks about his wife is love, not fear. No, he isn't afraid of her knowing — he doesn't want to be forgotten.

— You'll want to ask about children next, Mara says.

— I will?

Yes, you will, dumbass. Kids left behind and all that.

— But I'll just say again that I don't want to talk about it.

— And this time you'll mean it.

Mara's face relaxes and he lets out a low, tired laugh.

— Exactly.

— So I shouldn't push.

— No, that'll just make me mad.

— We'll save it for another time, then.

Mara doesn't answer, just motions Boy towards the door.

Boy stands on the white-covered stones outside, zips up his coat, and shoulders his pack. It has stopped snowing. The grey sky only dropped another few millimetres of snow, softening the edges of Boy's earlier footsteps. He steps in them as he walks out to the service road, stumbling in exactly the same places he did on the way in. The bottom of the loose fencing cuts a brief arc in the snow as he holds it back and steps through.

— Looks like we'll be coming back, he says. It wasn't so hard to convince him, eh?

As if you were the one doing the convincing.

CHAPTER 10

When his alarm goes off at 4 a.m., Boy's first thought is of the approved forms on his desk from Millhaven, the ones he sent off as soon as he turned eighteen. The ones Misty discovered first and challenged him about. He reaches for his phone and silences the alarm. Squints at the too-bright screen in the darkness, the first nervous pebbles in his stomach beginning to grind together. He dresses himself by the glow of the screen. He grabs the forms and stops at his door, listening. Quiet. A house breathing its easy way towards a Saturday reveille. Breakfast is a muffin and a banana. He slides the forms into his pack, as well as a water bottle and another muffin for the bus ride. The bottle further crushes the two letters and the STI pamphlet that have formed themselves to the bottom. He is tempted to take them out and flatten them against the counter but doesn't. There are thoughts of RMC, Morgan, babies. A corrosive heat in his gut.

The temperature plummeted overnight to an unseasonal low, perhaps the city's last blast of arctic air before being warmed by spring. Outside, the cold blanches the skin of his face and he breathes through his nose to warm the air, his sinuses aching. He softly closes and deadbolts the front door, turns, and nearly walks right into Charlie, who is waiting for him on the front step.

— Shit, he hisses, his heart stumbling to reclaim its rhythm.

Aww. Did you forget about me?

— No. Yes. I just wasn't thinking about you right then.

What were you thinking about?

He walks away from the house instead of responding, his footsteps crunching on the ice and snow and slush that has flash-frozen overnight. Cynthia's car is nowhere to be seen. Maybe she just doesn't work weekends.

The streets are deserted, the stoplights making eyes only at each other along Barton Street. Occasional pillars of steam rise from sewer grates. Every house is dark. The cold distracts him from thinking about Millhaven, the temperature low enough to think about the cold itself. Freezing all the wet snow into ridges and sculptures at the curb. Pasting the moisture to the roads as black ice. The air molecules seem to have actual weight as he walks through them, suspended heavily, moving almost reluctantly aside.

He arrives at the bus stop with a few minutes to spare. He could have waited and taken a late-morning GO bus right from here, but he prefers the quiet. Leaving before anyone is awake. He'll take the first city bus to the old Hunter Street station, an express GO bus to Union Station in Toronto, a train from Union to Kingston, a cab from the Kingston station to Millhaven. About six hours, leaving plenty of time to clear security. He opens the maps app on his phone and zooms into Millhaven in satellite view, its diamond shape and tri-spoked, radial wings stark against the Crown land surrounding the institution.

— Give me your phone. And your boots.

Boy looks up from the bright screen, blinking against his ruined night vision. In the orange glow of the street lamps, he can make out the shape of a guy in a hooded parka. His face is just a shadow deep in the back of the fur-fringed hood. He's short. Boy bends his knees to see his face, his assailant given bulk by the big coat but not an iota of extra height. *A strange, bold move, robbing someone who has at least four inches on you,* Boy thinks, relaxing slightly.

— Come on, man, Boy says. I'm just waiting for a bus here — it's cold.

— Don't be stupid. Give them to me. Now.

There's a flash of metal as a shaking, chapped hand draws a hunting knife from a pocket. It's a good knife, Boy sees, with a thumb stud draw and a locking blade. But then there is a change. The knife is perfectly still, held halfway out from the guy's body, the steam from his breath motionless in front of the deep hood. The sound has stopped. And the few cars moving lazily along the pre-dawn streets.

— Mara, he says, looking around.

Charlie begins to move away, towards the strip mall across the street. He follows, leaving the guy threatening only an empty bus stop. Mara is nowhere to be seen, although Charlie seems to have a sense of where to go. They round the far corner of the mall and see Mara walking up a side street, his khakis bright underneath a navy peacoat. Hands pushed deep into his pockets, pulling his shoulders forward and in, like the coat is swallowing him up against the frigid morning. His feet crunch along the flash-frozen slush and snow, the sound sharp then dull, like it can travel only so far before being arrested like everything else. He stops at a bright red mailbox and draws out a white envelope, looking at it a long moment before dropping it in. The door slams shut, the sound thrumming across the street like a heavy stroke on a deep bass drum before fading. He turns from the mailbox and sees Boy. Briefly looks around as though to escape. Boy walks over. They stand in the splash of light from the street light above.

— You saved me, Boy says.

— What are you doing here?

— I don't think he would've used the knife, but still —

It wouldn't have been his choice — did you see those hands shaking?

— What knife?

Boy tilts his head towards the bus stop and the unmoving thief. From across the street, he looks even smaller, like an action figure forgotten in the yard when the kids are called in for dinner.

— He wanted my phone, Boy says.

— Strange time for a mugging.

— You're out and about, though.

— You, too.

— I'm off to see my dad.

Our dad.

It feels strange to say it aloud. When was the last time he referred to Corny with such intimacy? Had he ever? Had Charlie?

— At Millhaven, Mara says.

— Yes. Wait, how did you know?

— You said your dad has been in prison a long time, which means federal custody. I just assumed it was something bad, which would put him at Millhaven.

— You know a lot about prisons.

— My ministry took me all over.

— Jailhouse confessions?

— Something like that.

Mara and Boy simultaneously stamp their feet against the frozen concrete, as much habit as to keep away the chill. They look at each other and smile, then immediately look down, as though their action has revealed too much.

— Is it your first visit?

— Yes, Boy says.

— Are you ready?

No.

— I think so. I got the forms back weeks ago, and I've wanted to do this for a while, so …

Mara opens his mouth like he wants to speak but closes it. Instead, he just nods slowly, holding Boy's gaze. Boy looks away, feeling as though something he can't see or know has been passed to him. Like trust. Mara coughs and stuffs his gloved hands into his coat pockets. Turns to leave. Boy doesn't want him to, somehow.

— Is the letter for your wife?

— Yes.

— Why not email or call?

Mara chuckles.

— Everything stops, even the electrons that run those things. The screen might stay on or the dial tone might hum, but there'd be nothing behind them.

— From the culvert, you could —

— I prefer the stillness when I do this. I like to take the time. It's just me out here, mostly.

— Doesn't she see the postmark when she gets the letter?

— Probably.

Confirmation. She's content to leave Mara be. He wonders what kind of person she is, what kind of family has such patience and willingness to give a father and husband that kind of space. For Boy, it's beyond imagining, like contemplating infinity.

— She must be something.

That's an understatement.

— Where sin increased, grace abounded all the more.

Mara's voice elevates, as though the words demand their own way of speaking. *They're familiar, too*, Boy thinks, but before he can ask, Mara walks away.

— Good luck today, Mara says over his shoulder.

A few minutes later, the icy intersection begins to move. Boy can see the thief move towards the space where Boy had just been standing only to encounter nothing. He whirls around, confused, fearful that his mark has somehow gotten the better of him. There is a whispering sound that might be Charlie laughing at the would-be thief's predicament. He doesn't see Boy still standing in the accusing glare of the street light. Dazed, he stumbles away, the knife in his hand forgotten at his side, looking for the tall guy with the expensive phone who has disappeared, mid-robbery, into the cold.

CHAPTER 11

— I'm sorry, but you hit positive, the guard says, folding his arms. It's below threshold but still there.

— So what do I do?

— If you want an open visit, you can come back another day —

— But I came all the way from Hamilton.

— Or submit to a strip search. It's late, though, so I can't guarantee you'd get in today.

A body cavity search would be an adventure, little brother.

The extra time he built into his timetable is gone. A delayed bus. An empty taxi stand. A call from Misty, where she rambled for a few minutes in a thick voice, apologized, then hung up. Signing in, storing his gear, unfamiliar security protocols. Then a positive hit from the ion scanner, the machine's insistent alarm. He'd worn clean clothes and wiped everything down with anti-bacterial wipes but still.

— No, I don't want to do that, he says.

— Because the levels are so low, I can pass you through for a closed visit. Have you handled money today?

— For the cab, Boy says.

— Next time, try to avoid cash, especially bills — most of them carry traces.

The guard gives Boy an orange card, tells him to give it to the next guard he sees, and buzzes him through. Another guard, another claustrophobic windowless space. She takes the card, scans the barcode on the visitor pass clipped to his shirt, checks his name against the computer. Directs him down a light green hallway to a waiting room, tells him to listen for his name. Charlie follows him in and assumes a position against the wall. Here, the ceilings and walls seem even closer. There's one other person in the waiting area, a stocky guy with long black hair streaked with white. He nods. Boy says hello, hoping he's not breaking an unwritten rule. He folds and unfolds his arms. Reaches for his phone to text Mark a few times before remembering that his pockets are empty.

— Your first visit, the man says.

— Yes.

— Who're you here to see?

— My father. My dad, I mean.

— That's good. You're a good son. Your band-aid, though —

He taps his forehead. Boy's bandage is sticking only on one side and won't re-adhere.

— I'd just take it off. The stitches look ready to come out.

But before Boy can respond further, the man nods and closes his eyes, sinking his chin to his chest. Not relaxed. Not sleeping. More like praying or meditating. Accompanied only by the rustling of Boy's movements on his own seat, the buzz of the fluorescent lights in their ceiling cages.

Boy's name is finally called. It feels like at least thirty minutes have passed. The other guy went through a few minutes ago, accompanied into the next section by a soundtrack of heavy locks in steel doors. Until this point, the doors were regular industrial inserts, with slit windows covered in translucent privacy film. Remotely controlled locks backed up by regular keyed deadbolts and electronic pass card readers. But the next door Boy will pass through has no windows. One visible lock, an oblong opening for an unusual key. He'd expect to see rounded rivet heads around its periphery, peeling paint, rust. He feels the clanking of the tumblers in his chest. Then the slow, measured opening of the door itself, automated, strong motors.

A burly guard with a clipboard and ill-fitting stab-proof vest pokes his head through.

— McVeigh?

He raises a hand. The weight of where he is settles in his throat.

— This way, please.

The guard walks Boy down another bright green hallway. Where every door is as heavy as the one he's just walked through, although these are barred rather than solid. Every window covered in steel mesh.

And you're the free one. He's in here, even though —

Boy stops and looks back at Charlie, moving along the hallway a few steps behind. She's been silent since the ion scanner.

— Even though what?

The guard asks if he's forgotten something.

— No, I just —

Laughter.

— Inside joke, the guard says. What could you forget — you can't bring anything in, right?

— Right, I guess.

— There's something about that door, though. Almost everyone looks back, especially on their first visit.

Before another heavy door, the guard pauses to adjust his uniform ball cap. Boy reaches up, too, towards his own long-absent wedge cap, a subconscious gesture. Idleness is uselessness, to be avoided at all times. Nerves are easily distracted and concealed by attending to the details. The perch of the headdress. The hang of the tunic. The shine of the boots. Dress and deportment like a dust-free, pressed armour.

The hall takes a final turn before entering a large room with grey cubicles lining the far side. Inside each, a metal stool is fixed to the floor beneath a narrow counter. Black telephone handsets rest in bolted-down cradles at the right side of each space. Thick greenish glass looks through to an identical room on the other side, the same colour scheme and depressing lighting, with only the glimpse of bars on a door differentiating the view. Each stall deep enough that, from the door, he's unable to see which of them is occupied.

— Number seven, the guard says, and sits at a steel desk near the door.

Boy moves down the numbered spaces — all empty — and stops in front of the empty cubicle.

— Guard?

— Yes?

— When will he be here?

— Not long. They called him in as soon as you cleared security.

Boy sits, the metal stool slowly warming under his backside. The hall is quiet, with only a distant, industrial humming of ventilation and other internal building processes. The guard's chair creaks as he rustles papers across his desk. There's a low murmuring from somewhere off to his right. The other guy, he assumes. Boy reaches into his pocket again for his phone, catches himself, shakes his head, and places his hands between his knees to keep from fidgeting. Charlie remains against the wall right behind him, her loose sweater reflected brightly in the glass.

Waiting. He's never been good at it, preferring an organized, bustling life even when it means a lack of downtime. The exception is his place on the rocks, but even there his mind is often unable to slow down even as his body is soothed by the action of the waves. He traces his silhouetted reflection in the dark green glass, trying to discern his own features within his body shape. At home, sitting at the kitchen table on a cloudy day, the glass on the sliding doors that overlook the backyard creates the same effect. On a bright day if he's wearing a white shirt, or at night when the vertical blinds are open and he has the light on his face, he might see himself. When he was a recruit, his cadet instructors sent them home with a homework assignment to interview their parents. *Find out about their decision-making processes, learn something new about your own home.* Boy could have gotten out of the assignment by playing the dead-sister-father-in-prison-grieving-mother card, but he was eager to please his new comrades. The plan was to ambush Misty before she dove into her gin, but he chose a night where she decided to work late. *Work late* were her words, of course. The sickly sweet smell of breathed alcohol, the slurred speech, the bloodshot eyes told a different story. *No, no, let's do this,* she'd said, and Boy had sat with her at the table for almost an hour as she rambled, her reflected movements in the door's glass exaggerated and dark.

Movement on the other side of the glass. Boy sits up straight and rests his elbows on the shallow ledge, perhaps a foot deep, and watches as a guard points at the stool opposite before moving to stand at the rear wall. A tall, gaunt figure appears, dressed in a loose sweater and jeans. His hair is threaded through with grey, and he wears a pair of thick, too-large glasses. He sits and looks at Boy for a long moment.

Boy can't decide which surprising feature to rest his eyes upon. How thin the man is. His greying, curly hair. The thickness of the glasses frames or the wrinkled face behind them. Or the clothes — why had he assumed there would be a prison uniform? The man reaches for the handset and brings it to his ear. Boy does the same. Mirror images in the thick glass, a father contained within the reflected outline of a son.

— You've changed, Boy says.

— It happens.

— I don't remember you wearing glasses.

— I always needed them, but never did enough reading to notice.

— You have a lot of time to read.

— Plenty.

Boy's few prepared questions disappear from the front of his mind, and he falls silent. Most of his preparation has been willing himself onto the bus, imagining what it would be like to pass into the institution. Trying to imagine the direction the conversation would take felt too academic, forced. So this part, where he actually interacts with his absent father, is a big question mark. Will there be stories to share? Information to exchange? Memory to plunder? A long moment passes before Boy finds his voice again.

— Thanks for agreeing to meet with me. My request must have been a surprise.

Corny shrugs.

— It's a nice break in routine. Gets me off the range.

— Misty didn't want me to come. She was pretty pissed I put in the paperwork.

— Why are you here?

Boy opens and closes his mouth, unprepared for Corny's bluntness.

— I just wanted to … I mean, I turned eighteen this year, and —

At the mention of his age, his father looks briefly away. In partial profile, Corny's changes become even more apparent.

Forty-year-old features that could betray a much older man. Skin so pale it's almost translucent, purplish shadows under his eyes, loose skin on his throat, etched crow's feet from the corners of his eyes, fanning out like the exaggerated rays children use to draw sunshine. A scar, new enough to retain its pink anger, is visible at the angle of his jaw.

— It's been more than eight years, Boy finishes, awkwardly.

— Yes, it has.

— And Misty never talks about you or gives us any information.

— This isn't a place you share with family.

Yet here we are. You can't hide away forever.

— I met your mother, Boy says. She's been watching our place. Says she's worried about us.

A snort.

— Cynthia always liked to pry into my business. I bet Carter still buys her a fur coat every Christmas and tells her it's from me, too.

— She said he died a few months ago.

It's out before he can stop himself, a rush of breath forced out from the lungs upon hearing Corny refer to his parents by their first names. Like a fist to the gut. So that's why he and Charlie never used Mom or Dad. Corny's eyes open wide for an instant before he shakes his head again.

— Fucker. Good riddance.

— Why would you say that?

— I don't want to talk about them.

— Because she seemed nice. I mean, they set up a fund for Charlie and me for college. Since I got into RMC, they said I could have Charlie's portion.

— They set one up for her, too?

— Yes.

Corny looks like he doesn't know what to do with the information. Visible pain at the mention of Charlie's name yet burdened by a flash of pure annoyance. The indignity of having someone else do a better job of providing for his children? He rubs his forehead with his free hand, his eyes narrowing.

— RMC, eh?

— I wanted — want — to go air force.

— You get the full ride?

— Yes, but —

— Don't take Cynthia's money. You won't need it, and you don't need them.

— It might not happen anyway.

— No?

— The squadron gave me all sorts of recommendations, and my marks were enough to put me near the top of any list.

— The cadet squadron.

— 742. Yes. You didn't know?

— How could I?

— Oh. Right. Sorry.

— Don't be sorry. You said your marks *were* good enough?

— They've fallen. I don't know if I'll be able to keep my spot.

— Something to do with those?

Corny nods at Boy's forehead. Boy raises a hand, winces as his fingertip snags on a suture knot. The bandage must have fallen off somewhere between the waiting room and here.

— No. Yes. Not directly.

— RMC, though. Not an easy admission. Losing it has to hurt.

— Yeah. It's all I've wanted since joining up. But everything's been so up in the air lately. Between Jay getting born, and my —

Boy stops himself before mentioning Morgan and the pregnancy. Not ready, or sure how, to give it voice.

— Who's Jay?

— The baby.

— Whose baby?

— Misty's. My half-brother.

— Misty is seeing someone?

— She and Nick have been together since —

— Who's Nick?

— Sarah's dad.

Boy falls silent as the slow crawl of understanding crosses Corny's face. Misty moving on. Whom she had chosen to move on with. A baby boy. Then painful acceptance, like silt settling to the bottom of shallow, still water. A long, heavy exhalation. Boy waits. The closed visit area has become quiet, as though the guard and the other visitor are holding their breath like Corny is. No, not holding — you can't hold what's already been driven out.

He didn't know. About any of it. Fuck.

— I know, I know, Boy snaps at her.

— What the hell are you talking about?

Corny misinterpreting Boy's words, that they were meant for him. His father holds the handset away from his ear and strikes the ledge with the other hand. The guard on the other side of the glass reaches for his radio, and starts to move. Corny turns towards him and Boy hears a low, crackly apology, enough to reassure. The guard says something Boy can't hear and stands back against the wall, more watchful now. Corny returns the handset to his ear, shoulders tense, knuckles white.

— I'm sorry, Boy says. I thought you knew.

— No, Misty never —

Corny pauses, considering. Relaxes.

— How old is — is —

— Jay. Jason, actually. Eight months, almost nine.

A sad smile.

— It's a good age. You were almost walking, if I recall. Earlier than most. You were so tall. Babbly, too.

Bits of his past laid in his hands with unexpected gentleness. An oddly paternal display from a parent who was never effusive in praise or emotion. Boy mostly remembers the things Corny let him do, holding tools while his father fixed and built things, with little recall of what was said or meant. Like a muted video. Corny goes quiet, his eyes shiny and rimmed in red, his skin even paler.

— Charlie always said you were a good little brother.

You're a good big brother, too.

— 'A damn good brother,' she said once.

— I'm sorry to dump all this on you, Boy says.

— I feel like I should have known somehow. Look, thanks for coming, but I'm going to go — it's a lot to take in, you know?

A father as distant touchstone. A conversation after eight years of silence, familial emotion locked away like a dangerous thing. Inside and outside this hard penitentiary. It feels good to talk to him, and Boy isn't ready for the conversation to end. It feels like those desperate times he'd follow Corny to the door, plying him with stories just to have him stay and listen.

— Wait. I need your advice, he says.

— What for?

And out it comes. Jay. Misty's drinking. Morgan's letter. His failing grades. And then he surprises himself by talking about Mara. Whether he should ask the man in the culvert who can stop time for help. To keep his scholarship and offer of admission, realign everything that's been jarred apart. Corny listens, intently at first, as though he was eager to have something to offer, but then cuts Boy off in mid-sentence, his anger returning.

— What the hell are you talking about?

— Maybe he could help. He seems like a nice guy, so I thought ...

— You're serious. Now, how would he do that? Stop *time*, I mean?

Boy doesn't catch his father's now-mocking tone.

— I don't know. It's not time, really … it's just what he calls it.

He went deaf after hearing about Mara. He's not ready. You should stop.

— Jesus Christ, Corny says. What is this?

— I was wondering what you'd do. If you were me.

— To start, I'd stop making up stories.

— I'm not. He's —

— And then I'd get my head back on the goddamn ground.

Corny gives his son a long hard look, shakes his head, and hangs up. He turns away from the glass, nods to the guard, and is led away, even as Boy pleads into the silent circuitry of the handset for his father to stay just a bit longer.

PART II
LATE APRIL

CHAPTER 12

Boy is eating his cereal on the back patio when his phone buzzes.

— *im here*

The clock on his phone tells him that Shi's twenty minutes early.

— *give me 5 mins*

Quiet. Now unseasonably warm. Breakfast on the patio a welcome escape from the dusty interior of the garage. He's been awake since five, working to finish his extra credit assignment, a papier mâché model of the Citadel du Québec to accompany the essay his teacher assigned.

By the time he gets dressed and is out the door, more than fifteen minutes have passed. Shi has turned off the minivan's engine and is hunched down behind the steering wheel, probably crushing jewels on her phone. He slides opens the rear door, startling her, and lays the model across the seat. Her eyes widen at the emerald ramparts and the intricate fortifications.

— It's so detailed, she says.

— I got a bit carried away with the model — the essay isn't nearly as good.

— Will it be enough, do you think? Will he even accept it now?

— I don't know. I hope so.

The project is well overdue, lost in life's jet-powered flyby. He's been occupied by weeks of worry about Mara and Corny and Misty and a million other things instead of his schoolwork. His teachers have gone silent about his progress, an ominous sign. Misty has been home and sober, so he should have been redoubling his efforts. But the culvert is a powerful distraction, calling his name right when he opens his laptop or makes a move towards the library. Spring fever, maybe. Bushes and trees filling in for the season. The rocks taking on more of the sun's warmth with each visit, the lake calmer and a promising blue.

The inside of the van is immaculate, like Shi detailed it just before driving over. Vacuum patterns on the carpeted floor and seats, a spray-polish shine on the dash. Even the vents are dust-free. Charlie has made herself at home in the rearmost part of the van, not sitting, not standing, just being there.

Jesus. You'd almost be afraid to sit in here.

A couple of trinkets dangle from the rear-view mirror. Jauntily out of place. The first is a faded, diamond-shaped knot, intricately woven, with three tarnished coins woven into the thread patterns beneath. The other looks newer, three red paper balls connected by twisted red thread and decorated with golden Chinese characters. About eight inches long, they swing with every movement of the van. He can't stop looking at them. Shi shakes her head.

— Those are my father's, the only things he leaves in the van at all, she says. I'm sorry; they're so ugly.

— I don't think they're ugly.

— *I* can't even leave sunglasses in here, or a tube of lip gloss.

Such frustration in her voice. He and Mark have commented on her usual stoicism, how easily she absorbs the nudges and twists of high school life. Boy introduced the two of them a few weeks ago, and she has blended into their dynamic so quickly and easily Boy is regretful that they didn't speak earlier.

— What do they mean?

— The balls are from Chinese New Year.

— Wasn't that a long time ago?

Shi's tense, leaning so far forward it looks as though she could rest her chin on the steering wheel. Nods.

— I don't know why he won't take them down.

— And the other one?

— From their wedding.

— What do the coins mean?

— They're good luck. Both charms are for luck.

— I didn't think church pastors —

— Every Chinese person believes in it. My father says luck has been around longer than the church.

There's an edge to her tone. Not convinced by her father's proclamation. Boy doesn't ask any more questions. He turns to look out the window, watching the suburbs scroll past as they get closer to school. A few minutes later, her phone lights up and buzzes in the cupholder beneath the dash. He reaches for it so she can keep her eyes on the road.

— It's from your mom, but it's in Chinese.

— Is it a long message?

— Just one character.

At the next stoplight, he holds it in front of her. A brief smile flits across her features.

— Well, she apologized. I guess that's something.

— Trouble at home?

— No, not at home. At church.

— What's wrong?

— My father's old boss …

She stops, as though considering how much to say. But before he can tell her it's all right, it's probably none of his business, they arrive at the school. Shi circles the parking lot, looking for a space, but it's full. She exits to the street and pulls into the drop-off roundabout in front of the school.

— Don't wait for me. I have to find street parking.

He gets out, slings his pack, and reaches into the back for the citadel model.

— Thanks for the ride.

— It's my pleasure.

He watches the rear of the van as she drives away.

He sits in the echoic cafeteria, almost alone apart from a few grade nine or ten students whose parents dropped them off early. The serving staff have emerged from their kitchen cocoon, rattling up the steel shutters, looking as though they'd rather be anywhere else. Steam rises from the counter and swirls around nitrile gloves and hairnets. He closes *The Outsider*, the class novel he's been staring at off and on for the past few weeks. Not really seeing it. Pretending to read, maybe.

Impressive effort, as always — you're really outdoing yourself.

— It's a book about nothingness, for God's sake, he says.

Amazing what you pick up even when you don't get past the first fucking pages.

— Maybe it'll be enough to BS my way through the exam.

Mark arrives with a mumbled greeting, throwing his backpack onto the table and heading over to the serving area to get himself something to eat. Shi arrives immediately after, unslinging her bag and reaching in for her own tattered copy of the novel. In just a few moments, she's lost in the book, pausing only to jot things down in an open binder. Impressive time management skills. Mark, his mouth already full, slides his tray onto the table and sits.

— Who were you talking to when I came in?

— No one, Boy says.

— He was just talking to himself again, Shi says without taking her eyes away from her book.

— I was just going over what I'm going to say to Essère.

— How you're going to beg, you mean, Mark says.

— I'm not going to beg.

Boy resists the urge to scan the cafeteria to see where Charlie has ended up. Had he spoken to Charlie aloud again? He's always been so careful only to respond to his sister when they're alone. Misty talks to herself, or did when she was at her worst. He used to make fun of what she said, the drugs and alcohol dissolving her verbal filter. But then it's easier to point at others than yourself, isn't it? Just last week, he'd embarrassed himself in front of the squadron when they asked him to come back and talk about the process of getting into RMC. All those bright eyes and eager cadets, imagining what they could aspire to. When he'd been introduced by the new WO1, a capable but shy cadet who'd been selected to fill Boy's slot, and saw Mark in the corner, he'd become flustered. His friend had been promoted to WO2, but he wouldn't look at Boy. He stumbled through his presentation as though his notes had been rearranged and rewritten in Swahili. The new WO1 had stepped in to cut him off.

The first bell rings, a flat electronic tone with as much verve as a safety lecture, and the three friends gather their things and get to their feet. Boy balances the citadel model on one hand like a serving tray. He turns to see Kyle moving towards them, breathing hard. Humiliated by the hallway incident a month ago, he's remained out of sight, much to Boy's satisfaction. The ease with which he laughed away Kyle's attempt to intimidate him has been enriching hallway gossip for weeks. But here he is.

Message not received.

— What do you want? Boy asks.

— We have to get going, Mark says.

Kyle looks at them for a long moment, as though deciding, his mouth opening, closing. Boy turns away. Kyle steps forward, grabs the model, glances down at it, and heaves it at the wall. No time to react — they can only watch as the model hits, bending, shuddering, splintering. The model falls to the floor, its spine broken, in a pathetic half-lean against the painted cinder block.

— What the fuck did you do that for? Mark asks, stepping towards Kyle.

Kyle brushes Mark aside with one arm like he's no more than vapour and walks away. A tiny smirk lifts the corners of his mouth as though he's just made his own day.

What an unbelievably shitty thing to do.

— Maybe we can fix it, Mark says.

— No, it's ruined, Shi says.

The citadel lies on the ground like a broken soldier. Split across its centre, the balsa wood buildings splintered, the papier mâché ramparts torn and ripped open. Flecks of paint, green from the simulated grass and aqua from the broken barrack rooftops, rest on the concrete floor like tiny islands of colour. Boy presses the tip of his index finger onto one, which adheres to his finger. A single rub of his thumb. Friction. Bright dust in the whorls of his fingerprint.

The second bell rings. Shi and Mark look at Boy, waiting for him to say something. He's moved by their willingness to stay, though there's nothing to be done. He grabs the sides of the model, pulls. The halves separate fully with a cracking sound and a shower of paint and flour dust. He lays one half on top of the other and picks them up.

— Here, let me help, Mark says.

— No, you two are already late. I got this.

— Don't be stupid. Let us help.

— I can't believe he did that, Shi says.

— Should we tell someone?

— No, Boy says.

— But —

— It's an extra credit assignment. It's not like there's a policy for this.

— Boy, it's still your work, Shi says. And he assaulted you. Kyle should —

— I'll be fine. I'll just show Essère and tell him I fell.

Mark rubs his forehead, frowns.

— He shouldn't get away with this, he says. We should tell someone.

He's more upset than you are. That's not right.

— I'll take care of it, Boy says. Besides, now it's easier to carry, right?

He performs a single spin, the citadel's broken halves held high, like he's delivering drinks across a crowded dance floor. Shi and Mark exchange glances.

A bit much, don't you think?

More protests, more offers to walk him to the office, somewhere he can store the broken work until Essère's class, but he deflects. There's nothing more appropriate than to carry the pieces on his own. The project still looks like a citadel. Maybe his teacher will focus on the achievement rather than the loss, the attempt rather than the failure. Or not, he allows. No guarantee that his project or any of his efforts will matter anyhow.

• • • • • • • •

On his spare period, after Essère's class, he exits through a side door and stops, savouring the warmth of the spring sun. The broken halves of his project have been shedding paint and bits of hardened paper with every step. The door closes behind him, its metallic sound echoing across the schoolyard. The yard is empty. In a few weeks, when the grass greens up and the ground dries, students will make the yard their preferred location for study, gossip, and all forms of spring procrastination. Last period, especially, for the scores who can't yet sign themselves out like he can. There is a lot of waiting for the bell happening during last period.

Now what?

— Now we get rid of this thing, he says.

He steps onto the soft ground, moving towards the back of the school. Boy stayed back to show Essère the project and to submit his essay. The teacher had been impressed by the citadel and had spent long minutes in silence, poring over every defensive angle and gun port. *I know it's late, sir,* Boy said. *More than late — it was due weeks ago,* Essère replied, watching him for a reaction.

Boy, feeling the birth pains of an angry response, focused on the floor precisely two finger-widths from one of the desk's legs. The ideal space between a cadet wedge cap and the eyebrows. Hard to argue the point, really, but it was hard not to be angry in the instant when he saw that all his work might be for nothing. Felt the ache in his gut for a grade twelve year being pulled away like intestines being unravelled one coil at a time. But here, anger would solve nothing. *Keep control, Cadet. It will only get worse if you lose control.* Better to level things out with precise contrition. *Yes, sir, I'm sorry,* he said. Essère grunted and held his hand out for the essay, taking it and sliding it into his briefcase with barely a glance. *I haven't decided whether or not to grade it — I just don't know how many more chances I have to give,* he said. Then he dismissed Boy with an irritated wave.

As Boy walks along the outside of the school, he passes the classrooms lining the side of the old building. He feels watched. Teachers. Distracted students. He can't see them because of the bright reflections in the glass but feels it anyhow. Every window has been opened a few inches at the bottom. In spring, everyone looks outside as often as they can, seeking any portal to the warmth, even by lifting dusty windows up for a few inches of fresh air.

He turns back towards the entrance, then reverses himself. Stops. The citadel awkwardly aloft, teetering. Just moments ago, through the slit window in her classroom door, he saw Ms. Vos marking essays at her desk, her face inches from the papers, as though she forgot her glasses this morning. He didn't pause then, but he now wonders if she might still extend grace, or whether she has hardened herself like Essère.

— Maybe I should go back in and beg her for mercy, he says.

All you can do is ask. What's there to lose?

Depends, he thinks, *on what value you place on pride, whether a person has enough to keep laying more and more of it on the altar of expectations.* Strategically crawling back for another chance after he has squandered so many feels dirty, too. And begging? The word is vinegar, its aftertaste just as foul.

— Not a chance.

You're not thinking straight.

— So you keep telling me.

He imagines every pair of eyes in the building looking out at the same instant. Seeing him standing in place and talking to himself. He makes his feet move to the rear of the building, to the fenced-in area the teachers use for their cigarette breaks. The ground here is packed earth, compressed by a thousand brief escapes. A stale tang of tobacco smoke in the air. In the corner stands a cut-off oil drum for extinguishing cigarettes. He throws the halves of the citadel into it, hearing the dull crunch of the project's corners sinking into the sand at the bottom. Imagines a harried teacher sneaking in a few drags before class dropping a barely smoked cigarette onto the papier mâché, the citadel smouldering.

If only he could stay and watch.

But no, now that Essère's project is done, there is another bit of unfinished business. Corny's bike has been locked to the racks for over a month, miraculously escaping the attention of the maintenance crew's hungry bolt-cutters. He misses the old, orange monstrosity, preferring the consistency of pedal power to the unpredictability of bus schedules and the slowness of walking. He walks over to the racks, digging through the envelopes and papers at the bottom of his pack for the key. The bike has suffered further indignities. Tubes stick out from between rubber and steel like long, limp tongues. Handlebars twisted sideways, grip tape askew. Gear and brake levers wrenched free, dangling to the ground at the end of their cables. Spokes kicked in. A sharp object has been dragged across the finish, scoring the orange paint down to the metal.

He pulls out his phone.

— *got bike where are you?*

Shi's response is almost immediate.

— *teacher let us out early meet at front*

The bike wobbles as he wheels it away, the rear wheel squealing, echoing against the school's high stone walls. A number of senior students are sprawled out across on the wide stone steps at the front. A few heads turn towards the sound, smirk at the sight of the gangly giant wheeling it along, and return to flirting, reading, and various states of un-study. Laptops, binders, pens, phones, clothing scattered around like the debris field of a strange tragedy where students explode when they leave the school. One of the massive front doors opens, and Shi walks out, shouldering on her backpack, and tying her black hair up in a ponytail. She smiles.

— We never get out early, she says. I'm not sure what to do with myself.

— You should get into some trouble.

— *We* should get into trouble, you mean.

— I'm not sure now is a great time.

— How'd it go?

The natural question. Genuine curiosity. Sideline cheering. He briefly entertains the idea of telling her about Essère's non-committal response, deciding against the conversation with Vos, dumping the citadel in the teachers' guilty fortress at the back of the school.

— Fine, he says. It went fine.

She looks down at the bike.

— You weren't kidding. It's in rough shape.

— Some family heirloom, eh?

Being new to the area and school, she hadn't known about his family's history. A couple of days after their introduction on the bus, she found him in the cafeteria and presented a laptop full of Google research, telling Boy he'd led a fascinating life. He'd never googled himself. All those fragments linked together, crawling up and down the screen. Cadet stuff. School board scholarship lists. Family tragedy. *I'm sorry about your sister*, she said.

— So your dad left it to you when he went to jail?

— I kind of adopted it, he says. It just sat in the garage all those years. I never saw Corny ride it.

— Corny?

— My dad. He and Misty always insisted we use their first names.

— Misty, I've heard, but I've only heard you call him Dad.

— Huh. Strange. Corny's from Cornelius, which is my middle name, too.

— I didn't know that.

— Charlie could never just use his name, though. Fucking Corny, she'd always say.

— That's the first time I've heard you say her name, either. Or swear. I read about her, of course, and the other girl.

— Sarah.

— Right, Sarah. Would you —

Looking down at the bike's defaced yet bright frame, she falls silent. Any death, even the most tragic and most in need of purging, might as well be a forbidden topic. For the awkwardness it breeds in conversation. He wishes it wouldn't close people's mouths, that there was just the easy interactions you rely on in friendships. They walk to the van in silence. He looks for an opportunity to help her move past the moment but doesn't find one, even as they drive. She parks the van in front of the shop and from the driver's seat watches him drag the bike onto the sidewalk.

— I can wait and give you a ride home afterwards, she says.

— I have some other things to do while I'm out, but thanks.

— Okay. See you tomorrow.

As he walks in, standing behind a fat, middle-aged man who insists on making small talk with the bike store guy behind the cash, he realizes he never thanked her. He pulls out his phone to text her but is interrupted by another employee emerging from the back of the store, wiping her hands on a greasy rag. Asking how she can help.

When he walks out of the store some time later, King Street is quiet, without a car or pedestrian in sight. He looks around, folding the yellow copy of the repair invoice in half and then in half again. Along the old building's facade, the bike shop's tinted windows are dotted bright with cycling brand stickers and taped-up notices. Clouds, brilliant against the blue sky, scud into their own dusty reflections. He slides the repair slip into his wallet and heads towards Niffin Street, where he'll cross and head over to Main to get the bus back out to Stoney Creek.

The quiet is unusual. This is a busy but rundown stretch of King, just east of downtown, where rents are low and the neediest can put down roots. Aside from the family-run bike shop, the only other building tenants are a pawn shop, two loan and cheque-cashing franchises, and a reptile store. The remaining spaces are vacant, windows papered over and smudged from neglect and time. New development is devouring land east and south of the city with a bland, wealthy appetite but not much has changed in this part of the city. When his parents needed to buy pills or weed, they'd put the suburbs in their rear-view mirror and head into the core. No one knew Misty here, and she could score without tainting her image. Corny always drove. Misty navigated, seeking out addresses scrawled on small, damp pieces of paper. Boy and Charlie sat in the back and nudged each other at every interesting person and occurrence, pointing, keeping their hands out of sight.

A murmuring sound rises as Boy nears the intersection. Around the corner, on Niffin, a lineup, perhaps two dozen strong, has formed next to a nondescript door and stretches along the narrow sidewalk. Some have their heads together, smoking and chatting. A few have their phones out, tapping away and ignoring everyone else. Others lean against the wall and stare. The building, freshly stuccoed and clean, looks at odds next to the crumbling brick and cement of its neighbours. *The Niffin Street Clinic* engraved above the door in black capital letters. *It makes sense now*, he thinks. The newness of the facade. The long lineup. The hollowed-out expression on every face. The clinic is a methadone treatment centre that made the news a few months ago, forced from its downtown home when the neighbourhood's rents shifted tenants towards the upscale. Lots of traffic. The distance not decreasing the need.

His phone thrums in his pocket. A text from Mark, out of class and looking to meet up. Boy's thumb hovers over the screen. How to let Mark know he has other plans — going to the culvert — without sounding dismissive. Or repetitive. He's become creative with the language he uses to blow off his friend without making his friend feel blown off. Another vibration.

— *was essere happy to see project?*

— *happy not the word*

— *thats great! i hope you get all a's*

Not what he meant. He starts to thumb out a further reply when his eyes are drawn to a woman wheeling a rickety baby stroller along Niffin. Slightly built, in old jeans, tattered trainers, a peeling Ti-Cats jacket. Cries from the baby in the stroller. A baby boy. His filthy face peeking from a tiny blue hoodie is a sickly hue of jaundice. He sounds weak, like he's already used up his life supply of volume. The men waiting beside the clinic make way, just enough to allow passage before returning to their places. Temporary displacement, like air moved by a plane's wing. She pushes the stroller up the access ramp, the clip-clip-clipping of the chipped wheel almost drowning out the baby's voice, and disappears inside. Surprising how easily they let her by — chivalry, manners, universal deference to women with babies are often no match for addiction's chemical need.

And what a thing, bringing a baby into such a place. He is overcome by the urge to rush into the clinic, scold her, grab the kid. His feet carry him across Niffin and into the clinic past the men who still say nothing. Inside, everything is stainless steel and frosted glass, softly lit, soothing colour shades. Every chair occupied. The mother leans towards the window to register, her child now on one hip. The baby has quieted, exhausted, eyeing the people in the waiting room. Boy stops. What exactly could he do? Turn the mother away from all her troubles? Share the magic elixir of parenthood, so the baby boy is nurtured and provided for? Boy, the saviour? Fixed to the wall is a display full of medical pamphlets in their little Plexiglas holders. A veritable education in tidy, folded packages. All for free. Maybe he'll walk her over and arm her with the knowledge she'll need to meet every immediate demand with grace and vigour.

There's no point, you know that, right?

Charlie's right, of course. It's not about what can be offered, but the willingness to take it. To change. And sometimes even then the strongest will cannot change a thing. He should just go.

A pamphlet on the wall unit draws his eye. Titled in various neon shades, a signal-flare assault on the eyes. *Have You Been Tested?* He slides out the bright trifold, opens it. Colours bright enough to illuminate his hands and fingers in an improbable glow. Tiny, jarring text. He closes the pamphlet, puts it back into its slot. Looks again, closer this time, at the title, which seems to have changed. *STIs: What You Need to Know.*

Not so vague, then.

And it comes back to him. The other pamphlet, the one given to him by Dr. Kamat listing the locations where anonymous testing can be done. *Well, why not*, he thinks. Settle a big question right here and now.

As he takes a step closer to reception, the baby cries out, a long, thready wail. Heartbreaking. Then a hitch, a snuffling sound, silence. The young, strung-out mother has finally brought the baby to her breast. His yellowed skin distinct against her pallor, his eyes closed, his suckling deep and content. She is bent

over his head, whispering into his ear. Is she lending secrets and
wisdom he might need later on in life? Boy wants to know. But
can't. He turns away, walks out of the clinic, and heads towards
the bus stop. If his timing is right, he won't have to wait long for
the eastbound express bus heading across town.

Mara takes the white plastic bag from Boy and looks inside.

— What is this?

— I stopped by the supermarket on the way back from —

Boy stops himself from mentioning his moment in the clinic.
His own burden to bear, even though the urge to spill it to someone has been building. *Buck up, Cadet — push it down, lock it up,
take the pain.*

— From school.

— You shouldn't have. I don't —

— You have to eat.

— I don't need your food. Take it back.

— No. It's for you.

Mara walks out of the culvert and places the bag on the
stones outside. He sits at the table and picks up the book he was
reading when Boy arrived with the food, a few snacks and pieces
of fruit. Why is he being so stubborn? Apart from a blue camping
water carrier and a couple banged-up hiking bottles, Mara seems
to keep nothing around for nourishment.

— The animals will get it out there, Boy says, turning towards
the entrance.

— Don't, Mara says.

— Why?

Mara carefully places a worn cloth bookmark between the
pages, closes the book, folds his arms against his chest, and looks
at Boy for a long, uncomfortable moment.

— Thank you for thinking of me. But I do a lot of fasting. In fact, I'm fasting most of the time. You wouldn't understand —

— In cadets, we learned about rationing food and making it last.

— It's not about preservation. I can get food whenever I want. But more a spiritual process. Self-denial. Submission.

A rote response, Boy thinks. Learned in a book and recited verbatim when a certain question gets asked.

— I don't know why you'd deny yourself if you don't have to.

Instead of replying, Mara gets up from the table, stretches, and walks to the back. A long, thin box leans against the concrete wall. It looks like it's travelled a long way to get here. Battered edges, numerous scuffs and scratches. He kneels and takes out a razor knife from an old metal toolbox and begins slicing through the tape along the edges of the box. Nods towards the toolbox.

— This was my father's. It never left the trunk of the car, so every time we'd hit a bump, they'd clank around back there. Drove my mother crazy.

The toolbox contains a number of basic tools, screwdrivers, a hammer, wrenches, pliers, clippers, a spirit level. Old tools. Chipped, hand-darkened woods, oxidized and rusted metals, the muted colours of old things. No plastic anywhere.

— Why do you need to fast so much?

— Give a hand, will you?

Mara unpacks the box. A small white booklet, stamped in foreign words and line drawings, falls at his feet. Mara tosses over a plastic pouch containing a selection of dowelling, plastic things, and fasteners. Boy has no choice but to catch it.

— You're in charge of those.

— Mara —

— I don't want to talk about it.

— Now or ever?

— I don't know.

Mara goes silent, leaving Boy to hold the pouch and watch him work. After a few moments, Boy crouches down and lays it on the floor. There's a rag stuffed inside the toolbox. Boy takes it out, shakes it free of metal filings, sawdust, and the tools' rusty remnants; lays it flat on the culvert floor; and begins sorting the extras into ranks by size and type. Mara stops unpacking the box and watches him.

— I don't get it. How can you be so disciplined and have the instinct for that kind of precision and still be failing your courses?

— Anyone can —

Mara holds up a hand.

— Maybe, but most people wouldn't. They'd just dump everything out and get building.

Boy carefully places the final pieces and waits for a proclamation, a nugget of wisdom meant to inspire, to realign. When he told Mara a couple of weeks ago about the danger of losing his RMC acceptance, Mara didn't make any proclamations and hadn't mentioned it since. Boy figured he must be waiting for the right time, but the priest just studies the instructions without comment. He's grateful for the space. The respectful silence. Still …

— I didn't tell you about the girl in Washington.

— No, you didn't.

So he tells Mara about the last night on the cadet trip to DC. The drugs, the sex. Morgan's letter. About how he had been managing to hold everything together until the envelope arrived like a bird strike at altitude. His inability to reach out to her.

— Have you told anyone else?

— The doctor at the clinic knows what happened but not the pregnancy. Corny at Millhaven —

— How did he react?

Boy just shakes his head, stopping himself from telling the complete story. Not knowing how Mara would react to Boy telling Corny about his ability.

— So she hasn't reached out again?

— No. And I bail every time I think about contacting her. What should I do?

— I'm not the one to —

— You're a priest. What would you say to someone in your parish who was going through this?

— Pastor, remember? We don't do confession.

— I'm not confessing. I just need some advice.

— Are you sure you want it? You might not like it.

— Yes.

— Wait.

— Just *wait*?

— If she wants you involved, she'll tell you.

— For how long? What if she never …

His words trail away. Even if he does reach out, even if she receives his overtures, he still can't expect to be involved. It isn't up to him.

— It's a hard reality, but it has to come from her. For the baby's sake, too. If it's her initiative, she'll paint you in a more favourable light.

Mara grabs a few bits of dowelling and starts inserting them into holes at the ends of the boards. One slips from his grasp and skitters across the concrete. It comes to rest against the far wall, the wood bright and warm against the cool grey cement. They work in silence for a few minutes before Mara speaks again.

— How did the project go, the one for the history teacher?

— I handed it in today.

— Great. And?

— And nothing. He couldn't guarantee I'd get a mark.

— That's fair, I suppose.

— How is that fair? All my work, with nothing to look forward to?

— It's called grace for a reason.

— Oh, that's rich. You're in fine form today. Fasting? Grace? I thought you'd be on my side about this.

— I am on your side. But your teacher's actions don't seem unfair to me. I'm sorry you aren't —

— That's it? An apology?

— You aren't seeing it from all sides.

— Useless. All useless.

— I don't understand. What's useless?

— You. This. All of it, Boy says, waving his arm around to encompass the culvert and the scrub and the rocks beyond. I mean, what good is a priest who can stop everything when he just buries himself away? You could fix so many things.

Mara takes a deep breath and stands.

— There's nothing to fix.

— You could do anything!

— You think what I have is a tool I can use for whatever I please.

— Yes, or —

— Or that it can help.

— Of course.

— Well, it can't. That's not how it works. It can't fix anything; it can only hurt more. It's a curse. Why do you think I'm here?

— Because —

— You can't possibly know.

Mara moves towards the mouth of the culvert, his jaw set, his eyes hard, the lines on his pale face etched even more deeply. Mara grabs his jacket, moves through the hung plastic, and walks down towards the lake. Boy waits a long time, the realization that he needs to apologize settling into his bones along with the cooler air near the entrance. But Mara stays away. In the end, Boy heads out, pausing at the entrance to look out at the dusk-darkened lake. Sensing Mara out there somewhere, just waiting for him to leave.

Leave the lights on — it gets dark so quickly these days.

CHAPTER 13

In his dream, he's a cadet at a parade night in his induction year. He's wearing his first uniform, issued to him without proper fitting, the one he wore before his growth spurt. But he's as tall as he is now. Every movement constricted, like he's been stitched into a tortuous support device. Every step small, to avoid splitting his seams and tearing himself into nakedness. Sitting is impossible, so he stands at the back of the classroom, awkwardly attempting to take notes in a navy blue notebook. The nervous sergeant — obviously giving his first lecture — has forgotten to put the class at ease, so all the cadets remain at attention. Boy is the only one without a seat. Charlie is there, too, her uniform hanging on her like a sack. She sits at attention like everyone else, her back straight and shoulders back, hands fisted beside her thighs, thumbs resting on the first joint of her index finger. The sergeant can't seem to string even a single sentence together in a cohesive way. Boy is just about to rescue him by simply taking over, the embarrassment of his own tiny uniform be damned, when he becomes aware of a strange sound in the classroom, rising in intensity, only he seems to notice. Eventually his awareness evolves and he wakes up to the realization that his phone, on silent, has been buzzing away on his table, inserting itself into his dream. He rolls over, squints at the display. Shi. Just after six in the morning. He groans, closes his eyes, and brings the phone to his ear.

— Well, this is a first, he croaks.

— I woke up to study, and his text was waiting for me. Did you get one?

— Have we ever actually called each other?

— Boy, listen —

— I mean, I can't even recall the last time I've phoned someone —

— Mark's in the hospital.

Boy sits up, awake now, and looks again at the screen. Sure enough, there's a notification there, pulsing like a tiny heart. It arrived just after midnight. He reads it aloud.

— *am at the general, will be here for a few days. kyle got me after school. im ok.*

— That's the message I got, too, Shi says.

— Oh my God. Did you call?

— No, he's probably sleeping.

— Yeah.

— We should go see him. I'll ask to borrow the van again.

Boy can't help but feel pulled towards the door, as though he should go to the hospital right now. *Slow down*, he tells himself, *there's no way they'd let you in to visit this early.* Family, maybe, but not just anyone, even a best friend beginning to ask himself if they should have waited for Mark after school. And why did Kyle hurt Mark? Sure, he's the amped-up high school cliché, but actual, physical violence?

— I don't know, she says. He's more of a nuisance than anything.

Shit, he thinks. *I must have spoken aloud.*

— I had the same thought about staying longer yesterday, Shi continues. Maybe we should have.

— We couldn't have known, right?

— I was just so excited to leave early.

— Me, too.

— Should we go visit first thing?

Boy gets out of his bed and stretches as they discuss logistics, trying to get his blood moving. Another abbreviated rest. It took a long time to fall asleep, the conversation with Mara moving around his mind in circuits. Then those unsettled dreams.

After they end their call, Boy hears Jay crying tentatively, like he can't decide whether he's hungry enough to wake up. Boy goes into his brother's room and is greeted by a yip of delight and the rustle of excited movement. Jay raises his arms to be lifted from the crib.

— Morning, little man. Miss me?

Jay buries himself against Boy's neck.

— Let's get you something to eat.

Jay babbles their way down the stairs. When Boy shows him an empty bottle from the cupboard, he reaches for it, immediately trying to pull off the lid while Boy takes out the carton of formula. When he brings Jay into the family room, he can barely settle onto the sofa before Jay is working the nipple.

Boy is worried about Mark, but also angry about how long he waited to tell them. He wants to fire off a quick, sharp text, one that carries the lightness of banter as well as the clear weight of rebuke, but the phone is back in the bedroom. Probably a good thing. Mark's text really said nothing at all. Maybe he made it light to cover a far more serious reality. Internal bleeding. Surgery. Worse. That would be just like him — Mark's a good cadet, a good leader. He'd know when to understate things to keep panic in check. He has had the same training. *They'll look to you when it all falls apart — keep it together, for everyone's sake.*

— I should know that, too, right? he asks, his voice low.

Jay stirs and looks up at Boy with sober, serious eyes.

— But it's not looking too hopeful at the moment, is it?

Jay's only response is a contented grunt. He closes his eyes again. *To have such simplicity*, Boy thinks. *Such contentment*. Yet he isn't living simply, is he? He's already faced more tough moments than most suburban kids face through their entire lives, and the contentedness is more in spite of his environment than because of it. A message to the universe in his own language. Too much to see and wonder and do to let neglect get in the way. *Keep it simple, Cadet, and thrive, that's the secret.*

Keep it simple, he thinks.

Simple.

The simplest of solutions comes to him, clear but as diffused as a sonic boom reaching the ground thirty thousand feet below. He doesn't need RMC. He'll enlist in the regular forces.

It's not elegant. Unlike the direct path through RMC, he'd have to work his way through the non-commissioned ranks. Start as a private recruit, the lowest of the low. Low pay, low responsibility, low opportunity to shine. But the good always rise, don't they? At first, whenever he trained at 742, Charlie's dream was always there, reminding him that he was marching where she would have marched, marking her parade ground. But he quickly grew into his own uniform. Didn't see her face as often in the mirror-gleam of his drill boots. Service and discipline, so uncomfortable at first, fitting themselves to him as comfortably as sized leather gloves. And now? Surely he could reclaim his discipline enough to attract notice, even amidst the mud and grit of an enlisted life. Climb a little quicker than everyone else. Serve notice of his potential. His dream of becoming an air force pilot would not be eclipsed; promising enlisted personnel can and do make the leap to become officers. His cadet successes and squadron connections would fast track him through the recruitment process. An ideal candidate. Bright. Healthy. Clean. Motivated.

Plus, he's eighteen, so he doesn't need anyone's permission. He could walk into the Bay Street recruiting centre and walk out with a handshake promise, a backpack full of forms and literature, an earful of encouragement to wait for the call. So simple. Why should he create so many barriers to break himself against when he could sweep them away so easily? Why worry when a new life, a good life full of the adventure he's always craved, is within reach?

— Good call, Jay — simple it is.

His whispering voice seems to disappear into the darkened family room. He smiles, closes his own eyes, and leans his head back against the sofa's cushions. He and Jay are asleep within minutes.

— We'll be fine, Misty says, yawning.

— Are you sure?

— I've told you before: this isn't my first rodeo.

— I know it's sudden. It's just that —

— You can't plan for these things. Go see your friend.

Boy hears the minivan before it pulls into the driveway. Shi has her music up, and he can feel the muddy vibrations even in the house. Like he has ears full of cotton. The tune is distantly familiar, a pop anthem that slid off the charts months ago. He gets into the passenger seat and sees that Shi has been crying. He has to yell to be heard.

— Are you all right?

Shi twists the stereo's knob down, clicking off the music.

— Just loud enough to be a good distraction, she says.

— We couldn't have known Mark would —

— Oh, Mark, right. Him, too.

— What's going on?

She wipes her eyes and waves away his question, says it's nothing.

Fuck that — she's hiding something.

Boy laughs, surprising her.

— I'm sorry, he says. That was harsh — but it's clearly *not* nothing.

— My father, he —

And she pauses, looks at her hands in her lap, wrestling with how much to say. Boy is used to her reticence. At first, he assumed it was a Chinese thing, like saving face or a Great Wall of family secrets. No. Shi just controls her words and emotions. Strengthening herself, like rebar strengthens concrete. Still, she does open up to him and Mark, if infrequently and in her own time, so he waits.

— Some people from my father's old church, the one that sponsored him to come to Canada, are making nasty allegations about him.

— What are they saying?

Shi simply shakes her head in response, her eyes filling again.

— I can't even say it.

— All right.

She performs a precise shoulder-check and backs into the street. They drive to the hospital in almost silence, the morning traffic outside a pleasant white noise. By the time they arrive, her eyes have dried. In the elevator, Shi pulls out her phone to find the text Mark sent with his room number.

— I asked him to send a selfie to prepare us, she says.

— Let me guess — he hasn't.

— No. And I was all ready to reply that it was a big improvement.

Deadpan delivery, deliciously unexpected, given everything going on. Boy tries to keep a straight face.

— Well, that's just inexcusable, he says.

— Selfish, right?

They trade a look and burst out laughing just as the elevator opens to the recovery floor. Startling an orderly who has fallen asleep waiting for the elevator. Put out at having his rest interrupted so rudely, he pushes past, glaring at them with red, shadowed eyes set deep in a stubbled face. They approach the nurses' station smiling, savouring such a rare light moment.

— It's early, the duty nurse says. You're family, then?

— Oh, yes, Shi says and giggles.

The nurse looks like she's going to make an issue of it, these two teenagers who are clearly not family, but then thinks better of it and directs them to Mark's room near the end of the hall.

Mark is asleep in the bed next to the south-facing window. He has the four-bed room all to himself at the moment. The blinds have been drawn, and an untouched breakfast tray sits on a swing table over his legs. A trio of studious machines blink and glow silently next to the wall. He's pale but looks otherwise fine — no bruises or lacerations mar his exposed skin. Hands resting peacefully on his legs, one wrist bangled by ID tags and a taped intravenous line. Boy is relieved to see how well he looks.

— Maybe we should text him and let him know we've arrived, he says in a stage-whisper.

Mark's eyes open, squinting against the morning haze.

— It's just us, Shi says.

— Hey, guys.

His words, drawn out across a second and a half, are light and wispy, barely his own. His smile is too broad.

— They've doped you up pretty good, Boy says.

— Yes, sir, they have indeed.

Shi lays a hand on Mark's sheeted foot.

— How are you?

— I'm fine, fine. How about you two?

— Have they told you how long you need to stay? Boy asks.

— No, not yet. They use the word observation a lot.

He shifts, pushing himself to become more attentive to his guests. His face twists in on itself, its placid glow replaced by a rictus of pain. A quick new pallor. He gasps.

— Fuck, that hurts.

Boy and Shi exchange concerned glances. Mark's all-is-well veneer stripped away and thrown into the room's dim corner by one movement and a precise swear word.

— Sorry about that, he says and reaches for a button on a long cord tied to the bed next to his hand. He squeezes it, waits, and closes his eyes a moment later.

— Self-medication — best idea ever, he says, dropping the control.

— What happened?

— I remember waiting for you, hearing Kyle's voice behind me, and then waking up here. With these.

He lifts his shirt. Boy and Shi take in a sharp, audible breath. Mark's abdomen is covered in abrasions and bruises. He begins giving a guided tour.

— This one is a broken rib, this one here is my contused liver, under here my spleen may have been ruptured, and they might have to remove it today.

— Mark, we're so sorry. If we'd been there —

Boy's voice trails off. Mark drops his shirt and shakes his head.

— I'll be fine. Hey, Shi, are you okay?

— I need to step outside for a few minutes, she says.

— I'll go with you —

— No, stay with Mark. I'll come back in when my stomach settles.

And she's gone before Boy can protest any further.

— It was my fault, Mark says after a moment.

— Why would you say that?

Mark is quiet a moment before responding.

— I threatened him.

— Kyle?

— After the citadel thing, I found him later, and —

— Mark, that was stupid. He's —

— I'm just so tired of how much of an asshole he's being to you.

— But threatening him? That's just going to piss him off.

A distant smile.

— Apparently.

— Did anyone see it happen?

— No. Vos found me, though, and called my folks. No one knows anything.

— I'll ask around today. What happened to Kyle?

— Nothing. I haven't told anyone it was him.

— What? Jesus, you have to say something.

— I don't know. What if —

His voice fades.

He's protecting you.

— This is bigger than a shove in the hall or a broken model, okay? You're in the hospital, for God's sake. The police —

— No way.

— What would you say to one of your cadets?

Mark closes his eyes and takes a deep, pained breath. Shakes his head.

— No.

— Mark, come on.

— My mom stayed all night, but she must have stepped out for something.

— We have to —

— I'm sure she'll be back. You should go.

Mark's last few words are slurred, and his eyelids begin to drift together. Boy stands at the foot of the bed, watching his friend give in to the painkillers. Within a minute or two, he's snoring gently, riding a painless cloud of sleep, his face relaxed. How different a day can look when you're thrown into it so early. He had just resolved to tell his friend today about his decision to enlist in the regular forces. Rip off the bandage. Deal with Mark's disappointment, knowing it will eventually turn into support. But not now.

A nurse arrives, checking the machines and making a show of looking at her watch. Boy walks into the hall, where Shi leans against a closet door.

— Mark's asleep. Did you want to go back in?

— No. I'm still not ready. Let's just go.

Official visiting hours are still some time away, so the ward is quiet, with only the occasional snoring and mumbled sleep-talk filtering into the hall. They don't say anything as they wait for the elevator, each lost in thought. Boy's phone begins to vibrate, its buzzer sounding loud in the hushed atmosphere. He answers but for a long moment hears only the distant hiss of the open line and fragments of distant voices.

— I'm sorry, a scratchy voice finally says. I'm so sorry.

Boy looks at the screen. Area code 613 and a number but no other information.

— Who's this?

— I was angry when you left. I made jokes about what you said. About that guy, stopping time —

A pause.

— I didn't realize he was paying attention.

613. Kingston? Millhaven?

— Corny?

— They got it out of me. I'm sorry —

And the voice hitches, tries again, breaks. The hiss of the line, those amputated voices again. A click. The phone beeping to end the call.

— I'd like to have seen it, Mara says.

— Didn't you hear me? The guy who broke the citadel is the one who went after Mark.

— I was disappointed the last time when you didn't offer to let me see it. You'd talked about it so much I felt almost like a part of the process.

— It's gone, Mara. Now will you help me or not?

Boy and Mara sit at the mouth of the culvert, looking down the stone spillway at the lake. Charlie is nowhere to be seen, having vanished as soon as he passed by the rocks on the way here. Mara insisted on bringing the chairs here to take advantage of the warm sunshine. He's in a strange mood, where everything needs to take twice as long — movements, words, responses — and Boy is becoming impatient. After the hospital, Shi drove them both to school but Boy didn't sign in, instead rushing over to the rocks with Kyle's violence, Mark's injuries, and Corny's cryptic phone call tumbling around his mind.

— I'm glad things have warmed up so nicely. The winter felt too long. The concrete really gets into your bones.

— Mara, please —

Mara crosses one leg over the other and leans back in the chair, closing his eyes and lifting his face to the sun. His hands are laced behind his head. *Relaxed enough to be on holiday*, Boy thinks.

— Tell me how I could possibly help, Mara finally says.

— You could stop everything, give me a chance to make things right.

— By doing what, exactly?

— He couldn't fight back.

— Boy, stop. Think about what you're asking.

— I have thought about it. Why do you think I'm —

— Look beyond the immediate. What happens afterwards?

— No one would catch me.

— Maybe not. But Kyle isn't really your biggest problem, is he?

— It was just a phone call. A strange one, but —

— I'm not talking about Corny's call.

— Quit tossing it back to me and help out with this one thing.

— No.

— But your ability, it's —

— I'm not here because I have to be, but because I want to be. If it was a matter of "fixing" things, I'd have disappeared a long time ago.

Boy watches Mara's face. His eyes have remained closed throughout the conversation, and his expression remains calm. But what he said, about need versus choice, that he remains here by his own will, hangs between them like a mist. Not a threat, but …

— This doesn't change anything, Boy says. I'd never betray you.

— And I've enjoyed your visits. I look forward to them.

— Well, me, too, but —

— What you're asking isn't a solution.

Boy starts to protest.

— Stop. Don't make me insult your intelligence by explaining the consequences of violence.

— This would be on me, not you.

— No.

— I have to do something.

— So do something. Press charges, support your friend, get that idiot expelled. But don't ask me to help. It's impossible to unmake a wrong, and I won't try it again.

Boy stands up angrily, upsetting the chair. It falls backwards, its metallic clatter swallowed in one direction by the culvert and echoing in the other across the stones.

— That's fucking weak.

Mara opens his eyes and regards him coolly for a moment. Then he laughs, quick and emphatic.

— That's the whole point of why I'm here. Of course I'm weak.

— If you won't help, I'll tell the police you're here.

— You can predict how that will go, too.

Mara is right: there's nothing to corner him with. And he's just stating a simple fact: he won't be cornered. Reminding Boy that when it comes to bad things there is only forward motion, imperfect though it might be. After a hurricane, you can rebuild, but there's no point in marching out against a storm long since gone. Still, there will be anguish and grief. Regret. He grabs his pack and starts to walk away.

— You're always welcome here, Mara says to his back. And I'm sorry I have to say this, but please don't ask again. If you do, you'll never see me again.

It's raining by the time he gets home. Despite the earlier, clear skies, a low, scudding bank of clouds has rushed ashore, first blanketing the area in a thick, damp fog and then dumping its swollen contents on anyone caught outside. The frigid deluge has dropped the temperature a few degrees and has soaked him through. An old instinct, driven into his subconscious by Misty's strident warnings about wet clothing on the carpets and hard-wood, stops him in front of the door. He shrugs the backpack from his sodden shoulders and takes off his hoodie, dropping them wetly on the step. A constellation of water droplets forms on the concrete around his feet.

Just get inside.

— Nice of you to show up, sis.

I'd worry about hypothermia more than Misty.

— I'll be fine.

Shivering, he opens the pack. Water has made it to the bottom, swelling the edges of his unread copy of *The Outsider* and sticking together the loose-leaf pages of his binder. He leans the books against the lintel post to dry and fishes in the bottom of the pack for pens and pencils. His hands brush against wet paper. The pamphlet Dr. Kamat's nurse gave him comes apart in his hand. The two letters, Morgan's and RMC's, are soaked through but intact, saved by a better bond of paper. He opens them as gingerly as his numb hands will allow.

Morgan's letter is almost translucent, her brief, blue-penned note barely legible. The RMC letter, though sodden, is still read-able, its laser printing enduring well against the wetness. He'll have to dry both letters out to save them. *But why save them at all?* he asks himself. Why not just ball everything up — pamphlet, envelopes, life-altering correspondence — into a fist, squeeze every last drop of water from it, toss the pulpy wad into the toilet, and watch it dissolve? Because doing so wouldn't change a thing, of course, and destroying documents without a good reason is irresponsible. Morgan's letter is irreplaceable, a one-of-a-kind kick to the gut. The RMC letter could simply be reprinted from a faceless server with a few mouse clicks, but this version still means something. There's something about an original. You want to keep the important ones, right? *Maybe*, his mind replies. *We'll see.*

He leaves the pamphlet and letters next to his other things and goes inside. Charlie remains outside, off to the left, barely visible in his peripheral vision. She doesn't say anything further. He ignores a brief pang of cadet conscience. *Police your shit up! Squared awayness is next to Godliness! A tidy space equals a happy cadet!*

The cuffs of his jeans drag a wet trail across the threshold and onto the hallway tile. He pauses to roll them up, his brief rebellion and subsequent reflections pushed aside by his instinct like rude stepchildren.

— You're going to clean that up, I hope.

Misty has appeared in the hall and is scowling at the water on the floor. He's surprised to see her in skinny jeans and a fitted blouse, as well as the conservative, carefully made-up visage she puts on for house showings and potential new clients.

— I will. I just need a hot shower and a change first.

— What're you doing home so early?

He doesn't have an answer for her. He hadn't anticipated her being home, even though lately she mostly has been.

— It's really coming down out there, he says. It'll be good to get dry.

— Fine, whatever.

She turns away from him with an exaggerated motion and stumbles, reaching out a hand to steady herself against the wall.

— Whoops, she says.

She heads back into the kitchen and sits heavily at the table. With one hand, she reaches for a smouldering cigarette balanced precisely at the edge of a small plate. With the other, she raises a tall glass, fresh with lemon and ice. The air has the unmistakable tang of gin.

— You're all dressed up, he says.

She looks down at herself and her eyes widen, as though she's forgotten about the clothes she's in.

— Shopping. Outlet malls across the border.

— Where's Nick?

— Fuck if I know. Took off right after Corny called, not that I blame him. Probably out partying somewhere. He'll come back, though. Always seems to.

— Hold on, Corny called you?

Misty exhales. Drinks. Repeats.

— Misty? When did he call?

— Eight years of peace, then blubbering and *I'm sorry, I'm sorry, I'm sorry*. Bastard. We had an agreement. No contact, no drama.

— You're sure it was him?

Misty gives him a look, drains her glass, and heads to the refrigerator for another can of tonic. She pours her drink awkwardly, spattering the table. Juniper-scented droplets catching the light like dimes on a sidewalk. He waits a long moment, but she doesn't offer any more, just stares out into the backyard, sipping.

He has a bout of strong shivers, spasms almost, his core becoming aware of the cold. He runs up the stairs to the bathroom, twists the shower knob almost to its highest setting, and frantically sheds layers. Steam begins to fill the space. The scalding water feels like it's stripping away his skin along with the cold. He forces himself to endure, thinking about Misty's unsteady but remarkably controlled anger, the smoking and drinking. About Corny's words to the both of them. Distant apologies and things left cryptically unsaid. Near the end of the shower, right about the time he starts to feel warmed back to equilibrium, he remembers Jay. Wondering where he is, how he is, whether his infant mind can process the change in Misty against the stability of the past few weeks, or whether it would sadly just feel familiar again. Normal, like before.

— God, what a depressing thought, he says into the hissing water.

He shuts down the water, reaches for a towel, and steps out into the steam of a shower gone on too long. Skin red. The vapour cool in the space of the bathroom. Towel around his waist, he walks to Jay's door. His brother is asleep on his side, breathing deeply, knees drawn halfway to his chest, hands tucked between them, curled up like a question mark, perfectly content. He closes the door and goes back to the bathroom. As he lifts his sodden, heavy clothing and drapes them over the shower bar to dry, his phone tumbles out and clatters to the tile. He thumbs it on, wondering if Mark or Shi has texted with any news. The screen flickers on and then out, leaving a ghostly rainbow hue. Condensation clouds the inside of the screen. A slight tang of ozone filters up to his nostrils.

Perfect, he thinks. *Now this.*

He looks at the phone, wondering if it's ruined. Probably. The thought of having to walk into a store to buy a new one seems so pedestrian and mundane it threatens to take everything over. He clenches his fists, a frustrated shout mere microns from his mouth, tempted to whip the phone against the wall and be done with it. But he doesn't. He goes downstairs and takes an old bag of rice, a good two years past its expiry date, from under the counter. Jams his dead phone deep into the grains. Seals it. Tucks it under an arm. Next, he retrieves the backpack, novel, binder, and letters from the front step, bringing them upstairs to his room. Grabs a clean towel and lays it flat across his desk, smoothing the wet letters across it. Rests the bag of rice on a corner. Watches the

desk for a long moment, wondering about drying time and the
worthiness of preservation.

CHAPTER 14

Mark is laughing at him.

— An actual landline phone call. Imagine. Like a connection from the past.

— Knock it off, Boy says. What did I miss?

— Not much. I'm still bored out of my mind. I sent a few texts, mostly updates from the docs.

— And?

— Apparently my insides are more stable than they were worried about. I should be out later today or tomorrow.

— That's great news.

— Yeah.

But he'll be expected to go back to school. Mark's parents are easygoing, but even they'll make him head back sooner rather than later. Mark isn't one to let his grades and assignments fall too far behind, either — he claims boredom, but there's probably at least one schoolbook draped across his lap right now. Of course, going back means seeing Kyle, too.

— Mark, have you thought about telling anyone —

— No.

— It was Vos who found you. Shi says the vice-principal has been talking to everyone trying to figure this out. They want to press charges —

— No one saw it happen, and I'm not telling.

— You have to say something. There are other kids —

— I said no, Boy. My mind is made up. And promise me you won't tell anyone, either.

— Come on. You can't ask me to —

— I just did. Promise me.

Boy wants to tell him, no, he can't promise anything of the sort. There are bigger issues at play. More people to consider. The right thing to do. And so on. But this isn't cadets. He has no burden of responsible leadership here. Against his friendship with Mark, the words sound hollow, even in his mind.

— Okay.

— Say it.

— Mark —

— Say. It.

— Okay, okay. I promise.

— Good. Thanks.

They fall into a brief silence. Boy has the cordless handset in his bedroom, where he retreated after putting Jay down for the night. Misty is asleep downstairs on the couch. She has spent the evening drinking and worrying and trying to call Nick. Her phone still rests in the corner where she threw it when the battery died, black and shiny like a huge beetle left to perish on its back. She passed out early. Boy fed and played with Jay until his bedtime. The kitchen is a disaster of lemon wedges, tumblers, empty tonic cans, and open containers of junk food scattered around. He dreads tomorrow morning, when he'll have to tidy up the wreckage of her sudden bender before bringing Jay downstairs.

Decide in the moment whether or not to go to school, depending on Misty's state. Then another option inserts itself into his thoughts. Cynthia. She had offered to help, hadn't she? If Misty is still hell-bent on grieving Corny's intrusion into her life and Nick's absence, wouldn't it be time to take Cynthia up on it? Her card is still in his bedside table, resting mutely, just waiting …

— Who's that? Mark asks.

— What? Who?

— Cynthia.

Boy groans — he spoke aloud again — and debates how much to say. But only for a moment. This time, he gives in to the desire to tell Mark everything. See if it will feel better. Get his friend's advice. Absolution, maybe, a phoned-in confession. So he does. After he finishes, Mark goes quiet, pondering this new information to a faint soundtrack of landline-to-mobile hiss.

— Jesus. That's a lot to take in, especially right now.

— Do you think I should call her?

A barking, exaggerated laugh.

— *You* are asking *my* advice? Boy reaching out? Will wonders never cease?

— Mark —

— I'm fucking with you. Wait until tomorrow to call. You're asking for more than just house help, right?

— Yeah.

— Funny how everything seems to happen all at once. Kyle's stupidity towards me, your predicament, Shi's issues —

— What happened to Shi?

— She stopped in again tonight. Managed to keep her supper down around me, ha. I guess there's serious upheaval at home, something to do with someone her father used to work with.

Boy curses the unexpected rain for killing his phone and causing him to feel so disconnected from his friends. Shi was wrestling with something in the van that morning that she couldn't or wouldn't go into. There is a pang of heartbreak — and a little envy — that he couldn't be there. Especially given Mara's refusal to help, his skittish rebuff and threat to disappear. He can't help but feel as though his trip to the culvert was a missed opportunity. Which sets him off on another round of mental wrangling, the choices and regrets he's made, the ones still to come. He's just about to share his decision to enlist when his friend yawns.

— I dosed myself again. Feels like everything is kicking in all at once. I'm flying.

— Night, buddy.

— I like flying. You like flying, too, right?

— You know it.

— So reliable. Push a little red button, and every time —

He starts giggling and can't finish the thought.

Of course, Boy thinks as he says goodnight and disconnects the call. *There are things you can count on and things you can't. Things you can't time or measure, a list that seems to be growing despite all my best intentions.*

Misty is actually awake before him the next morning, her eyes red but clear. The kitchen has been tidied, the table and counters clear from dishes and garbage. She sips coffee at the kitchen table and watches the morning news on the small TV on the counter. An all-news station splits the screen into a half-dozen flickering segments, from traffic cameras along the QEW to a live weather report to the scrolling stock ticker at the side. As he assembles his cereal and juice breakfast, Boy tries to watch but has to turn away when the studio anchor appears with a flash of chromed animations and whooshing sound effects. It's too early, he thinks, to have his senses assaulted this way.

With a low, dramatic delivery, the anchor promises that they will stay on top of the breaking news that police have laid a number of new sexual assault charges, and that they will have live coverage of the press conference later in the morning. He says the word *live* as though he could hang every viewer's dreams and expectations on those four letters.

— God, not another scandal, Misty says, shaking her head. Do any of them have a shred of integrity?

— Who's they?

— Religious nuts, all of them.

Yet she can't stop watching, even as the anchor switches to the other studio camera with an easy turn of his coiffed head and a well-rehearsed smile, transitioning to a local kitten's viral video. Boy blinks and carries his cereal to the couch, out of sight of the frenzied news program. Misty's commentary is oddly comforting. Feels almost like normal. She has sobered up to face the day, and although he can't imagine she'll remain this way, easing back into her morning news might be a good sign. Maybe Cynthia won't be needed.

Boy reaches for the laptop on the coffee table and goes to his favourite news website. He watches the screen for a few minutes, chewing passively, before realizing he's not actually reading. His mind has gone back to a time when Misty would leave the morning news blaring on the kitchen TV after she left in the morning. Boy would munch on his cereal until Charlie switched off the set, smacked him on the head, and told him to get a move on. A *fucking* move on. He closes the computer, feeling a painful twinge at Charlie's memory. How infrequently he thinks about those days anymore. She's there whenever he steps away from the house, of course, but beyond that …

— It's supposed to rain again today, Misty says. You might want to bring an umbrella to school with you this time.

He looks up. She's regarding him with a slight smile.

— A joke about yesterday? Really?

He gets up and puts his bowl and spoon into the dishwasher, noticing that there are still food stains and spills on the counter. He imagines germs and microbes, even though the surface appears to be clean, and grabs the cloth from the sink, wets it, and starts wiping with sharp, digging movements.

— I'm sorry about yesterday, she says. When your father called —

— He called me, too, you know.

— And when Nick left, I — wait, really? What did he say?

— It doesn't matter. At least I kept it together.

She winces and looks away.

— Nick's a big boy who can take care of himself. But Jay needs you sober. He's going to start seeing all of this really soon.

His voice is rising, and he stops himself before it can penetrate the ceiling and disturb Jay's final moments of precious sleep. *Like Charlie and I did*, he doesn't say, but immediately wonders whether he should. She raises her hands — he notices her age in the deeper grooves and sun spots there — and apologizes again.

— You're right. It's no excuse. But I'm fine.

— Damn it, Misty, it's not about you at all. How did I become the parent here?

He walks out, his last words charring the air between them, grabs his things, and begins the long walk to the bus stop. The satisfaction he hoped to feel at letting her have it never takes hold. Just the diminishing simmer of boiled water removed from its heat source and eventually the stillness of the cold.

Ms. Vos closes the door behind him, quietly but firmly. The conversation did not go well, much as he expected. *Little or no progress?* she asked, and he responded honestly. *None at all.* But he stopped himself just in time from using Mark's injuries as an excuse — he's ashamed with himself for even thinking it, much less almost falling on it like the refuge horns of a sacred altar. Still, almost as though she read his thoughts, she tried to find out more about the attack on Mark. But he held firm, even though Vos admitted that there had been no real progress in the search for his attacker.

Another one bites the dust — how many do you have left in your corner, anyhow?

He ignores Charlie and reaches for his phone before remembering that it's dead at home. Remarkable how much he misses it. He sees himself as a light user, unlike everyone else spending so much time hunched over their tiny screens it's impossible to imagine them any other way. Trying to find Shi is a strangely analog exercise without texting as a navigation aid. Only the distant odour of cooked food makes him think about the cafeteria.

On the way, he sees Kyle sauntering down the hall, trying to get the attention of a girl who obviously would rather be anywhere else. His backpack is slung low, his voice loud and indistinct amidst its own ringing echoes. That he is walking the halls with impunity is an insult to all things orderly and just. Boy wants to walk over and beat him down, a sampling of the pain Mark is experiencing. He clenches his fists.

Aaaaaaand Boy finds a solution to his dilemma, sports fans, the old hit-first-deal-with-the-questions-later strategy. A classic move if ever there was one.

Boy stops. Charlie's voice, normally so low and controlled and subtle he sometimes questions whether it's real at all, is loud and exaggerated, an old school radio sportscaster making up for lousy airwaves with volume and drama.

— What the hell was that?

But Charlie doesn't respond, leaving him motionless in the middle of the hall, caught between opposing forces, snagged with grappling hooks from all four points of the compass. Held with just enough force to keep him exactly where he stands.

— What the hell was what?

Shi is walking towards him, looking as put-together as ever, her black hair up in a tidy ponytail, a heavy stack of books clasped to her chest.

— Nothing, he says. It's just … nothing.

— Was that Kyle?

— Yes.

— What's he doing here? Shouldn't he be —

— He should, but Mark never told anyone it was him.

— What? Why?

— I think he's worried that Kyle will lash out at others. You. Me.

— But he can't just do anything he wants. Besides, when he went after you the other day, you just pushed him away. You could —

— I'm not the police.

— Of course not, but —

— Mark made me promise not to tell.

Shi tilts her head and narrows her eyes.

— That's dumb, Boy. What's wrong with you?

— Nothing. He just —

— This isn't like you at all. You know what we should do. When did you find out?

— At the hospital yesterday. While you were in the hall.

— You've known since then and haven't told anyone?

— Yes.

— We're telling someone. Right now.

He nods and follows her towards the office, still feeling as though this whole scenario is being lived out by someone else.

Next you'll try to stop her and suggest an anonymous fucking phone call.

They pass the senior lounge, where a flat screen TV mutters at low volume. Shi stops in the middle of the hall, eyes fixed on the screen high on the wall. The TV is set to the same news channel Misty was watching. The anchor's expression is grim as he reads to the camera, and although the volume is too low to really hear what he's saying, a scrolling ticker underneath declares new sexual interference charges against Reverend Raymond Dempster, the disgraced former head pastor of Jacob's Ladder, a Toronto mega-church.

— Shi? What's wrong?

— Dempster sponsored my father to come to Canada.

— Wow, I'm sorry. Your father's involved?

— Yes. No. Not in a bad way. The first charges came a few years ago when he was still a pastor there. There was a lot of trouble for the congregation, and when Dempster disappeared, the church broke up.

— And you came here.

— Yes. And our new church is having some difficulty with all of this, given my father's position at the time.

The news cuts to file video of Jacob's Ladder and shaky footage of a portly man in khakis shielding his face from the cameras as he walks into the church, digitally blurred photographs of the victims, stock images of the nearby police station. Then back to the studio, where the anchor sits across from an expert on abuse cases. Suspended between them, projected onto the green screen studio wall, Dempster's mug shot appears, miserable, unshaven, jowly, pale. Shi is saying something about her father's innocence, his being cleared quickly by the investigators despite his ties to the congregation and the fallen pastor, when Boy imagines how the man in the mug shot might appear years later, without the scruff and the defeat, a few pounds lighter, ages older.

Mara. Mara is Dempster. Dempster is Mara. Not a priest but a pastor.

— Oh my God, he says.

— And it's really wearing on my father. He's bringing it home, which sets my mother off —

— I have to go.

— But —

Boy leaves Shi standing in the lounge. All he can see is the fallen image of Mara — Dempster — holding up the numbered name board for the police. Shi, Mark, Kyle, and the thousand other things he's filled the day with disappear as he bolts from the school, passes by the waiting bus stop, and begins walking home, thinking about the strange but harmless man in the culvert he's come to view as a friend. But not harmless, is he? Boy has few thoughts for himself, but he does feel sick when he thinks of bringing Jay to see Mara, the proximity he allowed between a predator and the most vulnerable. And what a predator he could be. He reaches into his pocket to call the police, but his phone still isn't there.

CHAPTER 15

He watches the front of the house for a long moment, as though it will spit out all the answers he needs if he waits long enough. The blinds are open. They're usually closed, the house slumbering, eyelids shut tight against the too-bright world. Misty's SUV sits alone on the driveway. Nick's is still gone, its usual position marked by oil stains on the pavement. Charlie, a few paces away, has been quiet since their abrupt departure from school.

He gave up on his walk and took the bus almost all the way home. His whirling thoughts about Mara — should he call him Dempster now? — had been enough to propel him for a couple of kilometres but no farther. He stopped in front of a community policing station, a converted storefront in a strip mall. But it was locked when he tried to go in. Stymied by the closure, the odd hours the suburban officers observed from that little shop. Imagined what he'd say, had it all worked out. But farther along Jones Road, as he neared his neighbourhood, he changed his resolve. Questions about his own involvement, his choice to visit again and again. Complicity. And Mara had never acted threatening or given the impression that he could be dangerous. Moody and reluctant, but who wouldn't be? No, better to sit on this for a while.

The neighbourhood is quiet, with only the birds and occasional passing car breaking the silence. Even the hoarse whisper of an airliner cruising past at forty thousand feet reaches his ears. Everyone at work or school, houses sealed. When he unlocks and opens the front door, he is surprised by Jay's laughter washing around him and escaping into the neighbourhood. He finds Misty on her knees, relaxed in a pair of boxers and a T-shirt, tickling and blowing raspberries onto his pale tummy. An eighties mixed tape is on, filling the room with the Talking Heads. Jay, wearing only a diaper, squirms and giggles deliciously with each round of attention, eyes squeezed tight to keep his joy in while his mouth gapes, unable to contain it. Bright, first laughter, tearless, breathless, straight from his compact core. Misty sits back, flushed, and brushes her hair away from her eyes.

— Nick's still gone, Boy says.

A shadow moves across her face and she nods. At the sound of Boy's voice, Jay barrel-rolls to his stomach and squeals a greeting, before crawling over to his brother and holding up his arms. Boy scoops him up. Jay digs into his neck and begins jabbering.

— Not even a phone call.

— What will you do? Call the police?

She gives a short, exasperated laugh.

— No, he'll be back. He's done this before.

— Really?

— Not since Jay was born. But before — well, his shift work made it easy to hide.

— Does this change anything?

She fills a glass of water from the tap and gives him a long look over the rim of the glass as she drinks. Places the glass on the counter.

— You mean for us? As in, will I take him back?

— He shouldn't leave like this.

— I know.

Jay has shifted a little, his head now against Boy's shoulder, murmuring softly and worrying at Boy's collar with one hand.

— You're home early again. Anything I should be worried about?

She has no idea, he thinks. *About any of it.* He shakes his head. So Nick is a serial vanisher, even with a baby son on the scene. Boy learned early not to expect much from the grief-stricken firefighter who moved in so soon after Charlie's death. Wallowing in their family mess, always with an escape plan. Corny had always been the flawed but calming presence in Misty's corner, and it was like any sense of reason and responsibility had been locked up with him in Millhaven. Even ten-year-old Boy saw that Misty was prepared to lock everything away to move on. Her emotions. Corny's things banished to the garage. Nick moving in, like a willing captive in his parents' bed.

She drains the rest of her water and reaches for Jay.

— We should get changed, shouldn't we, baby boy?

Jay leans away from Boy and lets himself be carried upstairs. Boy watches them go, relieved that Misty is sober and alert to her responsibilities, and sits at the table, hoping to figure out what he's going to do next.

The sound of something heavy falling to the floor upstairs interrupts his thoughts. Immediately, the siren-wail of a hurt baby bleeds through the floor, and Boy is standing at Jay's door before he even knows he has stood from the table, watching Misty clasping his keening baby brother to her chest. Jay is inconsolable, squirming, twisting his head, pushing away from Misty, and screaming. Her eyes are red, wide, fearful.

— He fell from the change table. I just turned to put the diaper into the pail, and —

— Did he hit his head?

Jay reaches out his arms towards the sound of Boy's voice. He takes him from Misty, who sits back on her heels, hands on her thighs, looking at the floor but without really seeing anything.

— I don't know. I just heard the sound of him hitting the floor, and then his crying, and —

He screamed right away, so no loss of consciousness, he thinks. *No visible bruising or open wounds. Fantastic volume. Take charge, Cadet. Get him to the hospital.*

— Misty, get dressed. Get your keys.

— Wait. Maybe we should call an ambulance —

She stops, looks at her hands, and up at the boys. Makes a decision.

— No, we'll drive him over, she says. Get him buckled in. I'll be down by the time you're done.

And she is. Boy sits in the back with Jay who, by the time they stop in the Emergency drop-off, has stopped crying. His world shifting from the all-encompassing panic of fall and pain to snuffling, wide-eyed observance of the things they pass on the way.

Jay likes the doctor, a mousy-haired woman in scrubs with deep smudges under her eyes. He smiles and grabs at her stethoscope, her pen, her ponytail as she leans over him in the chrome and plastic crib, presses, manipulates, listens, and asks a battery of questions. A small patch of swelling has appeared on his forehead, red and warm. At the end, when she stands up straight, he reaches his arms out to her. She smiles and tickles him under his chin. Clicks open her pen, makes a few notes on an aluminum clipboard.

— His responses are all excellent. And he seems in good spirits.

— And the swelling? Boy asks.

— It's minimal, and there's no disfigurement.

— Meaning ...

— He's fine. Ice will help with the swelling. I will order an x-ray for his right wrist — there was discomfort there — but I'm not concerned about the head or spine.

— Thank God, Misty says.

The doctor smiles tiredly, makes a final note, and leaves. Eventually, another nurse comes in and hands Misty a form and gives her directions to radiology. When Misty stands to walk out with Jay in her arms, the sour smell of alcohol drifts off her. Boy's stomach falls, even though he hasn't seen her drink and she hasn't been out of his sight since home. Still, the smell gives her away; perhaps she had a nip when they were getting out of the car.

— Here, give me Jay. You just focus on walking.

— What?

— I can smell it, Misty.

— Smell what?

— The booze.

— I haven't been drinking.

It's tiresome how little we can rely on what our parents say, isn't it?

Misty stands there, her lips set in a thin line. Then realization.

— It's my shirt. I grabbed it from the laundry.

— Come on —

She stops, looks at him, and nods down at herself.

— Go ahead, smell it. The left shoulder is where I drooled on myself.

For an instant, he's tempted to do just that. But, no.

— I'm not going to smell you.

— Can we just go to radiology and get this over with?

Jay is asleep by the time they register. There is a rough-looking couple in stained clothing waiting for their scans. The guy is leaning back, eyes partially closed, holding one swollen ankle up on a nearby chair. The woman taps at her phone, only stopping to stare at Misty. Misty doesn't notice. Boy does, though, and looks right back at them until the man closes his eyes and the woman returns to whatever had held her attention on her screen. He's resigned himself to the looks, keenly aware of how everything appears. Drunk mom. Abused baby. Enabling older son. But he can't ignore the sting of misplaced disapproval, either. Restless, he stands.

— Go get yourself a drink or something, Misty whispers. I'll call you when we go in.

— My phone's dead, he says, explaining about the rain.

Misty waves him away.

— Who knows how long it'll be? Go. We'll be fine.

— Are you sure?

— Yes.

Boy spends a few moments in front of the vending machines just down the hall before realizing that he's not really looking at the drinks and snacks. He feels tired, as though his body realized long before his mind that exhaustion is knocking. He stretches and wanders through the main floor of the hospital, feeling the blood in his veins thinning out and moving more freely. Hospitals are not places to move quickly — everyone is at half speed or slower, even the healthy ones — so he heads outside into the late afternoon sunshine. Barton Street is busy with cars and buses, the sidewalks bustling with the earthy people of East Hamilton. Charlie moves along the sidewalk a few paces in front of him.

— I don't know what to do.

About what?

— About Mara. Dempster. Do I just stay away?

I think it's your only option. But you already knew that. Why revisit the same question?

— I have no idea. I'm so tired.

He rubs his eyes. Combined with Mark's injuries, the tug-of-war Shi must be feeling between her family's strife and her own daily needs, Corny's odd intrusions into his own and Misty's lives, and now Jay's fall adding new worry to his load, there's little wonder his eyes feel so full, the rest of him sluggish. It's like a long bout of shadow-boxing, where his opponent never makes contact but continually pummels the space where he just was. Exhaustion by proximity and his own sweating self.

He passes a mobile phone store decked out in neon pinks and reds. Stops.

You're not going to find many answers here.

— Ha, ha. I do need a new phone, though.

Need, want …

He goes inside. The walls and pillars are studded with blinking phones and mute accessories. He asks the clerk about cheap smartphones but instead is given a lengthy sermon about the ridiculous features and free upgrades he could have if he makes a two-year commitment. He waves away every offer, knowing the pimply student is just angling for a bigger commission. He can't imagine what his life will look like in two years. In the end, a basic phone with no further obligation seems the best choice, so he cuts the clerk off in mid-sentence and points at the model he wants to buy. The clerk links the new phone to Boy's old account without another word, sulking behind his computer screen. Boy pays with his debit card and walks out, almost colliding with a homeless man shuffling along the sidewalk who barely registers the near miss at all.

Misty and Jay haven't been taken in, nor have they moved. Jay is still asleep, limp and content against Misty, who has also closed her eyes. The rough-looking couple is gone. Boy quietly sits down a few seats away and gets out his new phone. He opens his messaging app to text Mark and Shi, let them know he's connected again. But there are no contacts on the new device, no phone history, no apps aside from the ones installed by the manufacturer. Useless to him until he can recompile all those little scraps of data. A blind start instead of a fresh one.

The double doors leading into radiology open with a loud click and a hum. The rough couple comes back into the waiting room, arguing about something. She stops in front of Misty and looks down at Jay.

— They'll sleep through anything, eh?

Although at a low volume, her voice is strident enough to reach Jay wherever he is. He stirs and groans loudly before falling silent again. Misty smiles up at her.

— Just about, she says.

— You weren't going to do this, Maureen, the man says.

He's annoyed at having to stop, his injured leg lifted from the ground and dangling heavily. The crutches creak as he shifts. He's pale from the pain, eyes bloodshot and weary.

— Let's get back to Emergency. The doc said —

— I remember you now, she says, her eyes locked with Misty's.

— I don't think so …

— You came in looking to score. Years ago. With some guy.

— Wait, Misty says. That can't be —

— No, it was you. Saw your car parked outside. Thought it looked too nice.

— We —

— Did it feel good?

— I'm sorry?

— When you hit this beautiful boy.

Misty's smile disappears.

— You should be ashamed of yourself.

Then the woman hawks up from deep within her throat, and Boy and her husband watch, fixed to their spots as they wait for her to spit on Misty. At this sound, big and ugly and wrong, Jay wakes up, his sleep-dazed eyes squinting and searching around the room. But the woman just snorts, swallows, and walks out, her husband following and apologizing weakly. Boy gets up to follow them out and tell them how wrong they are — Misty is short of many things, but this one is not on her — but stops, caught between telling them off and remaining with his family. Jay makes a plaintive wake-up cry, and Boy turns back to find Misty taking a small bottle from her purse on the seat next to her. Her shaking hand can't twist the paper-taped lid from the mickey of gin, and she spends an agonizing moment caught between her need for drink and the instinct not to drop her son.

It's a sickness, after all. It isn't about willpower. Corny was sick, too, you know.

Boy stands and goes to Misty's purse to grab her keys but stops. Jay still needs his x-ray. He sits and feeds his brother snacks from the diaper bag while Misty sips from the bottle, looking miserable and staring at the ground. *Good*, he thinks, *you should feel terrible about all of this.* But he doesn't say anything, focused on helping Jay grab the cereal and bits of dried fruit. His brother has learned this new skill over the past couple of weeks and is pleased to be involved with his own feeding. Within moments, he is happily pasting crumbs to his chin with drool. *It probably doesn't make a difference*, Boy thinks, *whether the mickey was already in her purse or whether she was able to pause in the midst of her worry long enough to grab it from home.*

CHAPTER 16

Two in the morning. Boy walks north, towards the lakeshore.

The all-clear from the doctors sent him, Misty, and Jay home to a quiet, darkened house with far too much room for conflicted feelings. As soon as he closed his bedroom door behind him, his new phone was out and he was dialing the police. But he didn't connect the call, the green icon and ten digits staring at him from the screen like an accusation. He lay in bed for hours, his mind assembling and disassembling all this new information over and over, until he swore at himself and got out of bed. On his way out, he paused at Jay's door for a moment, listening to his brother's regular, deep breathing, envying him his contented sleep.

He shivers as he walks. He's wearing the same things he always wears in the winter, yet they seem inadequate. The cold feels different at this time of night, as though it has extra depth, and it soon finds its way to his core. He ducks into a twenty-four-hour diner at the corner of Fruitland and North Service and orders a cup of coffee with two creams and two sugars. The place is all red vinyl and chrome, with booths and a walk-up bar, the floor a checkerboard of black and white. Truck parking out back. A fifties atmosphere trying way too hard to stay interesting.

— You look familiar, the server says when she returns with his coffee.

— I'm sorry, what?

— I'm having trouble placing you, though.

— I don't recognize you.

— I'll figure this out. You just wait.

She walks away, stiff in her polyester uniform that has been fit to the tight side of the scale. But her voice was cheerful, and her ponytail swings with her mood. Hair dark brown. Her eyes are brown, too, bright and unshadowed, as though the night shift suits her. *She does look vaguely familiar*, he thinks. She's attractive enough to be a draw for the driving crowd, evidenced by appreciative, lingering looks as she passes by the other customers.

That's Janice. She was in my class, but I forget her last name.

— Really.

I don't see many people I recognize from before.

— Except me.

Except you.

He wants to ask how well they knew each other — it doesn't seem odd that a twelve-year-old might not know a friend's last name — and what interests they shared. Did Janice have a foul mouth, too, and was it Charlie's inspiration, or the other way around? Did they get into recess mischief together?

— Everything all right over there?

He looks up. Janice is looking at him from behind the counter.

— You were talking to yourself.

— I'm fine, thanks.

A strange connection to make, meeting a former friend of a dead sister, so late on such a random night. He glances at Charlie, who has placed herself against the diner's window, bright against the darkness outside. She doesn't say anything further, though. Doesn't look at him, in fact. He pulls out his phone. The screen is full of notifications, emails, texts, calls and voicemails. Earlier, in bed, after his failed police call, he'd fiddled with the new device, retrieving the damp SIM card from his old phone and sliding it into the new one. It must have made some kind of authorization, and now all this lost information is his again. Snatched from the ether, blossoming on his phone. Strange connections, indeed.

A few minutes later, he looks up to find the server standing next to his booth, coffee pot in hand, ready to warm up his coffee.

— You're Janice.

— Right! How did —

— I'm Boy McVeigh. You knew my sister Charlie.

She gasps long and slow, like the breath has been pressed from her lungs.

— Ah, shit. Right. I'm sorry.

She puts the coffee pot on the table and slides into the booth. She folds her arms and studies the advertising placemat she laid in front of him when he first sat down. Her face is pale.

— I haven't thought about her in years. Jesus, that was a shock.

— It was.

— We were friends. Good friends, actually. Not like her and Sarah, but —

Her eyes fill. She wipes away a single tear with a delicate movement of her fingertip, saving her mascara.

— You were at the funeral, he says.

Both funerals.

— Both funerals, she says.

— Right.

More silence. More of the kind that seems impossible to fill in any meaningful way.

— God, she could swear, Janice says. It was embarrassing, but also so —

— Perfect, in a way.

She laughs.

— Exactly.

They spend a few minutes trading small talk and updates, bits of lives lived. After a while, she looks up at bright lights flashing across the window, the sound of air brakes being applied. The driver walks in, a short man with a huge beard and a shirt at least four sizes too large. *Like he lost all that weight and needs to put it back on in this diner*, Boy thinks, watching him brush dried mud from his scuffed black boots after he sits at the counter. The driver looks around for service. Janice gives him a wave and stands, smoothing her uniform, telling Boy she'll be back in a few minutes. The driver places his order without looking up from a zippered binder he's laid on the counter. Papers and envelopes migrate across the faded surface. A logbook, charting distances travelled, drive and rest time.

— I can't believe she knew you, Boy says.

I didn't leave many friends.

He feels the desire to tell Janice everything rising up his esophagus like bile. Surely the release would do him good. Get the neutral advice of an almost stranger. But her rounds of coffee refills, dessert orders, and serving the diminutive trucker the biggest breakfast Boy has ever seen keeps her away for several long minutes. By the time she returns, looking as though she'd be content to sit again and continue their conversation, the desire has passed, deciding to remain in his gut like a cluster of leaden grapeshot. Also gone is the desire to go to the rocks and confront

Mara about the accusations, a ridiculous idea, given the weather and the hour. Arrived is the need to walk home, jog if need be, crawl back into bed, and wait for morning.

— I can't believe you're back already, Boy says.

— Docs said I just had to take it easy, Mark says. Besides, you know I'm Superman.

— That doesn't sound like enough —

— And what about Kyle? Shi asks.

— He still won't tell anyone, Boy replies.

Mark glares at him.

— Boy …

— Come on, it just feels so wrong that he's walking around, Boy says.

— And no one is talking about it, Shi says. Teachers, other students —

— It's better this way, Mark says. It might sound strange, but it is.

— We should have gone to the office, Shi says. I was going to, but after you left —

— When was this? Mark asks.

— Yesterday, Shi says.

— Guys, promise me —

— You don't have to say it, Shi says. If you don't want us to say anything, of course we won't. But it's like it never happened.

— Again —

— Yeah, yeah, Boy says, rolling his eyes. It's better this way. We know. But —

A piercing chime from Boy's new phone interrupts him, sudden and loud enough to make the three friends jump.

— Sorry. Haven't found the time to figure this thing out.

It's a text from the bike shop, telling him Corny's bike is ready and quoting a price for the repair. He lays the phone down between him and his two friends, who've watched him retrieve the messages with interest.

— Bike's ready, he says.

— Do you need a ride this time?

— No, thanks. I'll take the bus over after lunch.

— On your spare, you mean, Mark says.

Boy just shrugs.

— So that's it? You've just given up?

Mark's tone is scoffing. Boy hesitates for an instant, then lays out his plans for entering the enlisted ranks, trying to sell the optimism and security of his plan. Shi's expression betrays nothing, but Mark becomes angrier and angrier.

— That's fucking stupid. You'll never get very far if you don't get your diploma.

— It's a stable life, and I'm more than qualified. I should have no trouble getting in —

— You're an officer through and through, you dumbass. You'll regret it every day.

— RMC isn't an option anymore. With my grades —

— Right now, maybe. But take another year, do some equivalencies, and apply again.

— What else can I do? The teachers have given up on me, and I'm running out of time.

— You're too smart for me to even think about answering that question.

He's not wrong, you know.

— You'd be throwing everything away, Shi says.

Her, too.

Shi's face is still neutral, but her dark eyes are hard and refusing to look away. They've never locked eyes this way; in fact, he's never really looked in her eyes at all. She always seems to be reading or working, or keeping her gaze lowered when she's not, as though she needs always to be ready in case something to study or write happens by. But not now, and it's unsettling. He feels dissected by her. Charlie had the same ability to pin him down with a big-sisterly look, smack him upside the head, and pummel him with the perfect insult-cuss combination until he spilled whatever toxic secret he'd been holding. *Change the subject*, he thinks. He says how great it is that Mark is back, asks Shi about her family challenges, but receives only monosyllabic responses. Eventually, he gives up and collapses his attention on learning the features of his new phone while they focus on the schoolwork they were happy to ignore moments earlier. Eventually, the bell rings to signal the end of lunch. Mark and Shi grab their things and head out for their afternoon classes, their goodbyes perfunctory, leaving Boy to stare at their backs as they go.

Corny's old ten-speed rides like a different bike. Boy flies east down Queenston Road, the rush of wind almost cooling away his worries. He gets a few looks — or imagines he does — as he pilots the bright orange frame towards Stoney Creek, jeans tucked into socks, pack cinched tight around his shoulders. Heart rate rising, core warming, beads of sweat evaporating on his upper lip and trickling down his chest. The bike mechanic gave Boy a conspirator's smile and a wink when he walked into the shop. The bike had proven more of a challenge than she'd anticipated, the bent frame supplying the best moments of agony and triumph, something about the old steel frames holding up better to welding and old-fashioned force than the newer ones. She changed out the most problematic components for new ones — bottom bracket insert, chain, wheels, tires, brake and shifter cables, brake pads. She even rewrapped the drop-bars. When Boy asked how it was possible that the price was lower than the quote, she just shrugged and smiled, speaking cryptically about labours of lost love.

With that sort of setup, Boy is feeling compelled to ride fast and put the old bike through its paces. Past Eastgate Square, he turns left, up Centennial and onto Barton, where the traffic thins out and he can ride more freely in his lane. He makes great time along Barton, industry stretching off to his left towards the QEW and the lake, and residential areas to his right nestling against the escarpment. The streets aren't busy. Kids still in school and the labouring crowd deep in their afternoon shifts. He signals a right turn into his neighbourhood at Dewitt, slows, and allows himself to sit back and ride through the streets with no hands. He dismounts at the end of his own street to walk the bike home, slow down his heart, delay his arrival, allow his worries to catch up. He passes the spot where Cynthia had been idling her car, but the curb is bare, the street empty. He is disappointed — how perfect it would have been to have her right there, making his request for help more convenient, if not easier. He thinks of her card still sitting on his desk and resolves that Jay will have a guardian angel, Misty's feelings be damned. *That little card will be his first stop*, he thinks, as he rounds the last bend.

There's a guy sitting on the front step, smoking. Boy dismounts, walks the bike up to the garage, and leans it against the wall.

— Can I help you?

The man stands, stretching as though he's been sitting there a long time, brings his foot up, and extinguishes the cigarette against its sole. He takes a silver case from his pocket and places the butt inside. The case closes with a confident click and disappears back into the pocket. Boy watches him, his alarm increasing with each silent, precise movement. He's short, perhaps just over five feet tall, and yet his movements are graceful and sinewy, making him appear bigger than he is. His simple clothes — canvas sneakers, fitted jeans, golf shirt — are all darkly coloured, contrasting with his pale face and reducing any definition, like a shadow or walking silhouette. He smiles and gives Boy a once-over with pale grey eyes completely unaffected by his smiling face or demeanour.

— I'm hoping so, he says.

He looks cut from stone.

Charlie's voice startles Boy, and he flinches. The man's smile falters for an instant, and he takes a half step back. Any illusions about the guy's relaxed state vanish. *She's right*, he thinks — there's something about how his tailored clothing fits him, as though the soft fabric won't let itself relax enough to drape properly on his hard angles. Boy moves towards the door, but the man blocks him from doing so with just a slight turn towards the house.

— Who are you?

— Call me John, he says, extending a hand. And you must be Boy.

The man — John apparently, although you'd wonder if it was just for today — would be fascinating enough to question, if not for the fact that everything he does demonstrates his control over the situation. Even the handshake is an exercise in restraint and restraining — Boy can feel power there like a barely shielded current of electricity. A platinum flash on his wrist draws Boy's eyes to an expensive aviator's watch. Breitling. Ten thousand dollars, at least.

— I'm a friend of your Dad's.

— I don't understand.

— No, wait, that's not quite accurate. I'm a friend of an *associate* of your Dad's. I've never met Corny myself, you see. I'm sorry for being so imprecise.

The obvious question — *What do you want?* — doesn't come. It might be fear keeping Boy from speaking or a sense that the man is on his own schedule and will reveal his purpose only when he's ready.

— You're taller than I thought you'd be. What, six-two, six-three?

— Six-two.

— Ha! Six-two, I knew it!

As he speaks, as pleased as a boy who has discovered chocolate, John punches the palm of his opposite hand. So quick it's a blur, the sound so deep you'd know he could move boulders with the same movement. Another display. Another reason for Boy to wait. Another moment for concern, although now he begins to worry about the man getting into the house, about what those fists could do to Jay or Misty. And yet, had he wanted to get in, Boy has no doubts that John would have those skills, too.

— Right, to business, he says. I've been asked to find you, and —

The sharp tumbling of the deadbolt behind him cuts John's voice off, and he makes another partial turn, his weight shifting slightly forward, his hands quickly up and held loosely in front of him. The door opens with the clunk-hush of weather-stripping against the hallway tile. Misty, in jeans and an old, shapeless T-shirt, hair dishevelled and eyes rimmed in red, peeks around the door.

— I told you to leave, she says.

— And I told you I'd be staying, Misty. You need to listen better.

— Please leave.

— But Boy and I have barely had a chance to talk. And I said we needed to have a little chat, right?

His tone is that of an old friend at a class reunion.

— I called the police.

— No, I don't think you did. If you had, you see, I —

But then a distant siren drifts through the neighbourhood. Coincidence? Had she really called? John frowns.

— That is so disappointing, Misty.

— Boy, come inside.

Her voice is minutely slurred. John makes a tut-tutting sound under his breath before laying a hand on Boy's arm. He tries to shake it free and move inside but the man's grip is titanium. John leans in and speaks softly, almost close enough for his lips to brush Boy's ear.

— I want to meet the man who can stop time. Corny offered him up to pay what's owed.

He releases Boy's arm and gives a jaunty little wave. His eyes linger on the neckline of her T-shirt, stretched to one side, the collarbone visible. Hungry.

— Sure was nice to meet you, Misty. I'm sure we'll meet again soon.

With a lighthearted, whistled tune, the man walks to the far side of the street and gets into his car, a nondescript silver sedan Boy hadn't noticed before. He drives away slowly, the unhurried engine almost silent in the neighbourhood air.

— Who is he? Misty asks.

— Have you been drinking again?

— What did he say to you?

— Misty …

— Nick's going to leave me.

Boy sighs and steps inside.

— If the police are coming, you better get cleaned up. They won't take you seriously if —

— They're not coming. I didn't have enough time to call, so I bluffed.

— I thought so. Where's Nick?

— I don't know.

— But how —

— He called me.

— And he said he's leaving you — us?

Her hands move to cover her face and she sinks heavily to the landing. Her shoulders tremble. He can't remember the last time Misty cried in front of him — at Charlie's funeral or in the days following, perhaps? He stands there for a few minutes, feeling about as useful as a jet without an engine, before heading past her and up the stairs to check on Jay, napping in his crib, laid out flat on his stomach, a small patch of contented drool soaking into the fitted sheet. Boy goes outside, stepping around Misty in the front hall. He looks for the silver sedan but sees only an empty street. He heaves open the heavy garage door and rolls the bike in, leaning it against Corny's sagging boxes. Fixed. Bright. Boxes and bicycle, new and old, together. Like they're all meant to be right there.

CHAPTER 17

This time, he passes through without so much as a peep from the ion scanner, and he's buzzed through to the large open visit area. He sits at a bolted-down table near the side of the room and waits. His clothes are stiff and still creased from his pack, which is sitting in a locker at the Kingston bus station. After a wipe down with a couple of Jay's diaper wipes, he changed all of his clothes, right down to his underwear, in the station bathroom's spacious wheelchair stall. He wiped down his ID and debit card and put them in his pocket, his cash in a sandwich bag that he wiped down also. He washed his hands again, walked out, and hailed a taxi to Millhaven.

He had to wait a few days to make the trip. After John left, he left the house and was almost at the downtown GO station before stopping himself, realizing that if he left then he'd arrive in the middle of the night and have to find lodging, and remembering Millhaven's visit requests taking a minimum of forty-eight hours to clear.

Although little else occupied his mind on the long bus ride, he still doesn't know what he's going to say to his father. He knows how he'll say it; he's angry and confused about the threats John made to him and Misty. He stands, then sits. Stretches. Fidgets. Realizes he's fidgeting. Thinks about his hands, how to keep them occupied when there's nothing to hold.

Most of the tables in the open visit area are occupied by inmates and loved ones talking in low voices, many with only two people, a few with children, a baby or child balanced on a knee. The paint on the walls is faded and peeling, the steel furniture nicked and scratched and worn. Old mop and wax scum gather in shadowed nooks wherever anything touches the floor. It all feels tired, beaten down. It's near the end of visiting hours, too, so the air is close from a day's worth of painfully restrained visits, uncountable disappointed breaths, and bodies at all stages of cleanliness. Boy would have thought that a bigger space would handle the air better — on his last visit, the closed visit room smelled exactly the same way.

Finally, at the far end of the room, a buzzer sounds, and Corny comes in. He's wearing the same sweater as last time, but it seems to have grown. Boy can see the angles of his father's shoulders through the fabric, and his throat seems thinner. *Has he lost more weight,* he wonders, *or is it just the effect of seeing him from head to toe, undistorted by the thick green glass they'd had to speak through the last time?* But when Corny sees him and walks slowly towards him, it's clear that his father has deteriorated since his last visit. There's new darkness to the hollows in his cheeks, the shadows around his eyes. His Adam's apple seems more pronounced, the skin on his throat looser. He doesn't look like he could handle much. How about both barrels from a pissed-off son?

— You should see the other guy, Corny says as he sits.

— I ...

— Didn't anyone teach you it's not polite to stare?

Corny snorts and laughs, a sandpaper-dry sound devolving into a bout of coughing Corny can barely contain with his skeletal hands. The coughs are so deep and wet Boy half expects to see spatters of blood on his father's fingers. Corny catches the look and opens his palms for Boy to see.

— Look, there's nothing there. I'm falling apart, but I think I have some time left.

Boy has the sudden image of his father in a hospital bed, hooked up to innumerable tubes and monitors, the barely registrable chest movement of failing heart and lungs. Serious nurses and doctors. The prospect of time you can never get back.

— Hey, Corny says, tapping Boy's hand on the table. I'm right here.

— I know, I —

— You looked at me like I was already dead.

— Are you sick?

— No, just tired. It was a surprise to find out I had a visitor. I thought your other visit might have been a one-time deal.

— Why would you think that?

— I'm sorry for walking away from you.

Boy sits back. Whatever Boy had tried to anticipate, an apologetic Corny wasn't a possibility. He'd pictured dramatic confrontation and apologies, awkward silences and long, drawn-out pauses. He can practically hear Charlie's scoffing snort.

You'd almost think he was contrite, or something.

— Your scar looks good, by the way, Corny says. Suits you.

— Scar?

His father points at Boy's forehead.

— Still looked angry the last time you were here.

— Oh. Right. Stitches came out clean, just snip and pull. I did it myself, actually.

— Bet they itched like crazy.

Boy nods.

— How would you know?

Corny laughs.

— If you haven't had stitches, you haven't done much living.

They fall silent for a few moments, Corny watching him closely, as though he's waiting for a response to an unasked question.

— I wasn't planning on coming back.

— No?

— Or I wasn't sure if I would or not. Truthfully, I've had a lot of other things keeping me busy.

Sharpness in the words. Corny nods, but there is hurt in those reddened, tired eyes, too. Boy was looking for a gentle lead-in rather than a salvo. Feels like he was channelling Charlie.

— Well, I'm glad you did. How's your mother?

Interesting. He's never heard Corny use the word mother.

— She's a mess.

— Why?

— Nick left.

An easy and quick response. Too much so? Corny draws a long breath. He doesn't look surprised, but what could he do? His family's universe has been inverted for eight years, and he's had time to imagine what they would have to do to survive without him. Does Corny find the progression of their lives surprising, or does all the drama seem like natural offshoots of the seeds he'd helped plant? Misty and Nick ending up together because of their mutual grief and her singular rage, their substance codependence creating a household in steady decay. Boy keeping his head down and embracing a surrogate upbringing in the air cadets. An unplanned but innocent baby boy being born in the midst of all of it. A lot of trying to forget. A certain volume of silence. It's easy for Boy to list these things, the tangibles he's lived through — there's no telling what Corny has managed to conjure as he waits out his time. But it doesn't change anything, does it? He still screwed up, leading danger right up their front walkway.

— But that's not why I'm here, Boy says. I —

— How's Jay?

— What? Oh. He, uh, seems to be doing really well, all things considered.

Corny gives a small smile.

— Good. I'm glad. And I'm sure you're a good big brother.

— Thanks.

Corny's compliment has derailed Boy's momentum. They fall silent again, allowing the muted nearby conversations to wash over them. Boy watches a family struggle to stay positive. The father, bald and tattooed, holds a young girl on his knee and tries to soothe the woman across the table, whose mascara has begun to smudge. Their words are clipped but correct, desperately trying not to let whatever baggage they brought into the visit affect the child's experience. Admirable and probably futile — children soak in the bad along with the good, even when it's glossed in proper language and best intentions. It all has to come out sometime. You can't hide away what you're essentially made of, can you? Can't delay what's already in motion.

Boy hears himself describing John. So far the visit has been a mix of positive and negative energy, Corny's concern and appearance nudging Boy from his intended path. But not now. Any positive energy that has been allowed to build up between them seeps out like water from peat that has been lifted from its bog. Boy can almost see his anger and confusion warring together in the muddy hole left behind.

— God, I'm sorry, Corny says. I didn't have anything else to offer.

— I don't understand.

— I didn't think they believed me. I was angry when you left and said a few things to my cellmate. A day later, they're cornering me in the yard.

— Who's they? And what've you done?

— I made the wrong deal when I first got here. I settled it, but they have long memories. Just give him up and they'll leave you alone. You'll be fine.

— Hold on. I can't just —

— I'm sorry, Corny says again.

And there it is. Another empty apology. Boy stands as if to leave but finds himself just staring at the diminished figure below him.

Stay, brother. There's more.

The inmate with the girl on his knee looks over and shifts slightly, as though he can sense the change in the father and son at the adjacent table, shielding his girl from whatever unpleasantness is about to come. It's a good instinct, and Boy has the urge to walk over and shake the man's hand and tell him exactly that. And ask him how much apologizing he has to do, whether his family ever seems to grow weary of the excuses, if they seem like they might just give up on him at any moment.

— McVeigh? Everything all right?

A guard has sauntered over, hands on his utility belt. He's looking at Boy with a stern expression, and Boy realizes that his own hands have clenched into fists and that he's pulled himself tight from toe to crown. He must look a sight, a son towering over his father, aggressive and tense, precisely the sort of bearing they must watch for to keep things from spiralling beyond control. He forces himself to relax. Visibly, at least; inside, he's boiling.

— I think we're all right, Corny says.

— You sure?

— I just gave him some bad news.

The guard stands by for a few moments, looking hard at Boy until he sits down again on the metal seat. The bolted-down arrangement now feels too small, as though his anger has swelled him. The guard gives them a final look, nods, and returns to his place near the entrance.

— How could you do it, Corny?

— Some things follow you wherever you go. I had no choice.

— No choice?

— None at all.

— He came right to our house. You put us in danger.

— And you won't give up the guy down by the lake to protect your family?

— He's not dangerous, and ...

No, brother, he is dangerous. Even you see that.

— Okay, maybe he is dangerous. But regardless, do you think you'll be washed clean? That they'll just forget about you? You shouldn't have given us up.

— You have no idea what it takes in here to survive, Boy. This isn't pick and choose.

— This was a mistake. I shouldn't have told you. I shouldn't have contacted you, either.

— But you did.

— Maybe I won't anymore.

In his mind, it reads like a threat, sounds like one. No father would pass up the chance to keep contact with his son, would he? Especially one in prison, with such limited freedom and opportunity to connect with those who are supposed to love him? But Corny just folds his arms and hardens his eyes.

— That would be on you, he says.

— If you can't even be trusted to keep a family secret, what's the point? You're just another guy doing time.

— A *family* secret? Jesus, Boy, what dream world are you living in? How the hell is this a family secret?

— Any secret, then.

— You're right. Maybe you shouldn't waste your time.

There's a squawking and squealing from the PA system, as well as garbled words that might contain a warning to wrap things up, that visiting hours are nearly over. Although no one rises immediately, there is a shift in the air of the huge room, as though everyone is taking in one final, contemplated breath, figuring out just the right words to string together as they part ways. Boy and Corny don't speak, watching the other families and visitors wrap things up and slowly trickle towards their designated exits. Finally, Corny gets up to go.

Stop, dammit, just stop. Don't leave things like this.

But Boy just stares hard at his father's retreating back. A few paces away, as though unprepared for the new weight of his son's disappointment, Corny staggers. He steadies himself and pulls out a photo from his pants pocket.

— Thank you for this, he says.

— What?

— It's the only one I have. I like the new deck. Misty was always embarrassed about the old one.

Boy knows the photo. Misty made Nick take it a few weeks after Jay came home, and although it seems to capture a rare glimpse of joy, Boy remembers it as his first moment of big-brother panic. He was dragged away from cadet paperwork for the photo while Misty and Nick argued about the photo's composition. They'd been drinking, and Misty nearly dropped Jay onto the boards as she clumsily thrust him into Boy's arms. She laughed then, a clueless sound, as one way as a clock tower bell. Thankfully, Jay slept through the entire ordeal — for the first few weeks he slept a lot, before discovering how much more interesting life is when you can take it in with open eyes, when you can grab almost everything in reach.

Corny's finger rests just below Jay's tiny face. His eyes display, if only for the briefest instant, the weight of how much he discarded the night he let himself get behind the wheel. Then he looks at Boy and allows an equally brief sad smile.

— I can see Jay trusts you, all nestled into you like that. And Misty looks good — tired, but good.

— I didn't send it, Boy says.

— It must have been her, then.

— Yeah.

Corny walks away, leaving Boy seated on the stool and thinking about the photo. Why had she sent it to him after eight years of dismissal and denial? When had it arrived? She never talks about Corny, aside from brief necessities and the occasional insensitive questions of others, preferring to pack him away in those mouldy boxes in the garage. The guard who spoke to them a few minutes ago coughs loudly, sharp in the massive, now empty space. Boy leaves the open visit room wondering if it's the last time he'll be there, thinking about the solitary, incomplete family photo taped to a cold, concrete wall.

I should be in that photo.

— Yes, you should, he says, ignoring the odd looks from the prison staff as he passes through the final security door.

CHAPTER 18

— Thanks for coming, Boy says as he climbs into Shi's minivan.

— I was up anyway.

Studying, as it turns out. The last bus to Hamilton blew a tire just east of Pickering and the riders spent an uncomfortable couple of hours on the shoulder of the 401 waiting for a service truck. Boy texted her when he realized that the delay would put him downtown well after the last city buses stopped running. When the bus finally pulled in, the city seemed to have emptied itself of all activity on the streets apart from occasional groups of drunk university students and a few hail taxis steadily trolling the bars for fares. Shi was passing the time by reviewing her study notes under the van's dim dome light, but as he climbs in, she clips them together and throws them on the console.

— So how is he?

— How's who?

Shi reaches up to flick off the light and puts the van in gear.

— It's the last bus from Kingston. Not hard to figure out where you were.

He shrugs.

— He looks tired. Older.

— Mark thinks you visiting him is a good thing. For both of you.

— How does he know about it?

Shi actually laughs.

— Of course he knows — you're not invisible, Boy. You really think your best friends won't see how crazy all of this is making you?

— I suppose.

They fall silent as the city slides past, the synchronized stoplights along Main moving them steadily eastward without pause.

— How's the studying going? he asks.

— Good.

— You're early.

— I always start reviewing about a month ahead of time. You should try it; you could use the extra brainpower.

— I should. You're right.

But the thought of doing so — or worse still, that it might be too late even if he were to try — paralyzes him. *If it can go all to hell, it will. When it rains, it's gonna pour. You can't stop an avalanche after it gets going.* Boy leans his head back against the headrest and looks out the window as Main becomes Queenston becomes Highway 8. Shi drives in silence. Boy hopes she's mentally reviewing her study notes rather than worrying about him; it's uncomfortable knowledge that his friends might try to help him bear his burdens.

— Thank your dad for letting you take the van out so late, he says when they pull into the driveway.

— I didn't ask him.

— No?

— He's not hearing much these days. Dempster has really …

She shakes her head.

— The church is thinking about letting him go, she says.

— He didn't do anything, so why would this come back to him?

— He was in a leadership position. Everyone's suspicious.

— But it happened so long ago.

— As Dad likes to say, *A stain is a stain is a stain.* Forever.

— That doesn't sound like a pastor.

— I know. But it sounds like him right now, if that makes sense.

— It does.

It really fucking does.

Boy eats a quick snack and heads upstairs to bed. Although the master bedroom door is open, there's no snoring coming out, so Nick hasn't reversed his panicked flight and come home. Boy looks in against the gloom, his eyes now accustomed to the darkness, and sees the empty bed, its covers askew and half on the floor.

— Misty?

No response. His voice feels loud. He heads back downstairs to the living room, calling her name. Again, nothing.

His fatigue begins to burn into worry as he moves around the house looking for his mother. Office. Family room. Basement. He walks back out the front door and confirms that her SUV is in the driveway. Just as he pulls out his phone, he smells the acrid and distinct smell of a lit cigarette wafting across the dark driveway. He follows his nose to the garage door, where the smell is even stronger. He lifts the door, barely registering its weight, and blinks against the sudden light. Misty is sprawled on top of a pile of clothing spread from Corny's old boxes, an ignored cigarette in one hand, tipped by a precariously long ash tube, and an almost-empty mickey of gin in the other.

— Boy, you're home.

She raises the bottle unsteadily, sloshing high an awkward salute. She tries to get up but stumbles, dropping the cigarette onto the pile of clothing. She leans over and tries to pick it up and extinguish it all in one motion, succeeding only in dusting Corny's scattered clothing with smudged grey ash.

— Here, Misty, let me —

— Nope. I can do this. Like riding a bicycle.

— You're going to start a fire.

— You sound like Corny. *You'll burn the goddamn house down, lover,* he'd say.

She laughs at her own impression of Corny and tries to rise again. The bottle falls onto the pile, the remnants absorbed by the old clothes. Pale, dishevelled, and wearing only a faded sports bra and outsized pair of men's boxers — Nick's? Corny's? — she looks like a bizarre, half-dressed mannequin trying to animate itself in the middle of a tragic garage sale. Boy doesn't move — help steady his mother or close the garage door? He's angry with her but concerned, too, about what impressions they might add to the ones already compiled about his fractured family. Finally, she manages to stand, swaying unsteadily.

— Well, he's really going this time, she slurs. Eight years and a baby and off he goes.

— How do you —

— He called, didn't say anything, just breathed into the phone like a fucking pervert.

— Let's get you inside.

— I told him I could see his number but he hung up.

— It's late —

— What'd you say to him?

— What?

— You've been talking about me, haven't you? To Nick, Corny, everyone.

— No, I —

— Some brother you are. I mean, Jay's right upstairs. He needs you, you know.

— You're his mother — how can you get so wasted with him in the house?

She waves away his words like she's shooing a fly.

— I put him down first. He's fine.

— It's not fine at all. He's just a baby.

— *I'm eighteen, I can do whatever I want. Badmouthing my mother, running off to see her husband in prison* —

Her tone is mocking. Boy doesn't know what to say. Husband? *Her* husband? He can't recall the last time she used those words. Misty's avoidance of uncomfortable labels is almost a science. Even Nick is just Nick, never *Daddy* or *Papa* or anything that could be confused with affection. Even around Jay, she uses Nick's first name, like he and Jay are siblings or friends rather than father and son. But this reference, well, it's —

— You sent the photo, he says.

— What?

— Corny thanked me for sending it, but of course it was you.

A snort and a fool's attempt to pick up the bottle sends her back onto the clothing pile with a giggle. She brings the bottle to her mouth and tongues away the gin remnants around its neck.

— That was fast. I sent it only a few days ago.

— What are you doing? Why send a picture now?

— It shouldn't just be your face he gets to see.

— And Jay? Why include him?

A long, lopsided grin moves across her features but only partially, like the full genuine article would be far too difficult. The result is a clown sneer.

— I wanted him to see how I've moved on. Thought maybe a picture of my new baby would do it.

My God, he thinks, *how torturous that photo must be — a master stroke of guilt.* How wonderful it would be for Corny to be able to see the two remaining souls he had once shared a life with. And yet heartrending, as only a visual reminder of a surviving child and a spouse driven away could be. He'd always be suspended between the opposing desires of destroying the reminder in order to move on but also the desire to protect and preserve it, too. You hang on to what you can.

— Hang on, nothing — he can choke on it, she says.

He'd spoken aloud again without realizing it.

Corny's better off without her, even if it's a prison keeping him away.

He looks out the garage door, squinting, the bright interior turning the darkened street beyond into blackness. Charlie's out there but he can't see her. He wants to, even if she's as expressionless as always. Misty, meanwhile, scrabbles around in the pile of clothing until she locates the crumpled pack of cigarettes and a neon green lighter. Lights up. Inhales. Lets herself fall back into the clothing with a groan. A forgetful sound, no memory of the terrible words she just spoke or the horrible state she's perpetually in. His sympathy disappears along with the faint tendrils of smoke drifting out into the dark. No one should be able to do the sorts of things she's done and still be able to breathe so easily.

Without another word, Boy walks away from her and back into the house, glancing at the light switch on the wall as he goes in and deciding to leave it as it is. He'll come back in a little while, after her inevitable passing out, to make sure the cigarette isn't smouldering in the musty clothing. There's no way he'll stand by and let her burn the house down as he and Jay try to sleep, but he's more than content to leave the light on all night. He'd like to believe that it will be like bathing her in shame but doubts she'll even think about it at all.

The next morning, Boy watches the whitecapped swells on the lake and wonders if the wind storm would rate being called a tempest. *Pilots have a funny relationship with storms*, his flight commander said. All the other science and measurements — pressure, humidity, wind speed, et cetera — have precise quantitative terminology, but what they combine to form have always kept their artful descriptions. Gale. Hurricane. Thunderheads and lightning. Squall. When he woke up this morning after an unexpectedly deep sleep, he lay in bed for half an hour staring at the ceiling and listening to the storm blow against the side of the house. *Go to the rocks. Don't go. Go.* Thinking about how a storm could batter the shore without any rain. He'd gotten dressed thinking about the magnitude of the waves they might see.

— What'd I tell you? he yells against the blow.

Jay, wrapped tightly in the chest carrier and facing the lake, babbles an indistinct reply that gets carried over their shoulders and back towards the QEW.

You fooled him, that's for sure.

— What?

You're not here to see the waves.

— You're right. I'm not. But now that I'm here, I'm not sure I want to go any farther.

You shouldn't have brought him.

He looks over at his sister, in her spot but unaffected by the unsettled air, her voice level. What else could he do? Misty's a wreck, so he couldn't leave Jay at home. Instead of responding, he closes his eyes for an instant, concentrating on the moisture in the air, droplets flung from the waves and carried up to where he stands. A kind of immersion. He is so immersed in those few seconds of sensory solitude that he doesn't react to the sudden lack of sound, the absence of wind cooling the pinpricks of moisture on his face. It's Jay's voice, loud in its isolation, that brings him back.

— Ba-ba?

When Boy opens his eyes, the stillness is jarring against how unsettled everything had been before.

— Ba-ba!

A new kind of wonder has taken hold of his brother. Jay is trying to make the transition between the extremes. His eyes are still wide open but now he's looking around, sensing in his immature way that something is definitely off with the world. Completely unaffected by the stoppage, just like he and Charlie are. Fascinating. Jay's head swivels towards the sound of footsteps on loose stones. Mara appears through the bushes lining the shore at the far end of the rocks and begins to climb, carefully placing each step on the storm-shiny rock. When he's only a few metres away, he smiles and waves. Jay laughs and reaches for Mara so quickly and with such enthusiasm it almost throws Boy off balance.

— I thought it might be Jay, Mara says. I don't get to hear such young voices anymore.

Mara steps towards them. Boy pulls Jay back and retreats a step, putting himself between Mara and his brother. Jay looks at Mara and then at Boy and bursts into tears.

— I'm sorry, Mara says. I didn't mean to startle him.

— Just stay there. I'm not sure I want you to come closer.

— Why? What's wrong?

— I know your name's not Mara.

Mara laughs.

— Of course it's not Mara — it's just a nickname someone gave me when I was living on the streets. You came here to tell me that?

— No, I came to ...

And what would he say, really? Now that the man is standing in front of him, it all seems so ridiculous. Confront him, demand a confession? Ignore all of that and ask Mara's advice about eighteen-year-old woes? And what was he thinking, bringing Jay along? He remembers the images on the TV, Dempster's face, the tearful testimonies by boys — now men — talking about the most horrible things, the glaring lights, riotous courtroom scrums, shaky camera shots, shouted questions, the pacifying defence lawyer.

— Your name is Dempster; it's all over the news.

Mara's face goes pale, his eyes narrowing.

— There are new charges against you. Did you know?

Mara relaxes, turning to look out over the still water and folding his arms.

— No, but they were bound to come out.

— Are they true?

Please let them not be, Boy thinks even as he speaks. Jay has stopped his squirming and studies Mara with remarkable patience. Charlie, too, has turned to face the three of them, and Boy notices how similar her expression is to Jay's. Mara is silent for a long time before he finally speaks.

— Yes, he says. They are.

— How many —

— All of them. Even the ones that haven't come out yet.

How short-sighted can a person be, Boy thinks. He feels dizzy, sick to his stomach. He turns to leave.

— There's never been anything for you to worry about, Mara says.

We're well past the point of not worrying.

— We're going, Boy says. Please don't follow us.

— Hear me out. I'm not going to try to say anything other than I'm a sick, bad person, but …

Mara trails off as he searches for what to say next.

— But what?

— I want to tell you it's best that you leave, but I can't. I've enjoyed getting to know you.

God, that's creepy.

It is, Boy thinks. *But also true.* Why isn't he feeling angrier? Resentful? Anything?

— I don't know what to do right now. There's really no way to turn this back, you know?

— I know, Mara says.

— All of it. You, me, this thing you do —

— You'd think it would be a gift. I did, for a long time.

— Did it happen — what they're saying you did — while everything was stopped?

— Yes.

— Do you still —

— Not for a long time.

— So you're better, then.

— No. I control myself by living away from everyone. That's all I can do.

Jay begins pushing against the pressure of the chest carrier, looking to get out.

— But you can't just vanish, Boy says.

— I can't. All I can do is stop things; there's no redemption when you've already taken what was never offered.

— Mara — Dempster — we can't stay.

— It's Raymond.

— Raymond, then. But you have to know I won't be —

— I know. I understand.

He has to.

Boy moves towards the treeline and the fence beyond. After a few steps, everything starts up again, the waves and wind resuming their bluster and nearly blowing him from his footing.

— Jesus Christ! He's just fucking there!

From behind a large sumac bush, a man emerges, pointing at Mara as excitedly as a schoolboy chewing bubble gum for the first time. On his wrist, a platinum watch. Breitling. Ten grand. John. Another man, who stands a head taller than John, emerges from behind another bush. John is shaking his head and speaking loudly against the wind.

— I mean, I was just thinking about leaving. How long can a guy just stare at waves and talk to himself, right? But then I blink and you're not alone. He's fucking real!

— Boy? Who are these men?

— I don't know —

— Now, Boy, let's not be rude. I'm John, an associate of Boy's father.

John tips an imaginary hat towards Mara. He doesn't introduce the other guy.

— What do you want? Mara asks.

— Boy told his dad about you, and Corny just couldn't keep his mouth shut. My man inside thought it all sounded a bit far-fetched, but I'm a bigger picture kind of person.

— I didn't say anything about you to him, Boy says to Mara.

— No, I just tracked your phone. Fucked by technology, am I right?

Mara moves a few paces closer to them and asks John again what he wants. John, still smiling, reaches behind him and pulls out a large silver pistol from his waistband.

— Easy, friend. Here's where I tell you what to do.

— I'm so sorry, Boy says to Mara.

Jay, watching the strange man pull out the gun but having no concept about what it all means, reaches for the shiny object and giggles. Boy pulls him back, again startling him — there's a squeak of surprise and then a rush of tears. John rolls his eyes and orders Boy to keep Jay quiet. Jay, perhaps in a baby fit of rebellion, only cries louder.

— What do you want? Money? Mara asks.

— No, no. Well, yes, actually — in the longer term. For now, you come with us.

— If I don't?

— Then I hope the storm is loud enough to cover three gunshots.

John's face is neutral, as though he was responding to an inquiry about the time of day. Jay, still squalling, has nestled into Boy's neck. *He'll kill Jay*, he thinks, wanting to vomit. *He'd actually kill a baby*. Boy sees Mara look at him and his baby brother with a tenderness that seems to burn through the storm. He stands a little straighter, turning towards John as if the gun isn't even there, his eyes tightening, his chin rising. Boy feels his own body tensing, his heart rate slowing, his body shifting to place itself between the gun and his brother.

— No, Mara says. No.

John and his associate trade looks. The threat of violence hasn't had the desired effect. John's gun comes up from his side as the other man steps towards Mara. But neither finishes his movement. Again, the waves and wind hush to a stop, leaving only the sound of Jay's crying and their breathing. The other two men are frozen in place, dynamic, sudden statues.

— I don't think they thought this through very well, Mara says.

Jay stops crying, again looking around the interrupted world with wonder. An amazing thing, to see things again for the first time.

— We have to get out of here, Boy says.

Mara shakes his head.

— They'll just find you.

— But not you.

— No, not me. I can always disappear, at least for a time.

— What should we do?

There's no response from Mara, just a long look towards the escarpment. As the moment moves on, it begins to feel familiar, this pause. One day after school earlier in the year, Boy asked Mr. Essère how he always seemed to get the best answers from students. *Wait time*, Essère said. Teaching 101. *No one likes silence — even the most hesitant people will instinctively try to fill it*. Mara is waiting, allowing a moment that Boy can fill with his own reflections. It doesn't take long for him to see what has to happen next. What happens within the stoppage can be controlled, but nothing else — there will always be consequences. And right here, right now, there must be a measuring of consequence between running away and hoping for the best and making sure that whatever happens when everything resumes cannot hurt any of them anymore. Only one thing — one final thing — can seal up the danger permanently.

— Jesus, Boy says. We have to —

— Not *we*. Just me.

— But this is my fault. I told Corny —

— I'm already beyond repair, Mara replies. If *you* do this …

He looks at Jay and then right into Boy's eyes and then waits again. And Boy understands.

— It's not about being found out, is it? Boy asks.

— No. It's about what you can or can't carry.

You wouldn't be able to carry this, little brother. There's too much conscience in you.

— Go now, Mara says.

Charlie moves towards the break in the fence line, passing by without so much as a glance. Boy follows, surprising himself with how easily he made the decision to follow his dead sister and take his brother away from harm, leaving Mara to deal with the two motionless men on his own. He wonders if anyone will miss them. He wonders if Mara doing what he has to do is the only way stopping time could be a gift. Though what's fixed, really? It's just another sort of delay. An imperfect solution. As it has been all along, of course, as imperfect as Boy's hope that Mara could use his gift to help him. A stalling strategy at best, regardless of whether it seems as though it might be helping.

Boy doesn't know how much time passes before the world begins moving again, but it feels like an age. As he weaves back into the labyrinth of familiar and anonymous streets, though the pausing of everything physical probably makes sound impossible, he listens for something that betrays the choice Mara has made about the two men. Not for a gunshot, or a scream, or even a noise exactly, but perhaps a slight adjustment in the sound of his own heartbeat, a break in what had been the continuous stream of an intact conscience.

CHAPTER 19

Later that afternoon, Boy studies the graffiti in a library washroom stall. Layers of scratches and marker and pen as well as the paint the maintenance staff uses in a futile effort to cover it over. Generations of graffiti. Rebellious history. He retreated here quite some time ago, trying to get away from Mark's and Shi's best intentions, to put structure on what happened this morning, to help him move through the fact that he is a part of the deaths of two people. He can't, though. It just feels too big. He is an accomplice, a willing one, an even bigger reality. The etched obscenities and mental musings of the stall's captive audience merely become a blur, part of the background as his mind turns over again and again. He exits the washroom and returns to his friends.

— Sorry that took so long, he says.

— No problem, Shi says.

Mark shrugs.

Mark and Shi showed up together a couple of hours after he returned home from the rocks. Boy's mind was still reeling. When they practically ordered him to come study with them at the library, Misty took Jay into her arms and told Boy to go. She was sober enough to apologize. It felt like the perfect intervention, the right amount of guilt coming from his two friends and the precise amount of on-the-spot pressure from his mother. He now finds himself enduring what seems like a marathon brainstorming session about what he can do to save his grades. Mark is growing impatient, frustrated by Boy's lack of enthusiasm. Shi looks tired.

— I don't know why I came, Boy says. My head's just not in it.

— You came because you want to pass, you dumb shit, Mark says.

— I'm not sure I have it in me to fight anymore, he says. The air force —

— Fuck the air force and your enlistment plan, Mark says. You're too smart to be anything less than an officer and a pilot.

He's not wrong.

He looks over at Charlie, who's arranged herself by the DVDs at the far side of the library. A few harried library patrons scan the shelves for just the right escape for the evening, moving along the shelves in kind of a sideways slide, heads tilted to the right to read the titles and barely missing each other as they get near. A middle-aged woman tapping away on her smartphone and mumbling to herself passes right through Charlie. Boy half expects the woman to shudder or stop, as though she has this subconscious sense of making contact with the spectral, like you see in the movies. But there's nothing.

— No, I'm fine, thanks, Shi says.

— I'm sorry?

— You asked if I was cold.

Mark watches Boy with a barely restrained, annoyed rage.

— What's with you? If you're not interested in our help —

Shi glances at Mark sharply, an unexpected glimpse of what might happen if she were to lose her remarkable restraint. Boy is

continually impressed by her poise, no matter the situation —
even her own issues, her family's stress at home, seems impossible
to measure behind her still features. He wonders whether his own
facade, the masks he has had to adopt — *Remember, Cadets, you
carry the squadron with you wherever you go*, he'd say at the end of
every parade night — have started to crack. But this is the first
time he has seen the glare of Shi's impatience. *There's fire in there*,
he thinks.

— Well?

— Maybe you shouldn't tie yourselves too closely to me, Boy
says.

— What?

— Sinking ships and all.

— What's that supposed to mean?

— All this generosity might just end up tarnishing your stars,
too.

Mark's mouth opens and closes, his face reddening. Boy's
two friends mean well but he's still picking a fight as though he's
helpless against himself. Probably easier to walk away, leave them
to their own success. Besides, even this argument feels forced,
almost to the point of being ridiculous. When he imagines trying
to win teachers back against what he just went through on the
rocks, it feels like making sure there's a new coat of paint on the
front door in the middle of a hurricane. *Sandbag, Cadet. Close
the door. Board up the damn windows.* He stands and grabs his
pack, mumbling something about grabbing a bus, not to worry,
and so on, and walks out, not even looking back to see if Charlie
has followed.

Nick's SUV, large and dark, is sitting in the driveway when he
arrives home. He walks in to find Nick sitting on the living

room sofa, a large but unidentifiable drink in one hand, his old BlackBerry in the other. He looks terrible. His clothes are limp and wrinkled. Days of unchecked beard growth, his skin loose and sallow. Jay is on the carpet at his feet, an army of stuffed animals besieging him. Every so often he looks up from the toys to scrutinize Nick with a serious look, as if to say, And what, exactly, are *you* doing here? When Nick tosses his phone to the side, drags his hand across his face, and curses loudly, Jay jumps, startled, and starts to cry. Boy lifts him up and soothes him close against his chest.

— Watch your language around Jay, Nick.

Nick ignores him and storms into the kitchen where he opens and closes various cupboards and the fridge without taking anything out. Cursing again, he returns to the sofa and grabs the phone, holding it close enough to his bleary eyes that Boy wonders how he can possibly read anything on the screen.

— Are you back, or just stopping in for a shower and some clean clothes?

— Not even a text message, Nick says.

— What are you doing here?

— What? I'm just — hold on, this is my house, too.

— It's Misty's house. *Our* house.

Again, unexpected solidarity. Why is he defending her again?

— Kid, we're not doing this right now.

— I'm sorry, are we somehow inconveniencing you?

Boy spits the question out like a mouthful of vinegar.

— Look —

— Where've you been?

— Out.

— That's it? You leave your wife and child behind without so much as a text message, and all you can say is *I went out*?

— She's not my wife. And he —

Nick tilts his head towards Jay and opens his mouth but then closes it. *Go ahead*, Boy thinks. *Say it. Joke about Jay not being your son. Or, worse still, give voice to the wish your son had never been born.* After a moment, Nick shakes his head instead.

— She's gone, he says.

Boy laughs.

— That's poetic, he says.

— No, I mean *gone* gone. She took her flight bag.

— But —

— It's like an overnight bag but with more clothes and things.

— I know what a flight bag is. I have one, too, for cadets, but with charts and maps. Survival gear.

— Oh, Nick says. Right. That makes sense, then.

— But why would she have one?

— We both do. For a quick getaway.

— From what?

— From you. And Jay. We put them together after he was born. *Boy's old enough now*, we said.

— You've got to be kidding —

Nick holds up a hand.

— It was a joke. A bad one, but just a joke.

Boy turns away from Nick and looks out the back window at the golden, late afternoon sun clipping the tops of nearby houses and trees.

— That's not funny, Boy says.

— I know.

Jay starts to squirm and cry. Boy puts him down amidst the toys, thinking that Jay just needs space, but on the carpet he only cries louder. Boy scoops him up, sniffs his diaper, and checks inside Jay's mouth for new teething buds. In the past few weeks, Jay has cut another tooth, this one on the top, on course to have a full set in record time. But all is pink and healthy, no new inflammation or telltale bumps.

— When did he eat last?

Nick shrugs.

— I got home about an hour ago.

Boy takes Jay into the kitchen for a snack. Jay makes short work of a yogurt squeeze pack with an odd blend of fruits and green veggies. Before long, his brother is gurgling and babbling again, the needed calories making their way through his baby-quick system.

Nick's phone rings. He answers. There's a brief exchange. He closes his eyes and speaks low into the handset. After he ends the call, he remains on the sofa for a few moments, looking out the window towards the late sun. He smiles a brief smile, pushes himself up from the couch, and heads towards the front hall, grabbing his car keys from the table.

— Was that Misty? Boy asks.

— I can't believe she's there.

— Where is she?

— I have to go.

Nick shrugs on a hooded firefighter sweatshirt and walks out the front door, leaving it wide open behind him. With Jay still in his arms, Boy follows him out, stopping on the front step and asking the question again. No response. Just the slamming of the driver's door. The cough of the still-warm engine. The sound of tires backing slowly across asphalt. The clunk of the transmission as it changes gears. The SUV accelerating. Leaving the cul-de-sac. The sound finally fading.

CHAPTER 20

— I'm glad you called, Cynthia says.

— They've left before but not like this. It feels different, Boy says.

— How so?

He tries to articulate, without going into too much uncomfortable detail, that spiralling sense he has. Of everything moving far faster than it should. But in the end, he shrugs and repeats how different it feels. They're sitting in the living room at the front of the house, the formal room with its good leather sofas, hardwood tables, precious glass lamps. Away from the everyday family room at the back, joined to the kitchen, with its dirty dishes and worn furniture. Toys strewn about in gentle chaos. The laptop Boy left open, tabs lined up in the browser, news sites that haven't said a word about two bodies turning up. Foul play. Et cetera.

As soon as he'd taken Cynthia's coat — after an awkward moment where it became obvious she was waiting for him to remove it from her shoulders — she stepped out of her low heels and walked right into the room, a place seldom used. She sat herself on the high-backed wing chair in the corner without so much as a glance at the loveseat or sofa. Jay, seated on her lap, is quiet and watchful. He sits with his little shoulders back and chubby chin raised like a king's puppet. She wears a deep red — merlot, almost — tailored dress and matching jacket. Expensive and stiff, reminiscent of conservative heads of state and British royalty. If it was a few shades lighter it would look cozy next to Mountie formal wear. No hat, though. An odd thought.

— Why would I need a hat? she asks.

God, not again, he thinks.

— Sorry, I was somewhere else.

— I never pegged you as a daydreamer.

— I'm not — not normally, anyhow. Lately, though, between Misty and Nick's stuff, the end of the school year rushing at me, leaving cadets, and —

— You feel like time doesn't matter as much.

— Yeah.

— You're probably not sleeping well, either.

— True.

Cynthia gives a quick smile.

— The joys of adulthood, she says.

Odd that he'd find himself daydreaming more as he gets into the later, more responsible period in life. Everything he'd been led to anticipate indicated that adulthood was a good opportunity to focus more, not less. Find your own voice and strengths. Success on the back of increasing wisdom and knowledge. Not a whiff or a thought of slacking off or failing, but now it seems as though those aspects are manifesting themselves quite nicely, and without any input or control from him.

— I thought it would get easier, he says. No, wait, not easier. Clearer.

— It does. It will.

He laughs and sits back on the sofa, the cool, seldom-used leather giving way with a reluctant groan. He's not quite sure why he laughed — it's not as though he has much faith in the brightness of adulthood these days. He watches Cynthia interacting with Jay, her own formal manner mirroring his seriousness back to him. Amazingly, he warms up to her, although not in the giggly, almost-manic acceptance most people hope for when they *goo* and *gaa* at the tiny humans of the world. No, he can see Jay's bearing relax just slightly, his hands wandering just a little more freely to Cynthia's pearl necklace and the expensive buttons on her blazer. He begins to make soft sounds through carefully pursed lips, ones Boy has never heard him make before. *Whispers*, he realizes. *My brother's first whispers*. Then his eyes are filling before he even has a chance to register the weight of Jay's response to Cynthia, an almost stranger. What a thing to be confronted by disquieting disturbances one minute — amazing how babies can survive so many traumatic firsts — yet be playing and whispering to himself in the next. Cynthia, pleased by Jay's curiosity, doesn't see Boy look away and blink the sudden wetness away from his eyes.

I don't want to move, he thinks. *I could just enjoy my brother's peaceful moment without another care.*

Yet there's no peace in this knowledge, which sits on his mind like a leaden helmet. Even if he takes advantage of right now, removing the heavy metal, he'd still have to find a place to put it. Where it would wait, grey and dull and necessary, until he could hoist it onto himself again. What would Charlie do with such a burden? *Fuck it*, she'd say, *What are we going to do? Run away? I don't fucking think so. We deal with this right here, right now.* Or would she? This could be the Charlie he thinks he remembers. So much could have changed across eight years, especially as she moved through her teenage years, making enemies and friends, finding success and occasional failure, leaving tracks in her life's mud. Deep, irregular, weaving tracks — the kind you make when you stomp through, unafraid to deviate from the path when obstacles loom.

— Boy! Did you hear me?

His head snaps forward and he opens his eyes, his vision blurry, his mouth cottoned.

— Sorry, what?

Jay laughs at his big brother's confusion, clapping in sheer glee.

— You're going to be late if you don't get moving.

— Late?

— For school.

— No, I'm —

— You're going to school. There's nothing more you can do, and worry is useless.

He pulls his phone out and looks at the time. Cynthia let him doze for at least fifteen minutes. He can't believe that Jay is still on her lap and still playing contentedly.

— Do you need a ride?

— No, Corny's bike is fixed —

— The old orange ten-speed?

— Yeah.

— He loved that bike. We …

But she doesn't finish her sentence, a shadow moving across her features and taking her voice. Boy wonders which *we* she's referring to. Cynthia coughs quietly and gets to her feet, hefting Jay with the ease of ingrained practice and telling him about snacks and toys, all the fun they'll have. Jay leans his head against her collarbone and exhales loudly, a contented, happy sound that undoubtedly pleases his new grandmother. But Boy thinks that perhaps it's meant more for him. *Go*, it says. *Worry is useless.*

· · · · · · ·

He can't say why, but the school's hallways feel different somehow. There's nothing visibly changed and yet the feeling of a shift is everywhere and unavoidable, like an unpleasant odour you can't quite place. The bike racks are still descending into their slow surrender to rust, anchored to the concrete by short and loose bolts. The side entrance nearest the racks is still a facade of crumbling stone and concrete, the steps still uneven and cracked, the afterthought wheelchair ramp still sloping away from the side like a tongue. The halls still yellow-lit from the fluorescent lighting, the floors still dingy yet shiny, too, the grime seemingly lacquered on.

Stopping and staring at it won't change a thing, you know.

— I know, he says.

His voice echoes. The halls are empty apart from the classroom noises seeping under doors and swirling around his feet as he walks. He stops at his homeroom door for a long moment before stepping inside. His homeroom teacher looks briefly up at him, half-heartedly tapping the watch on his wrist before returning to his crossword puzzle. The other students lounge, bicker, laugh, text, watch online videos to pass the time. A couple of the students glance at him before returning to their screens.

His phone buzzes in his pocket. Shi.

— *are you ok*

— *im fine*

— *marks pissed at you*

I know, he thinks. *And no wonder.*

— *are you here?*

He starts to tap out a reply but stops. He doesn't feel like small talk, his friends asking him every few seconds how he's doing. As he closes the messaging app, a bright red alert slides down from the top of the screen, the word "body" in the headline drawing his eye. He taps into the news app, his stomach clenching as he scans the story, looking for confirmation that two bodies have been found on the lakeshore. But the news is from Toronto, the body that of a jogger who'd been declared missing a few days ago. He can't decide if it's good or bad news that John and his goon associate haven't been found. Boy powers off the phone and slides it back into his pocket.

The rest of the day passes slowly. It's hard to focus in class, the uncertainty of what could happen if it turns out that Nick and Misty have indeed left for good. Could that even happen? Aside from the most glaring issue of what to do with an abandoned infant and newly adult son, there's the house and the bills and the zillion other things someone would have to sift through in that eventuality. He forces himself to take odd routes between classes and eats lunch in the library to avoid his friends, feeling guilty and the necessity of his evasiveness all at once, disparate emotions pulling at each other like twins fighting over the same scrap of blankie.

In Mr. Essère's class, he manages to get to his seat while the teacher is writing instructions on the whiteboard. The period passes in relative anonymity. Boy surprises himself by acing a surprise quiz about post–World War II land issues they'd covered in a previous class. After the students grade each other and hand the papers back, he realizes that Essère's material aligns with knowledge he'd gleaned from cadets. They pass the papers forward so the teacher can record the scores. After class, Essère asks Boy to stay back.

— Well, Mr. McVeigh, this is a hard conversation but a necessary one, I think.

As he speaks, he tabs through the quizzes until he finds Boy's, sliding the paper out and holding it aloft and slightly away as though he were handling a dirty plate.

— I'm not seeing any improvement ...

But then he sees the grade and stops himself. He shakes his head, a minuscule smile bending the corners of his mouth.

— I am surprised, he says.

— Me, too, sir.

— Really.

— I wish I could say I was ready, but it's a familiar subject.

— Ah, yes. Well, I'm glad something I've taught you has had some resonance.

Essère sounds like he's pouting, apologizing for how poorly his formerly promising student has done this year, as though seeing the quiz grade has struck a nerve, knocking him from the path he'd decided upon. *Shit*, Boy thinks, understanding where this conversation was supposed to lead.

— You read my essay, he says.

— I have.

— And?

Essère opens his drawer and pulls out the essay, the top page so scored by red marks it looks like it has run through concertina wire.

— There are glimpses of your potential here, he says.

He flips to the second page — more red — and the third, which he turns towards Boy. The red marks stop about a third of the way down.

— But seeing only glimpses through two pages didn't exactly send me into the third with excitement.

— You didn't finish? But couldn't —

Essère holds up a hand.

— It doesn't even read like your work, to be perfectly honest. Not that I'd worry about plagiarism, but I'm sure you'll understand why I had to stop.

— It's not worth your time.

— Or yours.

Essère hands back the paper. No mark at the top. And why would there be? It's an extra assignment; the teacher was under no obligation to assess it. Boy knows it was a poor effort, had known it since typing the first capital of the first paragraph, and feels again the urge to use his family hardship to get another chance. Or suck up to Essère, seek his advice, apply the last bandage, the old faithful, one labelled in black marker: *Playing to the Vain Teacher's Ego.*

No. He won't go there. He hears the overlapping voices of his overeager instructors from all the summers he spent at cadet camp at CFB Borden. Hearing his own voice mixed in as well. *No excuses, Plug. Don't make your problems their problems. Buck the fuck up, Cadet.*

Essère blinks, shakes his head.

— Well, that was colourful, he says.

This is becoming a bit of a crutch.

— No, sir, that's not what I meant —

— I'm finished, McVeigh. Academically, you're on your own from now on.

The teacher stuffs the quizzes and a few odds and ends into his briefcase, then stands and walks out. Boy follows. Charlie moves past them to the far side of the hallway, stops at the near end of a bank of lockers while the teacher locks up. The clunking of the heavy deadbolt knocks Boy from the last of the lingering excuses, strategies, pleas for further chances. He tightens the straps of his pack. Nods.

— Thank you, sir.

His teacher flinches ever so slightly, as though he too is unprepared for the finality of this conversation. When Boy reaches out his hand, Essère shakes it firmly but can't look him in the eye. Ill-advised investments all around, losses where gains are expected, resignation.

After the teacher is gone, Boy heads towards the exit and the bike ride home. For a moment, he savours the small victory of his extended hand, the nobility of the handshake he initiated. Feeling the bigger man, as it were. *Don't blow your bridges until there's no other way to keep the enemy from crossing.* Though by the time he unlocks Corny's bike, he begins to ask himself if the final gesture was worth it — whether he has sealed a new, mature understanding with the teacher or whether it just signals that he has well and truly given up.

As he rides the old ten-speed across jarring, winter-degraded asphalt, he imagines that although it is powered off, he can feel his phone vibrating in his pocket. Ghost vibrations. Mark and Shi must be wondering where he is, why he hasn't responded all afternoon. Or, for that matter, why he didn't meet up with them today at all. He ponders a few clichés — *Better get used to it, It'll toughen a person up, No tears, No drama* — though the sayings might not be for his friends. Until yesterday's frustrated words in the library, they've been so quiet around him, as though they're waiting for him to blow up first. Too quiet?

You're hoping, maybe, for someone to snap?

When he stops at a set of lights at Nash and Highway 8, he sees Charlie in the thin shadow of a stoplight pole.

— There should be some response, he says.

There is. They're mirroring you.

— No, that doesn't make sense.

Fuck, you're obtuse. No one's going to yell at you. They respect you too much. They know only you can claw your way out of wherever you've ended up. I can't even tell you everything —

She never speaks this way, he thinks. Never for more than a few words, much less with such passion. She's not looking at him, as usual, but her face seems darker, like her extended words have drawn something out of her she hadn't anticipated, either.

What's changed? A yelled obscenity from an impatient driver who sees only a boy on a bike speaking to himself — the light changed a few moments ago — prevents him from asking her the question. He steps on the pedals and gets up to speed quickly, mulling over Charlie's unexpected words for the remainder of the bike ride home.

There are two police cars parked in front of the house at the curb, engines off, quiet. Nick's SUV is in the driveway. Boy's stomach clenches again. *It's happening*, he thinks. *I've been found out.*

— What do I do?

Charlie stands next to the police cruiser, watching the house. Boy waits for her voice, her words, but nothing comes.

He lets Corny's bike fall to the front lawn. He nearly slams the front door into the back of a police officer in his haste to get in — there's a flurry of apologies and shuffling, rearranging in the hall to accommodate him. Then nothing. Boy looks at Cynthia, who stands with her arms folded, shoeless, her blouse untucked from her skirt.

— What's going on?

— This is Boy, Misty's son, she says to the officers.

The senior police officer, a sergeant, stands upright with her cap under her arm and gives Boy a slight nod as she introduces herself. He doesn't hear her name but instead looks her up and down, a ritual uniform inspection. She's at least six feet tall. Her dark uniform is immaculate, with not a thread loose or a speck of lint anywhere, her utility belt tight and clean, and her hair is pinned to the back of her head at the hairline in a tight bun that would do a drill sergeant proud. Her partner's uniform is equally impressive but looks out of place against his pale skin, greasy dark hair, and the shaving pimples on his throat. *He obviously steps up his game when he's with her*, Boy thinks, again looking at the woman approvingly. Ex-military, for sure.

— Army, right? MP?

A brief, grim smile, and another nod. He asks again what's happening. Cynthia lays a hand on his shoulder, her eyes heavy and rimmed in red. She gives a slight look towards the stairs. A white rush of sound begins to roar in his ears.

— Oh my God. Jay — what happened to Jay?

Cynthia starts, surprised.

— No, he's fine. Napping, actually. The police came here to see you.

So. They know. He can't imagine how it can possibly be, but they know about his relationship with Mara, about what he did to the guy who called himself John and his associate. Wait. It feels wrong. If this was about what happened to those two guys on the rocks, it would either be an army of police for the arrest or a quiet detective visit, an unmarked car. It's too soon. What a strange thought to have, as though he should somehow have prepared himself better for this. Readying himself, as though all of this was inevitable. *Redirect, Cadet. Delay. Give yourself time so you can work out the best course of action for you and your troops.*

— Did you change him beforehand? He sleeps better when he's dry, he says to Cynthia.

— He's fine —

— And after a snack, too, or else he'll wake up crying.

— Boy ...

— He won't understand why he's hungry. He'll —

The tall officer holds up a single hand. There's a strength behind the gesture, an authority Boy knows well. *I know what you're going to say and it doesn't matter. Now listen the fuck up and I'll tell you what's going to happen next.* He feels like a recruit again.

— Something has happened, young man. You'll need to —

— I can't tell you anything about him, he says. I wasn't there.

Cynthia and the two cops exchange a confused look.

— Do you mean Nick? Cynthia asks.

— What? No, I —

— Because he's upstairs, too. He had to lie down after he found out.

— Found what out? I don't understand.

The three adults take a deep breath and exchange another look. Then Boy, almost as though he's hovering outside himself, sees and feels himself being led into the living room, across the pristine carpet. His peripheral vision catalogues the bright, thick spines of Misty's precious cassette tape collection lining the upper shelves of a glass cabinet. Some of them, he knows, have never been played; many are even still wrapped in cellophane.

— I should take off my shoes, he says.

Cynthia sits down with him on the sofa. The police officers remain standing, put their heels together, and firm up their posture. Reseat the uniform cap under the left arm. Let the other arm fall straight down. Look straight ahead. They're standing at attention, he knows, to make sure there's no misunderstanding about who the focus is. *I'm here, but not here. This is all about you.*

Cynthia takes a deep breath, her lower lip trembling.

— Boy, your mother's dead. Misty's dead. I'm so sorry.

Her voice is thin, a thread stretched to its absolute limit from the spool. Boy says nothing, distracted by Cynthia's unexpected emotion. From now on, whenever his mind turns back to this moment, he'll be unable to recall how he reacted but he'll remember her tears. Eventually, he'll see that they aren't for Misty, but for him and Jay, half-brothers now without a mother. He'll remember, too, how she insists on including her daughter-in-law's first name when she tells him, as though sensing that he might need to hear a slightly different version in order to meet him where he is.

CHAPTER 21

— Misty's name was released today, Mark says.

— It had to come out at some point, Boy says.

There was a small flare-up of media interest after Misty died, when it came out that she fell from a Dundurn Street bridge, spanning the deep railway cut blasted through the western side of the city. A suspicious death. The authorities acted quickly, scheduling a quick autopsy, interviewing patrons at the last bar she was seen leaving.

— Do the police think —

— They're not assuming a suicide anymore, Boy says. Blood tests came back positive for alcohol and drugs. But aside from that ...

He shrugs.

A passing taxi driver came forward and said Misty was alone when she fell from the slippery handrail spanning the bridge. *Like a daredevil*, he said. The media, having little patience for news without an angle, allowed the story to fade away within a day or two.

— Well, her name is out there now, Mark says. Do you think they'll dig up —

— Yes.

Connections will be made to the news from almost a decade ago, two daughters killed, the guilty ex-husband still rotting away at Millhaven. But then there will be the new twists to discover, where the grieving mother shacks up with the other girl's father, the drugs and alcohol, an unexpected lovechild, the postpartum decline in her business, and so on. Boy glances at the landline phone on the kitchen counter, half expecting it to start ringing, hungry journalists smelling the hint of something tasty in the water.

Mark hands over his phone, lit up with a brief CBC update about Misty's death. Boy quickly reads the story — no new information — before swiping to other news updates, a new habit, looking for bodies and police tape, then returns the phone. Jay crawls around on the carpet with his favourite toy, a brightly coloured stack of rings on a spindle. He babbles quietly to himself as he practises his latest trick, lifting the rings carefully from the spindle then throwing them in every direction. He laughs as the rings bounce and roll around, then holds up the spindle to be restocked all over again. Boy slides down onto the carpet and stacks the rings. Jay repeats the cycle, making Boy and Mark smile.

— So what's next? Mark asks.

— I guess we take her, Boy says. No reason for her to stay in the morgue.

— Will there be a ceremony?

— I don't know.

For most, a simple question. But cadets didn't equip him for this kind of grief. No training, no lectures. No manual, algorithm, or instrument to measure sadness like a pitot tube measures airspeed. An artificial horizon to rely on when the clouds are too thick. *Trust the instruments — your instincts will fail you.* He wonders how obvious it is that he is indeed flying blind.

He thinks about Mara and about the two men, where they ended up, how safe he is. Then he looks at Jay and feels a pang of something sharp just below his sternum. Guilt, certainly. Projection, too, worrying about when Jay will have to confront the loss. Shouldn't Big Brother feel something when Baby Brother can't yet process it? Mark asked him yesterday how he was doing. *I think I miss her but I don't feel sad,* Boy told his friend. *Not yet, anyway.* There was nothing behind the words, though — it was more like trying them on.

Heavy footsteps on the stairs. Nick comes into the kitchen, opens the fridge, and stares at it a while. Finally, he grunts and reaches for a beer on the inside of the door before stopping himself and closing the door. But then he opens it again, reaches, pulls back, closes it. Repeats the cycle twice more before leaving the door closed and moving to the counter separating the kitchen from the dining area and family room. Finally he takes a glass from the cupboard and pours in a couple fingers of Misty's gin.

— It's twelve o'clock somewhere, he says.

Staring off somewhere above the boys' heads, he raises the glass as though saluting a distant, invisible companion and downs the gin in a single draught. He sets the glass down with surprising delicacy. He hasn't shaved, his facial hair now framing his chubby face in a full beard. His eyes and cheeks are swollen, hair unstyled. Grimy jeans and a moth-eaten fire-hall T-shirt do little to add to his appearance. He doesn't notice Jay's hopeful good-morning wave from the family room floor. He'd searched for a long time but never found Misty. She called him from that last bar, but by the time he arrived — apparently a favourite hangout when they fled the house pre-Jay — she was gone.

The front door opens and closes, and Cynthia walks in carrying a couple of cloth grocery bags. Stark contrast between her appearance and Nick's. Her hair and makeup are pristine, her jeans starched and her blouse immaculately tailored. She moved into the guest room the day Misty died and has been making sure meals get made, surfaces stay clean, and Nick does what he needs to do. She drove them to the morgue to identify the body, waiting patiently in the hallway while the attendant drew back the sheet. They'd cleaned Misty up well and aside from her pale, bluish complexion and a strategically placed drape over the worst of the head injuries, she looked almost normal. She helped Boy sign the positive identification form.

— Nick, you can't go like that, she says.

He doesn't respond, just grabs for the glass, and raises it to his lips before realizing that it's empty. Cynthia puts the bags on the counter and shoos Nick out of the kitchen, telling him he has ten minutes to make himself presentable. She starts putting the groceries away.

— What's going on? Boy asks.

— Nick has to meet with the lawyer today about Misty's will. You'll go, too, of course.

— Nick's next of kin?

— You both are. They've been living together for so long …

She doesn't finish the thought, but Boy doesn't need her to. The law he learned at school covered enough about common-law partnerships for him to understand they were effectively spouses.

Mark stands.

— I'll get your homework for you today, he says. Let me know how the lawyer thing goes, okay?

The lawyer thing. Corny's words, too, all those years ago, bathed in that yellowed, incandescent light memory recreates. Drunken conversation around the kitchen table. Misty and Corny playfully arguing between shots of liquor about bequeathing and beneficiaries and codices while he and Charlie watched TV in the family room. The piles of paper, the exaggerated courtesy when it came time to sign. *After you, m'dear. No, no, after you....* Today, he and the impostor father of his baby brother will discover the details of those frenzied conversations, whether his parents lined things up well or not. There is no preparation for a past that can assault you so unexpectedly, and a new sensation begins to grow, hot and acidic, as elevated as anything else he's felt in a long, long time. He wonders if this is grief or perhaps something more sinister, like resentment. He sees Mark stop in the hall and look hard at him, concern spreading across his friend's face. Boy can see the hesitation, the sudden urge not to leave, the urge to try to bear something for him. *No*, he thinks, *this is all mine* — who knows what could happen if he shares it too soon? He pushes it down and waves his friend away.

— Sure, Mark, thanks, he says.

Mark hesitates a long moment, nods, and heads out.

— I'm sorry, Nick, but the last official version of the will still has Cornelius as the primary beneficiary, the lawyer says.

— Sure, but —

— And they're still married.

Nick is dressed in better jeans and a collared shirt but still looks as though he is losing every skirmish in his battle against the unexpected. The latest salvo — Misty never formally filing for divorce — has beaten him back into the lawyer's guest chair. There will be no resolution today; aside from insurance money allocated for funeral costs that the lawyer says is easily obtained, the rest of her assets and the bulk of the insurance payout to be distributed to her survivors will probably have to be settled by a court-appointed executor. There are mechanisms for appeal, given that Boy is no longer a minor, Misty's state of mind, and her and Nick's long cohabitation, but until all the steps have been taken, there's not much else to be done.

— Of course it's your choice whether you want to appeal, Nick, the lawyer says. But you'd have to find another lawyer. I represent Cornelius, Misty, and Boy.

— What about Jay and me? Nick asks.

The lawyer admits that the baby will add layers to the process. Time. More lawyers. Money.

— Layers, Nick says. Christ.

— And Misty was incorporated, Boy says. As a realtor. What about —

— Nothing's been happening on that front, Nick says.

— But she was still doing showings a few weeks ago.

— Nope, not for a while now. She talked about getting back into it, but ...

But never actually did anything about it.

Charlie is in the far corner and inexplicably facing the wall.

— Do you represent her business interests, too?

— You don't miss much, the lawyer says to Boy.

— Sure, he's a regular brain trust, Nick says. But what —

The lawyer shakes his head.

— I can't talk about that with you. You might need to get involved at some point, but privacy laws keep me from answering those questions right now.

— All right, Boy says.

— No, it's not all right, Nick says. There's so much to figure out, and this guy —

— My hands are tied, the lawyer says.

— Fine, Nick says. What next?

The lawyer puts on an old-looking pair of reading glasses and flips through Misty's will.

— There is one provision I'm obligated to share. Misty has asked to be cremated instead of interred and expressly states that she doesn't want a funeral service of any kind.

Nick makes an exasperated sound.

— Well, that's one thing she made easy anyhow.

— What do we do with her ... uh, afterwards? Boy asks.

The lawyer puts down the papers and removes his glasses. He closes his eyes and rubs the bridge of his nose, even though the glasses had rested there only a few minutes.

— What to do with the cremated remains isn't specified, the lawyer says. Next of kin will have to make the decision.

Well, that's just convenient, isn't it?

Almost as though he heard Charlie, Nick makes another sound, the same as the first but drawn out across the span of a whole, deep breath. He stands. As he moves, the air his body displaces wafts over to Boy, smelling of alcohol, unwashed skin, unlaundered underwear. But above all else is another smell, one Boy has never smelled yet one he recognizes immediately. Defeat. Denial. Furious grief.

— I'll be damned if the ashes of my dead — dead —

Nick stops, looking caught between the certainty of the word he was about to use and the knowledge that he has never used it.

— There's no fucking way her ashes will sit on the mantle like a damn conversation piece.

He points down at Boy.

— You decide, he says.

— What, me? Why? Won't Corny have to —

Nick wrenches open the lawyer's door and walks out. Boy gets up, too, looks around for his backpack for a few moments before remembering he hasn't brought it along, then follows. He hears the lawyer behind him, pleading for them to stay and sign something or other, but he ignores him and keeps moving. Nick, moving faster than Boy has ever seen him move, doesn't stop until he gets to his SUV, which he parked crooked and straddling two spaces in the far corner of the lot. He pulls out his keys, unlocks and opens the door, and closes it again. He moves around to the front of the car, slaps at the hood with two open hands, and utters another infuriated roar, louder away from the confines of the office. Walks over to a shady length of curb and sits down. Charlie is already there, standing in the sun on a nearby patch of boulevard grass. Boy looks at her, waiting for her to make a proclamation, foul or profound, but she remains quiet.

Nick shakes his head slowly.

— What am I supposed to say, anyhow?

— Nick, I have no ...

Boy falls silent, again at a loss for how to explain the one-sided conversations others seem to be hearing more often, the ones he doesn't always realize he's even having.

— You and your mother. Two peas from the same pod.

Boy bites back his first response, the one where he declares that he's nothing like her, that he'll never make those kinds of choices, et cetera. Instead, without a word, he sits next to Nick. For the first time — *God, the timing*, he thinks — he also realizes that the heartbroken man slouched on the curb next to him is his stepfather. Nick seems to sense Boy's discomfort and turns towards him, clearly wrestling with his own role in the poor choices Misty clothed herself in.

— I don't mean the drugs, the booze, he says.

— Of course, but —

— I meant the zoning out, the talking to yourself.

— Oh.

— She told me once that she could see Charlie. Talk to her, too. She'd do a line or a shot and then run out, telling me she needed to go see her daughter.

She hasn't spoken to me in months. Not since Jay was born.

— Shit, Boy says.

— Exactly. Crazy, right?

Right, Boy wants to say, but doesn't. So Charlie followed Misty around, haunting her in the same passive way he's been haunted. Far stronger than the urge to placate Nick, though, is the immediate urge to dig for more information, grill him about the whens and wheres and hows. Yet before he can, Nick utters another long sound, deeper and rawer than the last, like a wind moaning through leafless trees, and covers his face with his hands.

My stepdad is weeping, he thinks, trying the label out as he waits to see what will happen next.

— No comment, Cynthia says. And please don't call again.

She ends the call, gives her phone a hard look.

— It's not a listed number, she says. How do they even get it?

Boy estimates that this is the third or fourth call Cynthia has gotten about Misty's death and connections to their family. Nick has fielded about the same number. Boy has received only two. But they're dwindling as the reporters discover, either by the lack of what they uncover or by the stony silence they've received from the family, that there's no angle to the story. Even if it was suicide, it's not news but merely tragic.

— I hope that's the last of them, Cynthia sighs.

— Me, too, Boy says.

— You can't just unplug the phone anymore, can you?

Boy, Cynthia, and Jay had arrived at the funeral home early, well before the time Misty's remains were supposed to be delivered from the morgue. Charlie was already there when they arrived, standing next to a huge, gaudy portrait of two sombre men in dark suits who had to be the founding partners. Brothers? The home's manager, a corpulent man in an expansive, almost-black suit and matching tie, had ushered them into the small room adjacent to the home's main foyer. He'd appeared a few minutes after they arrived, breathless and apologetic, his florid face and shiny brow suggesting that his attire had been hastily thrown on. The huge man had obviously been taking care of demanding — and likely gruesome — tasks in a sterile room behind one of the home's many unmarked doors. Coffee, tea, and milk were offered and presented before he departed again, promising he'd collect them when Misty's remains — *Your loved one's remains*, he said — arrive.

Cynthia and Boy fall silent. Jay plays with his toys on a receiving blanket spread out on the carpet. The silence of the home is absolute, as though between memorial breaths, so the clink and clatter of the few toys Cynthia packed for Jay on the carpeted flooring is sharp and loud.

— Ba-ba, Jay says from his spot on the floor.

— Hey, Plug, Boy says.

Jay smiles and reaches for Boy, who picks him up and sets him on his knee. Precisely three seconds later, Jay squirms with such enthusiasm Boy has no choice but to put him down on the blanket again.

— I wish you wouldn't give him those military nicknames. You never know what will stick.

You never know what name will stick. That's rich.

Boy doesn't say anything back to Cynthia, although inwardly he laughs. A few days have passed since identifying the body, but he still hasn't really felt any sadness about Misty's passing. He's started to wonder when it will hit him. *It has to, right?* he thinks. *She was my mother, after all.* His other concerns have kept him busy enough, but he wonders if he's just passing time. Caring for Jay. Helping Cynthia. Thinking about what Mara did after he was left with those two men on the rocks. Schoolwork, even, although more looking at it than anything else. How close he came to giving up and marching into the Canadian Forces recruiting office without telling anyone until it was all said and done and he'd taken his Oath of Allegiance. Whenever he has the urge, though, Mark or Shi, as though sensing the coming shift, appear or call or do something to stay his interest.

There's a quiet commotion in the foyer, rustling bodies and low voices. The manager, as pink and sweaty as before, opens the door and steps partially into the room.

— I'm sorry to disturb, he says. But the loved one's husband has arrived to pay his respects.

He steps to the side. A tall, thin man walks into the room, head swivelling, inspecting the furniture and fixtures, checking the windows. His movements aren't robotic exactly but absolutely efficient and without any wasted motion. His clothing — chinos, blue chambray shirt, light beige jacket — is so nondescript it has to be a uniform of some kind. A small golden badge with a red maple leaf in its centre and pointed borders winks from its position next to a few dark pouches along the man's brown leather belt. His only break from the inspection routine comes when he has to step around Jay on his blanket. He looks down and drops the slightest smile and a wink before resuming his circuit. Jay giggles, then looks over at Boy to make sure it's all right that he did. Boy and Cynthia watch the man move to the door and speak to someone outside in a low voice.

Boy stands when Corny is escorted in by the robotic man, accompanied by the low clacking sound of sheathed metal from the shackles at his ankles and wrists. Another man, in equally conspicuous civilian garb, follows and closes the door behind them. Two guards, one man. Corny is dressed in dress pants, shirt, and tie, likely what he was wearing when he was arraigned and when he pled guilty. The outfit is clean and pressed but it hangs on his thin frame, making him look tiny and shrivelled.

— My God, Cynthia says, rising from the sofa. Cornelius.

Corny looks at her a long moment.

— Mother, he says.

The first guard steps forward and introduces himself and his partner as officers from the federal correctional service before pulling out an index card and reading aloud the protocols for Corny's temporary absence from prison regarding their role, inspections, searches, and so on. The other guard unshackles Corny's hands but not his ankles before stepping away.

Starting to feel crowded, Boy thinks.

— How long do you have? Cynthia asks.

— Three days, Corny says. But it doesn't look like I'll need it, if everything is happening today.

Cynthia moves over to Corny and stands in front of him a long moment, looking him up and down. Without taking her eyes from him, she asks if touching is allowed. The first guard says it is but reminds Corny that he'll be searched before they leave. Cynthia hesitates another instant before reaching out and embracing Corny, a small, choked sound escaping her lips. She closes her eyes and hangs on. Corny just stands still and stares at the curtained window beyond his mother, his freed hands at his side. From his place a few feet away, Boy simply watches them, wondering how long it's been since Cynthia last embraced her only son. Years and years, his common sense tells him. But how many exactly? Finally, she releases him and steps away, pressing the unspilled tears from her eyes and wiping away the ones that have already coursed down her cheeks. Corny doesn't move at all, but Boy thinks that perhaps he's blinking a little more. But then he turns towards Boy and looks him in the eye, and they spend a long moment like that, with neither speaking. It feels like one of them should say something yet the words won't come.

Touching, right? Like a goddamn after-school movie.

There's a stumbling sound in the foyer and loud cursing. Nick limps in, as though he's stubbed his toe, and leans against the doorframe, wearing a rumpled suit, red-eyed and still unshaven. The correctional officers both take a step in his direction, unsnapping their belt-pouches. *Batons*, Boy thinks. *Nick is a threat.*

Nick points at Corny.

— What the hell are you doing here?

Corny shifts slightly, his ankle restraints clacking, and faces Nick in the doorway.

— She's my wife, he says.

— *Was* your wife. She's dead. But I'm the one who —

— Nick, stop. You're drunk, Cynthia says.

— Fucking right I am. But he —

Nick steps away from the door and lunges towards the shackled Corny. The first guard steps in the way and stops Nick in the middle of his motion, deftly and firmly pushing him back as easily as if he had no weight. Nick tries to wrestle with him for a few moments, but the guard apologizes softly as he holds him firm. Nick makes a strangled, defeated sound and steps back towards the door, reaching into his jacket pocket for a silver flask hidden there. He takes a drink and looks around the room.

— So, what happens now? Corny asks.

While Cynthia explains about the transfer of Misty's remains to the funeral home for cremation, Boy slips into the foyer, the guard at the door stepping aside to let him pass. The little room has begun to feel claustrophobic. He pulls out his phone, hoping to text someone, to secure a sense of normalcy. He feels the unexpected urge to reach out to Mara. Ridiculous. Mara made it clear there would be no more contact. Plus, he doesn't have a phone. Boy wanders around the spacious foyer decorated with a floral carpet runner, hung paintings, and walls a soothing palette of dusty greens and pinks. The pictures are bland landscape prints, hay fields and forested meadows. No people. Don't want to remind mourners of the deceased.

He hears the hush of the funeral home's front doors behind him.

Mark has taken a single step into the space but no farther, as though needing an invitation to come in. Although Mark in a cadet tunic is a familiar sight, Boy has never seen Mark in a suit before. Shi stands next to him in a fitted charcoal dress, her black hair falling to her shoulders, stunning against the grey. Both look years older. Like a glimpse into what they might become, responsible, important. Boy finds himself unable to speak. Shi walks over to Boy, reaches up, and gives him a quick embrace.

— You look tired, she says.

— I am tired, he says. This is all so weird.

— Is it all right we came? You didn't say specifically that we could, so —

I know I didn't, Boy thinks. *And I don't know if it's all right, not yet.* But he was glad when he saw them — that has to say something.

— No, stay, he says.

Mark and Shi trade a grateful look.

— How did you know about —

— My father knows the owner of the funeral home, Shi says.

— Pastor's privilege, Mark says.

— And he made me promise to ask if he could help in any way. With a memorial or anything.

— This isn't really that kind of service, Boy says.

— That's what I told him, too, but —

— It was nice of him to offer, really, Boy says. Please thank him for me — from all of us.

— I will.

Another unmarked door opens and the funeral director emerges again, his flushed face replaced by a studied sobriety, his tie knotted into a precise double-Windsor, jacket buttoned at the top. He tells Boy that the casket has arrived and has been prepped for the cremation. A moment later, everyone is in the foyer, standing around the director in a loose semicircle, listening to his instructions for what happens next. They'll follow him into the crematory chapel where they can pay final respects — the casket will be open — before the casket is wheeled into the cremation chamber. After, they are free to remain in the chapel while the loved one is cremated, which will take slightly more than two hours, and enjoy the light refreshments provided. Or, if they prefer, they can depart earlier and collect the cremated remains at a time of their choosing.

You can have a fucking cup of tea while Misty burns. Make small talk with the correctional officers. Wait for Nick to snap. How does that sound?

— I'll wait, Boy says. Everyone else can go to wherever they want.

— What about the ashes? Corny asks. I don't like the idea of her getting forgotten in a closet somewhere.

There is a flurry of looks between all those assembled. Nick nods at Boy.

— I asked him to take care of it, he says. I hope that's all right.

No, you told me to, Boy thinks, *because you can't deal with it yourself.* But Nick is looking right at him again, differently this time, his reddened eyes softer than before, and holds up his palms. *Will you do it?* Corny opens his mouth as though he's about to argue with Nick — he'd have every right to, given that he is, was, still her husband and next of kin — but he just looks at Boy and nods.

— Can you do it?

— Yes. Where should I —

— Just choose someplace nice, Nick and Corny say in unison.

The two men share a surprised look and utter a low, sad laugh. There's a collective exhaling of breath from everyone in the foyer, a shared relaxation of tensed muscles. The unexpected moment of grace catches Boy by surprise and, for the first time, he feels his eyes well up, as though his body finally has the means to let go of everything it has been holding. The trigger is the briefest thought of how Misty would respond to what just happened, how despite all of the shitty times that have passed, the confusion of the past eight years, and all of the family's abused and wasted moments, there could be a brief spark of unity.

I think she'd be at a complete fucking loss for words. That was unexpected.

When he feels Shi's hand on his own, he realizes that everyone else has moved into the chapel and that his thoughts have stopped him at the end of the carpet runner and in front of the now-closing door.

— Text when you're done, she says. If you want, we can —

— Only if you want to, though, Mark says.

Please come with me, he imagines himself saying. But his heart and mind blink out the thought almost immediately.

— Thanks. I'll talk to you later, he says and walks into the chapel.

He can't even rely on the mindless games installed on his phone to occupy his mind. He stands, puts his phone in his pocket, and walks over to the chapel's only window. In front of him, sprawled out across fields and tucked against the escarpment, are rows and rows of grapevines just past the spring flowering season; behind him, the empty chapel, the closed crematorium door, bare seats, and a small table bearing stale cookies and a cooling coffee urn.

No one remained for the cremation. After paying their final respects to Misty — laid out in the plain, cellulose casket he and Nick thought she'd prefer — everyone left quickly. Nick looked at her a long moment before leaving, flask in hand. The correctional officers stood off to the side while Corny shuffled up to the casket, laid his hands on Misty's, said a few words too low to hear, and walked away, his eyes red and full. Cynthia brought Jay up, but he couldn't figure out why his Mommy wouldn't move, no matter how loudly he called for her.

Charlie, though, has remained in the corner of the room, facing the stainless steel door in the wall behind which Misty is being consumed. Boy can't look at it, too disturbed by the reality of his mother's body being broken down to its most basic components behind the thin barrier door. Pondering the inevitable and uncomfortable. Last words said and unsaid. How he treated her, how she treated him and Jay. How to bear the incomplete manner in which she prepared him for adulthood.

Blame. Don't forget blame. There's so much of it we could spread around.

— But it would go both ways, right?

It might. Might not, too.

PART III
JUNE

Misty's ashes, resting in their cardboard box on the kitchen table and gathering a thin layer of dust, haven't been moved in weeks. Cynthia hasn't mentioned them. Her presence in the house is now a constant, to the point where Boy thinks of the guest room as her room, and it's impossible to ignore all the little pieces of her that seem to find their way into new spaces. Hairs in the sink. Slight adjustments of the creams and wipes on Jay's change table. The grooming gear and toothbrush in the bathroom. Coats, jackets, and shoes in the front hall closet. Meanwhile, Nick's presence seems to be fading, and his things have migrated to the master bedroom one item at a time, as though they, like him, need to hide themselves away yet still be near to their owner. When he's home, he retreats to the bedroom to drink, watch television, and look at photos of Sarah and Misty.

— So today was the last day of classes for the year, Cynthia says, looking up from her crossword.

— It was.

Boy gingerly puts his backpack on the table — it's heavy with the odds and ends he'd thrown into his locker over the course of the year — and moves into the kitchen for a snack. School days since Misty's death have been so full that the end of the year has almost caught him off guard. In sympathy, his teachers have banded together to help him prepare for his exams, hinting that his year might be salvageable if he does well next week. Nothing in writing, of course, but you can't just let a star pupil, whose grades may have been sliding but whose mother just died, fail his final year of high school. He's surprised himself by how willing he is to put in the hours of extra work. Charlie, in the middle of an intense and quiet library session just earlier this week, gave him the words to describe it. *So this is how you grieve.* Although her tone was neutral and he'd normally assume sarcasm or causticity, this time he sensed approval. *This is how I grieve*, he said aloud in agreement. Mark and Shi looked up at him, smiled, and returned to working on their laptops, well accustomed to his outbursts. *This is how I grieve.*

— And your exams are next week, Cynthia says.

— They are.

— Are you ready?

Boy shrugs and tells her he's been studying for a while now. She nods and re-immerses herself in her puzzle. A fresh cup of tea steams gently beside her, the vapour wafting lazily towards the box holding Misty's remains. She looks relaxed. Jay must be napping. *Good*, he thinks.

— I've decided what to do with the ashes, he says. I'll head out in a few minutes.

Although her shoulders tense slightly, she doesn't take her eyes from the little boxes on the page. She has completed only about a third of the puzzle, although there are no gaps in the solutions creeping from the upper left of the puzzle in a solid block of letters.

— All right. Do you need a ride somewhere?

— It's not far. I think she'd like this time of day, too.

— Sounds good.

He actually had the idea yesterday — to take Misty's remains to the rocks next to the lake and scatter them there — and surprised himself when he approached Nick about it first. *You should come along,* Boy said. Nick was pleased, although equally shocked, but declined. *No thanks,* he said, *but I think she'd like that the spot means something to you.* There were no other options, really, because Boy couldn't think of another place that would mean something to her. One with a strong enough association to Misty, a depth of memory, suitable to scatter the last of her.

— Jay should be awake soon, Cynthia says. His stroller's in the garage.

— I'm not taking him.

— Why not?

— He's not even a year old. It wouldn't mean a thing.

— How can you know that?

Would it be unforgivable to admit that he just wants to get going? That his resistance has less to do with Jay's age or ability to process or recall than the simple inconvenience of breaking momentum? That he made the decision and now waiting would feel more like stalling than extending courtesy to his baby brother? *Carry on, Cadet — you've passed refusal speed for this runway.*

— I'll see you later, he says, grabbing the box from the table.

— Let me know how it goes.

— I will.

As he puts the box in his pack and heads out to the bike, her words make him want to stay, discuss, change his mind. The box is heavy, adding a few pounds to the weight on his shoulders. Yet why do Cynthia's words, so gracious and understanding, feel so much heavier?

• • • • • • • •

The sky is mostly clear, with a few wispy clouds aligning themselves with high-altitude winds, the sun bearing hints of its future summer warmth. There's not much wind, just a lazy breath descending the Niagara Escarpment behind him, moving across the vineyards to quiet the waves coming in from offshore. It hasn't rained in a few days, either, so the rocks are dry and warm in the late afternoon sun. Perfect weather if he wanted to scatter his mother's remains over the lake.

Yet he can't. He's taken the box from his pack, opened it, removed the clear bag containing the grey-white ashes, and even unzipped the plastic seal. But from there he's stopped, overcome by a question that feels inevitable and universal, even though he'd been comfortably resolved to scatter the remains.

— Am I doing the right thing?

How the fuck would I know? This wasn't on Misty's list of things to talk about.

Charlie's right — there's no policy book for this, no flight manual. He reseals the bag, stuffs it back in the box, and repacks his backpack.

You could ask Corny.

It would give Corny the chance to speak to Boy's choice of location.

— Good idea, he says.

Tell me something I don't already know.

He shoulders his pack and walks away from the rocks, pulling out his phone to call Millhaven. He stumbles over a bright yellow grocery bag bounding over the rocks like suburban tumbleweed, swears under his breath, and stops to focus on the screen. He'll head to Kingston as soon as he can, like he did last time. The memory of the guy at the bus stop who almost robbed him makes him smile, how Mara had saved him without even realizing it.

In order to process Misty's death and to reinvest himself in his schoolwork, Boy has tried to push away thoughts of Mara. But here, in this space, he can't help but think about the man in the culvert, whether he made good on his promise to disappear. Boy moves towards the far end of the rocks, ending the call before anyone at Millhaven can answer.

What do you hope to see?

— I don't know. I just have to go.

He kicks at a still-greasy food wrapper and an empty pop can as he descends the far side of the rocks to the scrub. The presence of garbage is new, his pristine rocks having been discovered after all, probably by teenagers starting to look for places where they might spend the summer. A faint path has been worn through the grass and around the larger bushes. More bits of trash lie along the path, bright and conspicuous. He stops before rounding the head at the mouth of the discharge inlet to listen for voices. Who knows what kind of people would be staking out the culvert now? There's nothing, no voices, no sounds. He slips and clambers his way up the rocky inlet to the mouth of the culvert, which stands open to the elements.

— Shit, he says.

You said it.

Aside from the shape of the culvert's mouth, little else remains recognizable. It has taken almost no time for taggers to desecrate the place, covering the walls in spray paint. Mara's furniture and things lay smashed and strewn about the entrance, as though the culvert itself has purged itself of Mara's presence. Inside, broken furniture, splayed wiring, and smashed lightbulbs lay scattered about, filthy and stepped on. The back of the space is now a latrine, filling the air with the smells of urine and shit. Boy covers his mouth and nose with his hand and walks outside.

He took his clothes with him.

— And his books.

Nothing personal of Mara remains. He feels brief regret that Mara took his things, then banishes the thought. As though he could have expected the space to remain untouched, protected, like the rocks. He wonders why he imagined it would be any different. Everything crumbles, right? It all falls apart eventually.

When he arrives home, Cynthia glances at the box under his arm but says nothing. He places it in its spot on the kitchen table, watching Cynthia feed Jay a supper of an unidentifiable mash he can't seem to eat fast enough. His brother gives him a messy smile and a babbled greeting, sending bits of mash everywhere.

— How long has he been using the spoon?

— A few days now, Cynthia says. I thought he had it down pat yesterday, but today you can't tell he's ever held one before.

She reaches to take the spoon but Jay dodges her, digs it into the mash, and brings a mostly mess-free spoonful to his mouth. He grins as he chews. Cynthia laughs.

— Now that's more like it, she says.

It feels strange to sit in this kitchen and watch someone else work with Jay with the patience and good humour he deserves. The pang of missing out is stronger, though. Should he have known it was time for Jay to try using a spoon?

— It's a little early for cutlery, Cynthia says. But he always reaches for the spoon anyhow, so I thought, why not?

Jay receives another mouthful and smiles again, pleased with himself. Boy looks at the time on the microwave, hears himself say he should get back to studying. How strange. Is this what normalcy feels like, where teenagers can focus on their schoolwork, work part-time jobs, meet up with friends, and do a thousand things other than care for babies whose mothers have lost the ability to care? Had lost. Right. Misty's ashes are right there on the table, waiting to be scattered. His stomach clenches for an instant. Another new normal.

Nick stumbles into the front hall. His eyes are even more bloodshot than before. Permanent damage from the abuse he has sent through his straining blood vessels? Nick puts a finger to his lips.

— Shhhhh, he says. I'm not here.

Boy doesn't say anything.

— Hey, don't fucking look at me like that, Nick whispers.

— I'm not. I —

— Like I'm the one who's let everyone down.

He stumbles to the foot of the stairs and forces his way past Boy, knocking him against the wall. From the kitchen, Jay laughs, a sudden and pure expression of glee. As though the sound has physical force, Nick stops. He closes his eyes.

— Everyone expects so much from me. Even him, Nick hisses, gesturing towards the kitchen.

Boy wants to hiss right back, get in his face, dare him to stand up straighter. Tell him, How dare you pass off your baggage to your own baby? *Own your own shit, Cadet. Smarten the fuck up and get it together — they're looking to you for answers, not more questions.* But he doesn't.

Nick's eyes widen.

— My baby? How do I even know it's mine?

— What? Where did that come from?

— I just — I don't — Aw, fuck.

Nick stomps up the stairs and slams the bedroom door. Harsh. Boy doesn't give the words too much weight, though. Hard to come down to ground level when all it does is remind you of tragedy. Death. Grief. An uncertain future. Being a guest now in a home he had no part in building. Finances he's never worried about needing to be sorted out. Cynthia has been shuttling mail and documents back and forth to the lawyer, who's taking care of things at Corny's behest. A next of kin in prison an inconvenience for survivors but nothing to bureaucracies that still turn. And Nick has to watch all of it.

Cynthia emerges from the kitchen, wiping her hands on a dishtowel.

— Nick's home, Boy says.

— I heard.

— Really? And Jay?

— No. He was distracted by tickling and kisses from me.

— That's good.

— No, not good, she says. But it'll have to do, won't it?

CHAPTER 23

Sunday morning, early. Boy wakes up an hour before his 4 a.m. alarm but just lies in bed thinking and staring at the darkness. Second-guessing this trip to Millhaven. Hearing the distant voices of his teachers to use the time well, to dig in, yet hearing his own pride whispering much louder. Finish well. And why go to the prison, anyway? To ask about the ashes? Placate the ghost of his dead sister? Weak, weak, weak.

Finally, his phone chimes the alarm and lights up, bathing the room in its cool light. Boy dresses and grabs his pack, which is heavy with extra clothes, handi wipes to clean his ID and debit card, baggies for his wallet and cash. If he gets turned away from the prison, it won't because he neglects the details. The woman in charge of visitation slots was firm on the rule requiring forty-eight hours of notice until he mentioned Misty's remains and played the dead mother card. In the kitchen, he leaves the light off, preparing his breakfast and snacks for the road in the dim light of the open refrigerator door. He eats his cereal with his eyes closed, resting them against the long day to come.

A few minutes later, he opens his eyes to the sound of someone coming down the stairs. His night vision intact, he watches Nick stop at the bottom, out of breath, lungs wheezing against his load. Flight bag in one hand and a small suitcase in the other. His keys jangle as he walks down the hall and out the front door, leaving the door open, his car's yellow unlock-lights blinking him into silhouette. Boy sits still, listening to the low thunk of doors, the grumble of an engine, the hush of tires as Nick backs into the road and drives away.

For good? Probably. There's no other reason Nick would sneak away, luggage in hand, in the middle of the night. There's no out of town business to pursue, no red-eye flight out of Pearson. No distant relatives at the end of a long drive. No traffic to beat. His life is right here in Hamilton, his career, his new family. *Was* right here. Maybe more surprising that he's stayed this long at all.

Boy shakes his head, slings his pack, and walks into the early morning gloom. He is careful to close and lock the door behind him. Charlie waits across the road on a length of curb that is bright under the street lamps. Boy stops.

— Maybe I should wake Cynthia and let her know, he says.

Better to let them sleep.

— Leave a note?

Would it change anything?

No, it wouldn't, he thinks. But the morning will. Again.

Boy stares at Corny's right eye, which is surrounded by an ugly halo of purple and black. His father walks gingerly to the bolted-down seat and sits with a pained exhalation.

— Jesus, Corny. What happened?

— I screwed up, is all. Wrong thing said at a weak moment.

— Are you in trouble again?

— I told the COs I walked into a wall.

— And they believed you?

Corny shrugs, as if to say if they didn't, they're keeping mum about it. His eyes rest on the couples and families at nearby tables, all speaking in low voices — even the children — and doing their best to remain civil. Boy wonders about the volume of emotion in a place like this, how careful the attempt to restrain it.

Raises the question of how long it'll be before he's released, doesn't it?

— Will this affect your release? Boy asks.

— They'd need an actual investigation to change anything. Won't happen for a black eye no one talks about.

— Does it ever happen?

Corny looks at Boy for a long beat, nods.

— I've already had time added on. About a year in, I hurt someone pretty badly.

— How much —

— Well, in practical terms, it just means I'll probably get out near the original full sentence. I've kept myself out of trouble since then, but early release is unlikely.

— I had no idea.

— Why would you? I didn't even tell Misty.

Boy hasn't thought much about the specifics of when Corny might be spit back out into the world, but it bugs him that they didn't know.

— You should've told us, Boy says.

He has a right to move on, too. Can you imagine what he's carrying?

— I don't care what he's carrying, Boy says. He left, he fucked everything up, and he gets to mess around with his release?

Boy has turned to address Charlie, standing against the rear wall.

— What the hell? Corny asks, looking between Boy and the wall and back again.

Do you want him to get out?

— I don't know.

It's his time.

— No, it's not just up to him. It's selfish and not fair.

— Who are you talking to?

Boy ignores him. He's angry at the whole situation — not knowing, Corny's reticence to tell anyone, and now Charlie's defence of the man who killed her. She has moved away from her spot near the wall and stands next to the table, looking down at Corny, her eyes and features as expressionless as always but somehow focused on him, too.

Of course it's not fair. Nothing's fair.

— Stop. Just stop, Boy says.

God, the cliché of it, he thinks. *Life's not fair. Time as our own. Bullshit.* Yet Boy doesn't really know who he's speaking to, either, his dead sister or the chorus of confusion in his mind. Charlie inches close to him, her hand now extended, as though she's expecting him to take it.

Selfishness can protect, too.

— What does that even mean?

— You're talking to Charlie, Corny says, his eyes wide. Misty mentioned it in the letter she sent with the photo, but I —

— Shut up — everyone just shut up!

Boy slams his hands down on the metal table and stands. The room goes immediately quiet. The inmates glance over and then down at the floor, the habit not to draw attention to themselves or stare ingrained and instinctual. Their families, though, turn and look over at Boy hulking over a now-diminished Corny, mouths open, wondering what the disturbance will bring once the clanging echoes fade. The COs stationed near the exits move towards the table, heads tilted into shoulder-clipped handsets and speaking codes. Boy is about to storm towards the exit, not realizing that in a second or two he'll be seized and dropped to the floor, restrained, and practically dragged out. His visiting privileges having vaporized the instant he lost his temper. But he does see Charlie extending her reach with both arms now, grabbing his and Corny's wrists in an unbreakable grip. *She's holding me*, he thinks. But there's no substance to the grip, no icy drop in temperature in being held by the dead. Just an ineffable, invisible strength that immobilizes him and Corny the instant they lock eyes.

The room flickers, warps, goes black.

A dim nighttime world comes into focus. He's in a car. In the passenger seat. Outside, concrete sound barriers flash by, highway signs, concrete median blocks. Cars all around, colours odd and dark because of the yellow sodium lamps high above. There is the sound of laughter from the backseat, Charlie and Sarah chittering like sparrows. They've conspired to click free from their seat belts to slide back and forth across the seat as they babble. Charlie is deflecting Sarah's questions about her new sweater and jeans, everything loose and flowy, contrasting with her friend's fitted wear. Their hair is up in tight buns, severe, aging the girls along with the makeup they sneaked on just before getting into the car. Loud giggles, sharp. A growl from the front seat, Corny glaring at their silhouettes in the rear-view mirror and telling them to be quiet. Dismissive laughs from the two girls. His eyes are sunken shadows, his face rough, his hand shaking as it grasps a clear bottle between his legs. Empty. An awkward, swerving effort to throw the bottle out but the window isn't fully open, sending it clanking to the floor. A sharp swerve to the left. More giggles and incessant questions from the girls, demanding his commitment to be at parade on time. No answer. Charlie sliding forward, asking if Corny heard them. No answer. Charlie tapping on his shoulder. A barking retort to get away. Charlie's smile and lightning-quick move-ment, sliding her hands over Corny's eyes and pulling his head back, saying she won't let go until he promises to be on time. Corny roars, lets go of the steering wheel, and flails at Charlie's grip, his elbow catching the wheel, an unnatural sideways move-ment of the car as it catches the canted lip of the median, a sudden lurch, the sensation of the car flying and turning, a roof landing, sliding, grinding, turning around and around. A slow-ing. The blast of a huge horn, headlights splashing through the smashed side windows, too large and too high. Two brilliant, piercing screams. A massive sound. Nothing.

He still can't see, but Boy feels the pressure from his wrist release. The room swims forward, with Corny still meeting his gaze, although blinking and gulping breaths of air like he just can't seem to fill his lungs. Boy realizes he is doing the same thing, the sound of his own laboured breathing becoming louder and louder in his ears.

— Boy? Charlie? Jesus, I can't —

Selfish isn't always selfish.

Corny finally finds his breath, but it moves in and out of him with great difficulty. He leans forward and grasps the table with both hands and begins to weep, his chest heaving but mak-ing a pitifully inadequate sound, like the blast of foghorn passed through a hollow reed. He falls to the floor. Boy falls to his knees, too, his sinews and bone seemingly inadequate against gravity. Charlie stands over both of them now, her eyes again distant and cold. The COs rushing towards them, unsure, before stopping entirely, whispering back and forth about protocols, whether this is a medical issue or not. The rest of the room is still silent, watch-ing this bizarre production gather steam.

He protected me. My memory.

— Charlie caused the accident, Boy says, gasping. You're —

He stops. He was about to say innocent. But that's not really true, is it?

Corny shakes his head.

— Still my fault, he says.

— But Charlie did it, too. She —

— *Don't say it!* Corny shouts. *Don't you dare!*

There's a crackle of a radio on a CO's vest, a quick acknowledgement, a shared look between the guards, understanding. Another couple of COs enter the chamber and make a beeline for their table. One barks at Corny to get up and grabs him under the arm when he doesn't immediately respond. He is pulled roughly up to his feet and half led, half dragged away while Boy watches from the ground. The other guard kneels and asks if he's all right, whether Corny touched him or hurt him in any way. She calls him McVeigh, though, which Boy finds distantly amusing. *That's me, too*, he thinks. *And Charlie.*

And Misty.

— Wait, Boy calls after his father. What do I do?

Corny turns back, interrupting his and the guard's progress back towards the secure part of the prison. As though sensing the urgency and need of the question, the guard holding Corny stops, too, letting him face his son from a few feet away. Eyes red. Shadowed. Full of tears. His breath still comes in fits and starts.

— With Mom's ashes, I mean. And everything else, too — what do I do with — with —

What you now know.

— You'll find a place, Corny says. She'd trust you to make the decision. As for everything else, forget about it. It can't change anything.

And then he's gone, buzzed through the door and back into the warren of invisibility he's managed to create for so long. Boy wonders whether Corny will ever emerge when he comes to visit, whether he'll even allow contact after his sentences are served. He wonders where his broken father will go then, whether anywhere could be far enough. Boy is escorted through the gate and to the locker room to gather his backpack and possessions, a CO repeatedly asking if there's anything Boy would like to report. *No*, he says again and again.

Outside the prison, he pulls out his phone.

— *can you pick me up later from bus station*

Five seconds after he taps *send*, her reply arrives, making him smile.

— *yesssss!*

He surprises himself by falling asleep in the cab. The driver wakes him up, interrupting the beginnings of a meaningless, pleasant dream. He snaps at the man, startling him into silence, and his next thoughts, even before pulling out his wallet to meet the meter charge, are about Misty's sudden death denying her the chance to learn that she wasn't alone in seeing Charlie's ghost whenever she left the house, and what really happened in that car. She died thinking that her husband was still the villain. Corny can't claim innocence, of course, and she might never have offered him forgiveness. Still, never being given the chance might be much, much worse.

CHAPTER 24

Monday morning. Boy wakes to the muffled sound of Jay's cries in the next room. Sunlight through the blinds slashes radiator patterns on the wall. He and Jay slept in. Good. By the time Shi dropped him off, it was past midnight, so extra sleep is precious. He hears light footsteps in the hall and the low sound of Cynthia's voice, soothing and pacifying. Next, Jay's laughter. Boy stares at the ceiling, thinking about the day and week ahead. Today it's back to the rocks to scatter Misty's remains. Afterwards, more studying — exams begin tomorrow. And then? Who knows. He'll be free to make the next move, whether to enlist right away or wait until his results are posted in a few weeks to see if RMC is still an option.

He fell asleep with Charlie's vision playing in his mind. How his big sister was an active participant rather than a tragic victim. Corny falling on a kind of sword. Protecting her memory? Sure. Himself, too. And Misty, in a way, now also a memory. Misty. Boy called her mom for the first time he can recall. An unlikely kinship. She saw and perhaps understood more than anyone other than the two of them could understand. And died, leaving a strange triangle of understanding: teenage screw-up, incarcerated and failed father, sister and daughter's ghost. But with no one to talk to about it.

And he wants to. Back to Millhaven might be an option, assuming Corny will see him at all. Charlie, maybe, although she already knows. Cynthia? No way. Mark and Shi? Hard to say whether they'd understand or their friendship would be strained beyond repair. Mara, long reconciled to the impossible, would be great, but that's an empty wish.

He heads downstairs. Jay, finger-painting his face with the cereal Cynthia is attempting to spoon into him, squeals with delight when he sees Boy. Cynthia looks him over, toe to crown.

— How are you?

I have no idea, to be honest, he thinks, but there's no way to say so without having to reach and reveal more than he'd like.

— Fine, thanks.

— And Cornelius? How is he?

— He's lost more weight. Looks tired.

— Grief takes time.

— Yeah, maybe.

She falls silent and goes back to trying to feed Jay. Boy almost tells her about the extra time Corny will have to serve, but something keeps him from doing so. A mix of not wanting to burden her more and protecting Corny's privacy, perhaps.

— Perhaps what?

Boy cringes.

— I was just thinking about what today might look like, he says.

— Did Cornelius have any preference about Misty's remains? He shakes his head.

— He said she'd trust me to make the decision.

— That's good, she says. Trust is good.

How strange it must be to learn about your son's words through a second-hand conversation. And when that son is in prison for killing your granddaughter …

— Have you ever tried to visit him in prison?

— No. He wouldn't have allowed it. Although I did think about reaching out after his father died. I looked into it, had all the information lined up.

— But?

— I couldn't follow through.

She stops, again focused on the acrobatic task of feeding Jay. Talking about visiting Corny in prison has tightened the skin on her face, aging her. Boy tries to imagine what it would be like to have a son forced into circumstances that couldn't distance him any further, but can't. Even Misty, for all her faults, always came home. Not *there* exactly but not absent, either.

— You'll scatter the ashes today, I suppose.

— Yes. Right now, actually.

— May I ask where?

Of course you can ask, he thinks, flustered at the formality of the question, the courtesy it holds.

— There are some rocks that look over Lake Ontario. A good spot I always go to when I need to clear my head.

She smiles and nods.

— That sounds perfect. I'll clean Jay up and put a few things in the diaper bag for you.

He opens his mouth to object but stops himself, this time unable to imagine performing this last rite on Misty's behalf without Jay there, too. He crouches next to the high chair and finds himself reaching out to smooth a flyaway lock of hair back onto Jay's head.

— Up for a walk, Cadet?

Jay giggles and brushes Boy's hand away, leaving a constellation of baby cereal smudged across his fingers. He goes into the kitchen to wash his hands. He looks at the oatmeal patterns a long moment like he might read something there, an eleven-month-old's tea leaf fortune. As he washes and dries his hands, he also realizes that he hasn't eaten anything and is, in fact, not hungry at all. *Strange*, he thinks. *I always eat breakfast.*

It's good to be out walking with Jay again — it feels like a long time since the two of them conquered the streets together. The neighbourhood is mid-morning quiet, although the busy sounds of the surrounding city drift through it, the distant drone of cars on the QEW, the rumble of nearby construction, the rush of cars moving between stoplights. Jay has settled into his stroller with his favourite toy, a peculiar plush creature that looks like a cross between a rabbit and a grizzly bear. Misty's ashes are in a slung basket beneath the stroller. It's warm with a slight overcast, indistinct and grey.

As Boy stops at the end of their road to adjust the diaper bag slung across his shoulders, the insistently light sound of a bicycle bell shivers through the neighbourhood. Mark and Shi round the corner, riding bicycles. Mark waves and smiles. Shi rings her bell again. Jay laughs, extending his arms towards the two friends, who stop their bikes right beside them, sweaty and out of breath.

— What's going on? Boy asks. What's with the bikes?

— Well, we knew you'd be heading out to scatter Misty's ashes today, Mark says.

— How —

— You told me last night in the car, Shi says.

— We decided to come along, if that's all right, and —

— We thought we'd do it your way for a change, she finishes.

— You're early, though, Mark says. We thought you'd sleep in a little longer and we'd surprise you at home. Is it all right that we came?

Boy opens his mouth to say something but closes it. Simple thanks doesn't seem quite enough — his friends live far enough away that arranging and making the ride is more than sponta- neous support. This was discussed, decided, planned. All to help a friend take care of a necessary but difficult task. He looks away, moved. As though sensing his big brother's need to take a moment, Jay babbles a greeting to Boy's best friends, who spend a moment gooing, gahhing, and dinging their bells to make him laugh. Boy coughs and blinks away the slight blurriness beginning to mask his view of the nearby houses.

— It is, he manages. I'm glad you came. Although I'm walking —

— We didn't anticipate Jay coming along, Shi says.

— We just assumed it would be you and your ugly orange bike, Mark says.

— Corny's bike, Boy says.

— Oh. Sorry, I —

Boy waves away Mark's apology.

— I'm not sure I ever told you that.

Shi walks her bike over to a nearby hydro pole and unwraps the chain lock wrapped around her seat post. Mark rolls his bike over as well and lets Shi lock both against the pole.

— We'll walk with you, she says. If that's all right.

— Stop asking if it's all right. Of course it is.

They stand around for an awkward moment before Jay begins rocking forward and back, making puffing sounds with his mouth, impatient against sitting still. Boy looks around, struck by the odd and irrational feeling that they've left something behind. No, they haven't — they haven't been standing there long enough, really — but why is he now flooded by a sense of what's missing?

In his peripheral vision, he sees Mark tilt his head and give him an inquiring look.

— Forget something? he asks.

— No, but it feels like we have.

And then Boy understands why he feels so odd, like he hasn't fully assembled himself. Charlie. Where is she? For more than eight years, he has never been alone when he leaves the house and the neighbourhood, his sister's ghost always present, near enough to speak to. But she's nowhere to be seen this morning, not outside the house waiting for him when he stepped out, not waiting on a curb, not moving in her silent way to wherever he is going. In fact, he can't recall having seen her last night, either. He was so consumed by what she showed him and Corny that maybe he didn't notice her, but now it feels more like she wasn't even on the bus or in Shi's van on the drive home. Surely Charlie can't be gone entirely.

— Do you still think about her a lot? Shi asks.

— I'm sorry?

— Charlie.

— I do.

And I speak to her more than I should.

— I'm sure she'll be there in spirit, she says.

— Corny, too, Mark says.

— I'm sure you're right, Boy says, pushing the stroller into motion.

The lake is dark under the overcast sky. No wind. The foursome stands at the highest point, as close to the edge of the rocks as they can. Boy holds the clear plastic bag with Misty's remains out over the void with one hand and lets gravity carry the light grey ashes to the water. It's awkward. Although Shi offered to hold Jay while Boy scatters the remains, he insisted on strapping his brother into the chest carrier so he could be closer to the experience. He said, *I have to be able to tell him someday he was involved.*

Even though the carrier is clearly becoming too small for him, Jay just watches the proceedings, still, as though even he can sense the moment's importance. He has been quiet since arriving at the rocks, being wedged into the carrier, and even through the awkward and insufficient words Boy tried to say before scattering their mother to the lake and wind.

And then it's done, the lightest of the remains drifting out over the water, the heaviest falling almost straight down to the base of the rocks. What's left is a dusty plastic bag, oddly light, which Boy tucks into his pocket, unsure whether it's trash or something more.

— And that's it, he says, stepping away from the edge.

— Ma-ma, Jay says.

The three friends look at each other. How pregnant the statements from babies can be.

— This is a beautiful place, Shi says.

— I can't believe you didn't tell us about it sooner, Mark says.

— It's too bad about the garbage.

Boy remembers how pristine the place was. Or how pristine it seemed — he's found himself questioning whether he just couldn't see the flaws, as though Mara could pull a filter over his eyes as easily as he stopped the time, or whatever mechanism it was. Not that it matters, in the end. Mara is gone.

— So what next? Mark asks.

Shi rolls her eyes at him.

— We can stay, if you want, she says to Boy. It's your time.

— We'll get going soon, but there's something I want you to see, Boy says.

The walk through the scrub at the far end of the rocks has become more difficult, despite the new paths worn into the ground. Pushing aside branches and leaves slows their progress, like the vegetation has redoubled its efforts to reclaim the space, the bushes growing into each other with seeming urgency. Arriving at the shore near the mouth of the culvert's inlet is almost a surprise.

The place is even more derelict than the last time Boy was here only a few days ago. There's more graffiti and more refuse scattered around, and even the concrete itself seems to be crumbling. The smell is stronger, too, and Jay squirms against it. Boy decides not to go in, even though he is curious about what might remain, what might have been taken. Mark walks right in, holding his nose, leaving Shi standing with Boy and Jay outside.

— What is this place? Did you come here before? Shi asks.

— I did, Boy says. But it was different.

— How?

She looks at him, waiting patiently for his explanation. Until a few moments ago, he had been firmly resolved to tell both of them about Mara. But now all he can imagine is how much it might hurt her, given Mara's — Dempster's — connection to her family. She might press him for enough detail to decipher who the man in the culvert was. How would she respond, knowing that he had helped keep Dempster's secret, had helped him hide from his charges and justice? No, better to remain silent; the time to come clean was long ago. Mara has disappeared again. There's nothing to be gained by introducing it into their relationship.

— I just wanted you to see the rocks and the culvert, he says.

— I get why you'd come here.

— You do?

— To disappear. No school, no Misty, no Jay, nothing but rocks and water.

— That's about it, yeah.

— Too bad you have to go back to real life afterwards, though.

— How are things at home? I'm sorry I haven't asked sooner, but —

— Thanks, but we'll survive, she says. The church elders are pressuring my dad to resign, but he won't.

— But won't —

— He thinks calmer heads will prevail, when everything dies down again.

— It's a shame he's getting the blame, too.

— Guilt by association. It's not biblical, but it works.

— Right.

From the back of the culvert, Mark curses at top volume.

— I wonder what he found.

Boy tries to explain about the mess inside without being too graphic and fails. Shi makes a face.

— Charming. Thanks for sharing, smooth talker —

— Sorry. I shouldn't have —

She quiets him with a warm hand on his arm, smiling, her dark eyes bright.

— I'm kidding.

— Oh. Good. I —

Shi rises to her toes, placing a hand on Boy's shoulder for support. The other hand slips behind his neck and pulls him towards her, quick and awkward. Jay squeaks in surprise. She plants a soft, lingering kiss on the corner of Boy's mouth, then releases him and steps back, looking him up and down. He can't decide whether she looks more like she's daring him to say something or whether the look is an appraising one, like an artist assessing her work. Jay erupts into signature giggles, waving his arms and kicking his feet approvingly. *Well, isn't that something*, Boy thinks.

Mark emerges from the gloom, steps off the concrete and onto the stones, drawing a long, deep breath. His eyes are watering.

— That's fucking disgusting. You could have warned me.

Boy and Shi just watch him as he clears his lungs.

— It looks like someone lived in there, a long time ago.

Not so long, actually, Boy thinks.

But now Mark is looking at them, back and forth between their smiling faces, momentarily puzzled. From the corner of his eye, Boy sees Shi glance over at him. He begins to blush, heat creeping up his throat. Mark smirks and shakes his head.

— Oh, *that.* Good. It's about time.

— You knew?

— Of course I did, dumbass.

At Mark's words, there's a quick pain right below his diaphragm reminding him of Charlie's absence. The kiss was an amazing and welcome surprise, but he regrets he can't talk to Charlie about it. And strangely, Misty, too. Jay, for all his exuberance, has likely forgotten about it. Corny? Who knows. Family should be part of these things — good news, friendship, love — and Boy sees with two-hundred-mile visibility the word he will have to use from now on to describe his family. Incomplete.

CHAPTER 25

This is the last time he'll ever sit in this gymnasium under these lights. He's heard a few of his fellow seniors already talking about reunions, lingering over yearbook signatures as though the trite words they're writing will somehow be the ones that make the difference, not to be forgotten in a dusty box somewhere. But the thought of walking into what's next while constantly looking ahead to a date with reminiscence depresses him. No, better to leave and not look back. High school has not defined him.

Boy checks the time on the wall, satisfied with his performance in Essère's history final. The last period of the last sentence of the last essay question is still drying on the page in front of him, and there's thirty minutes to go. All around, students from every grade are bent over their test papers, writing madly, punching numbers and formulae into calculators, or pens hovering and thoughts paused. The gym has been transformed for the week. Carpet tiles installed over the hardwood. Desks brought in from all over the school, hundreds of them, strung out row on row.

He's done well on all his exams, much to his own surprise. The formal results won't be released for another few weeks, but he's left every session satisfied. Already looking towards his next challenge. He prepared thoroughly, even knowing that perfect scores wouldn't change the math of a failing grade. Still, although nothing is yet final, as he suspected, all of his teachers have said in low voices that if he gives a good showing on his exams, he'll pass his senior year. Merely passing won't be good enough to keep his admission to RMC, but at least he'll still receive his high school diploma.

He puts down his pen, lines it up next to the two backups he brought in, and waits. Soon, the proctor will announce that those who have completed their tests can leave. Ordinarily, right about now he'd wait for Charlie to pass along a crude or sarcastic epithet, an ironic proverb, to mark the end of an exam, but she isn't here. For the first two exams, he was conscious of her absence — she'd long been a constant, as reliable as the two-hour session feeling like four or the requisite sore hand from all the writing. Today, though, he doesn't miss her, which feels strange yet right. An understanding that woke him up a couple of nights ago from deep, REM sleep. What she revealed in the Millhaven waiting area was not just for him and Corny. It was enough to release her to wherever she needed to go.

There's a crackle and hiss from the PA system.

— *Ninety minutes have elapsed in this exam session. If you have completed your paper, raise your hand and your teacher will collect it, after which you may go. There are thirty minutes remaining.*

He smiles and raises his hand, unable to resist looking up and back to see who else has finished. No one has. There are a few disparaging looks from his classmates before they dig back into their own essays. Mark, sitting right behind him, whispers an insult against his manhood for finishing so quickly. He glimpses only the top of Shi's head, dark and lovely, right behind Mark. Essère walks slowly along the aisle towards him, accepts his papers, and goes back to the front without a word. Boy grabs his pens and walks out.

Finishing his high school career in such a fashion is anticlimactic. Other students, mostly younger ones with easier exams, come together as soon as they leave the gym, gabbing about how they did, which questions they aced, which they didn't. For him, it's just finished. No one's waiting for him. There are no more classes or assemblies to mark the end, just walking away from this final exam and returning in a few weeks for report cards and diplomas. He hasn't decided whether he'll attend the graduation ceremony.

As he leaves the gym, he tosses his three cheap stick pens towards a garbage can. And they stop in midair, along with everything else in a now-familiar absence of all movement and sound.

Mara. Dempster. Somewhere nearby. Boy catches himself looking up and down the hall to see if Mara has come into the school before stopping himself. Impossible. He wouldn't expose himself like that. No, he just wants Boy to know he is nearby.

A younger student has pulled a battered history textbook from his bag and stands, motionless, scrutinizing a page for confirmation that he got an exam detail right. Boy could walk right over and read it, too, if he wants. Pluck it right from his hands —

The exam, he thinks. Mara is trying to help him. A gift of time. He could read up on Essère's exam questions, return to the exam room, take his paper back, and answer every point, meet every expectation. A perplexing way to make amends, allowing Boy to cheat.

Boy won't, though. There have been changes to the plan. All is not lost anymore. He shakes his head and heads towards the exit and the bike ride home. And stops.

— Wait, he says. What if —

He bursts back into the exam room and walks to Essère's row. Passes his own desk, lonely in its vacancy. Glances at Mark's tight, precise writing, knowing the responses will be thoughtful and measured. Lays a hand on Shi's shoulder as he passes, enjoying her warmth, noticing her neat piles of loose-leaf and the single, half-filled page in front of her. Her ballpoint pen caught, mid-loop, in the second *e* in *however*. A conclusion, then. Almost finished.

At the back, wedged into the too-small final desk like an afterthought, Kyle leans over his exam. His papers organized, his writing unexpectedly legible. Boy reads the paragraph. A sensitive, in-depth treatment of a difficult topic. Structured. Balanced. Supported. Boy clenches his fists. Mark, whose bruises took weeks to fade, has maintained his silence. Kyle has not been named. How easy it would be to hurt him, give this idiot a reason to fear the sudden, blinding pain when everything starts up again. Boy stands a long moment before relaxing his hands. *Use your fucking head,* Charlie would say. Boy lifts Kyle's hand, grabs all the written pages, leaving only blank paper. He takes a blank page from every desk in the row and brings them back, stacking them neatly under Kyle's suspended pen.

He again walks out of the gym, smiling now, thinking about blank exams, wasted chances, taking something back for a friend. Deeper into the school, he wanders, moving down halls, passing classrooms and offices, familiar places. He runs his hand along the lockers, his own, Mark's, Shi's. At Kyle's locker, he stops. He folds the topmost page of Kyle's exam in half and wedges it into the gap between frame and door, the corner poking out like a white, pointed tongue. He turns away and exits through the nearest doors. Outside, he unlocks Corny's bike from the racks at the side of the school and rides away through a perfectly still world.

He pedals hard.

Along Queenston Road, Boy releases the rest of Kyle's exam a page at a time, his own speed enough to generate wind in the stillness and scatter them in his wake. He imagines returning to the walk-in clinic, this time seeking answers rather than leaving questions. Contacting a certain American cadet to see how involved she'd like him to be in raising their child. There will be difficult conversations to have with his new girlfriend, who will be looking ahead rather than at past mistakes. *Still, there* is *a girl,* he thinks. At home, in the garage, a long-absent father's things will need to be sorted through to figure out what to keep safe until he can reclaim them. There's a houseful of possessions and memories to explore in the light of a mother's passing, decisions to be made, what to sell and keep, how to move forward. A half-brother will search for care, and in giving it to him an older brother will have to learn to ask for help. There will be a question of money yet the certainty of not worrying about it at all. How to make amends for a school year almost lost and ensure that a dream of military service can still happen, even if it might mean serving on the ground for a while.

When everything starts up again, most of the world will resume pace, seemingly unchanged and unaware. Yet change always happens, even when nothing moves or breathes. No one sees him, but Boy laughs as he pedals, faster and faster, almost flying, imagining himself a flash of orange against all of it.

ACKNOWLEDGEMENTS

Thank you, thank you, thank you to my parents, Bill and Grace van Staalduinen, for your continued and unflappable support. It's an honour to be your son. I love how you love words, and how you have always modelled healthy reading habits: any writing ability I might have largely exists because you made our home a safe place to discover beautiful stories.

I owe so much to Dundurn's acquiring editor Rachel Spence, who saw the potential in this book and took a chance. Thanks also to the rest of the Dundurn team: it has been an absolute pleasure working with you, and I look forward to continuing the adventure together. Special thanks to Elena, Crissy, Tara, Stephanie, and Sophie, who brought this book into being in very particular ways.

Immeasurable thanks go out to the crew at UBC Creative Writing, who were there when Boy first woke up to discover time had stopped, and who continue to inspire. To my classmates in my fiction workshops, who pushed me hard and well, and especially to Geoff Cole, whose excellent suggestions caused the mid-writing crisis of conscience that ultimately made me re-think how this story should be told. To Annabel Lyon and Michael Winter, writers and fiction instructors extraordinaire. To Timothy Taylor, writer and thesis advisor par excellence, for your sharp eye and excellent comments, and for coming back a few years later to say nice things. To Ellen Keith, a writer I trust and admire, for proofreading and supplying a few of your words in support of the novel. And to Miriam Toews, my literary patron saint, for writing gorgeous books that move and challenge, for being my second thesis reader, and for unhesitatingly lending me a few of your encouraging words.

To my writer friends, my tribe, in Canada and beyond: you make me better. Thank you to Liz Harmer, who humbles me with her support, graciousness, and incredible craft. A massive thank you to the Canada Council for the Arts and the Ontario Arts Council, whose various grants at various times blur together but shine with one clear purpose: to make this life easier for me and countless other artists by funding our work and giving us space to create. There can be no greater gift for those who attempt to make the world beautiful.

And finally, thank you to family. To God, head of the entire show, for giving me everything and the desire to know more. Mom and Dad: again, my gratitude forever. To Kirsten, Dennis, and Sharon, for being the best siblings ever and your constant efforts to seek out the best for and in everyone. You brought some very cool people into our family, too, spouses and kids who build us up in every amazing way. To the faithful at SJE. To April, Stien, Rose, Nancy, and the rest of my rowdy cousins at HPL, saints all, who work so hard to create safe spaces in our city. To every kindred soul in my adopted hometown of Hamilton who struggles and changes and amazes and excels. To my daughters Nora and Alida, whose pure curiosity inspires me to seek out the delightful and the wonderful: I love being your Papa, and yes, I will read you a story. And to my first reader, Rosalee, my Left and my love, in this, our fifteenth anniversary year: your strength and faith in me gives me the strength and faith to keep doing what I do. I'm so glad we're facing all of this together, and I love you.

Brent van Staalduinen is the author of the novels *Saints, Unexpected* and the forthcoming *Nothing but Life*. His short stories have won numerous awards, including the Bristol Short Story Prize, the Fiddlehead Best Short Fiction Award, and the Lush Triumphant Literary Award, and have been published in *Prairie Fire, Sycamore Review, New Quarterly, SubTerrain, Fiddlehead, Litro, Event, Dalhousie Review*, and elsewhere. A former high school literature teacher, radio announcer, tree planter, and army medic, Brent now divides his time between writing, working at the public library, and helping other writers find their voice. He lives in Hamilton, Ontario, with his wife and two daughters. Follow him on Twitter and Instagram (@brentvans) and visit brentvanstaalduinen.com for more information.